G000124399

Not the Work of an Ordinary Boy

Victoria L. Humphreys

Stairwell Books //

Published by Stairwell Books
9 Carleton St
Greenwich
CT 06830 USA

161 Lowther Street
York, YO31 7LZ

www.stairwellbooks.co.uk
@stairwellbooks

ISBN: 978-1-913432-61-4

Layout: Alan Gillott
Cover design: Patrick Knowles
p18

In memory of my beloved dad, Leslie Humphreys,
the greatest of war babies.

Also in memory of Dr Carole Smith, writer, editor, mentor and friend.

For Ig, Hugo and Matilda: my be-alls and end-alls.

"Set in WWII, Victoria L. Humphreys' *Not the Work of an Ordinary Boy* is a kaleidoscope of a story, served in bits and pieces via transcribed interviews, carrier pigeon messages, interrogations, cartoons, Morse code, prose poetry, anecdotes, antidotes, and more. With a twist of the hand, Humphreys shifts her narrative vision through ever changing emotional textures and patterns, which blur and sharpen between grimness, playfulness, absurdity, humour, and pain. An original novel that offers unflinching glimpses into the inhumanity of this era." – Christine Leunens, author of *Caging Skies,* adapted into the Academy Award-winning film, *Jojo Rabbit*

"A refreshing new take on a war we think we know. Such a talented writer." – Dan Snow, Historian and Presenter

"This is not the work of an ordinary writer – Humphreys' prose is acute, playful, and compelling. She has some of the subtle, pin-sharp wit of Beryl Bainbridge yet can conjure a fictional world as immersive as Douglas Stuart's, both unflinching and warm. This is a new voice entirely in control of the story." – Will May, Professor of Modern and Contemporary Literature, University of Southampton

"Victoria L. Humphreys has brought us a new and captivating story which imparts to us a number of important themes. Not only does her work show to us how war and conflict can punctuate childhood innocence with coldness, abuse, brutality and darkness – it also strongly speaks of the tremendous moral courage shown by children in wartime. It demonstrates to us how the young, and the defenceless too, can make sacrifices for the greater good and often play a role beyond their comprehension, even in the face of unspeakable evil, thus becoming the great forgotten heroes of their time. Above all, Humphreys' triumphant tale now finally tells us the story of the greatest forgotten hero of history… perhaps, the most courageous of them all… the humble carrier pigeon." – Dr Joseph Quinn, project coordinator of 'Their Finest Hour', University of Oxford

Prologue

Confidential
Copy 3. Dossier on Boomerang   23 September 1943
To: C. Head of SIS
From: MI-14(d) Special Continental Pigeon Service

1. We have had some spectacular results with Boomerang.
2. Three pigeons have now undergone intensive training in the technique and are successfully demonstrating the capability to undertake two-way flights.
3. A pigeon named Ethelred the Unready has repeatedly flown between his home loft in Surrey and the agent (Earthstar) to which he has recently been assigned in Northern France. Although the intelligence delivered by the pigeon has not proved notable thus far, the value of carrier pigeons capable of boomeranging between two consistent locations in this way remains immeasurable and can no longer be reasonably contested: intelligence gathered in the field can now be received by London within hours rather than weeks or days.
4. Consider securing funds to extend the Boomerang programme forthwith.

1.

So that was the start of it all: the day Konstantin learned a person hanged by the neck will mess themselves either seconds before the event, or up to twenty-eight minutes after it. It was the day Konstantin discovered that his father murdered children, as well as adults. The day Konstantin decided that he had had enough of the war and the monster it had made of his father.

One boy of indeterminate age, but slightly older than Konstantin's fourteen years, and one youth, probably in his late teens by the look of it, dangle from the same branch of a Norwegian Maple on a dim February afternoon on the outskirts of a modest, but strategically important, village in the Picardy region of Northern France. A third, much smaller boy stands upon a chair, contemplates his unshod feet, wipes away the tears that have undoubtedly spilled down his grimy cheeks, and waits for the German soldier beside him to kick the chair from beneath him. It's a small observation, but Konstantin recognises the chair the smallest boy is made to stand upon. It is the chair that's been missing from his dining room table for some weeks. Its absence from the table is, I gather, a baffling response to the continued hospitalisation of his mother for pulmonary tuberculosis at a sanatorium somewhere in the German province of Brandenburg. That the chair's disappearance from the table did not coincide with that of his mother's – she was admitted to the sanatorium well before Konstantin and his father left Germany for France – was not a subject for discussion. When his mother returns to the family, the chair, it is promised, will return to the table, even though his mother has never occupied the prow of the table nor indeed the missing chair. In point of fact, the empty place at the table and Jugendstil chair is, and always has been, the province of Konstantin's father. But I digress. The three boys were probably brothers but were not necessarily members of the French resistance group that called themselves Les Gens Prévalent, as Konstantin's father claimed in the deposition (if there ever was such a thing). The image of this war crime was obviously taken by an expert in photography: the detail is keen and the composition first-class. How the image made it to Britain in such good order, Konstantin alone knows. I suspect we'll find an account of how it came to survive the war somewhere among the transcripts, if we're patient.

It might be supposed that I'm relaying a nightmare here. That Konstantin is merely experiencing one of those unsettling dreams that are wont to assail the sleeper moments before they awake. That the involuntary evacuation of urine behind the trunk of a neighbouring tree as he witnessed those boys being hanged by his father is but the climactic feature of his nightmare; a tactic employed by his brain to keep his body from wetting his bed sheets. But let it be known that I read the words of others, I don't write them. I assess words, I don't embellish them. And when I encounter words that you must never apprehend, I take my blue pencil and redact them with an even line that runs through the entire length and breadth of them.

Reading on, I have it slightly wrong, it seems. The youngest of the Les Gens Prévalent appears to have been hanged for *Espionage*; the middle boy for *Distributing Illegal Propaganda*; and the youth for *Sabotaging A Railway With Explosives*. This information leads me to conclude that the three boys might not have been brothers after all since they were accused of separate offences in wildly disparate locations and consistently denied knowing each other during the protracted interrogations. It's difficult to assess from this photograph whether the boys resemble one another. Death changes a face beyond all recognition. Perhaps the eldest two did have the same small nose, full lips, freckled face of the youngest one in life, but the truth is, in death, I cannot tell. What I can tell you is that each of the boys were equally malnourished. Perhaps Konstantin's father imprisoned them in the cellar of the large château he requisitioned upon arriving in France and withheld food until such time as the information he desired from each of them had been successfully extracted. 'Information buys food,' he may have promised. He either lied about that, or little information was surrendered because, as I have already said, each boy was painfully thin, and what's more, shabbily dressed, with ripped shirts, no berets, and holes in the knees of their trousers. Konstantin insists that he doesn't know the identities of any of the French people his father murdered during the German occupation of France, including the three currently under discussion here, and I'm inclined to believe this testimony, particularly in relation to these boys. It's not as if Konstantin attended the village school or spent summers building camps and lighting fires in the surrounding forest with them. Konstantin was the enemy.

The youngest boy was hanged for espionage but it wasn't just any old espionage. This boy was found to be *In Possession Of An Enemy Pigeon*. A British pigeon. Possibly an American pigeon. My magnifying glass is useless here. I'd have to see the pigeon to categorically determine its country of origin. As might be imagined, the American carrier pigeons were altogether bigger (though not better) than our pigeons having never had to endure grain rationing. From the transcript there is nothing to suggest that the Allied carrier pigeon was American rather than British, that it was plumper than the norm, but you should take the opportunity to read the relevant transcript for yourself if this sort of detail is important to you.

Transcript of Interview. Date: 11/09/44. Time: 11.48 HRS. Interview 1/7.
(**Informant:** Konstantin von Essen. **Interviewer:** Saunders. Also present: **Guardian:** Mrs Bloomfield.) Location of debrief: Combined Services Detailed Interrogation Unit, Latimer House, nr Amersham, Buckinghamshire.

Informant: The boy told Father that he found the pigeon in a potato field. 'What were you doing in the potato field?' Father demanded. The boy shrugged. Father slapped him. 'What were you doing in the potato field?' The boy began to cry. Father slapped him again. 'What were you doing in the potato field?' (PAUSE) 'Looking for potatoes,' said the boy. 'Looking for pigeons,' said Father. The boy said nothing. (PAUSE) Father slapped him. (COUGH) 'Looking for pigeons,' he repeated. The boy nodded. Father ruffled the boy's hair. 'This boy shall have soup today,' he said loudly, so the boys in the neighbouring cells would hear. (PAUSE)

Interviewer: Do continue, Konstantin.

Informant: The boy was looking for potatoes but found a pigeon instead. He should have surrendered it to one of Father's men, or better still, eaten it as he must have been very hungry to risk looking for potatoes in a farmer's field in the middle of the night.

Interviewer: What was the risk, Konstantin?

Informant: Ignoring the curfew, going out at night and waiting in a field with a torch. Naturally, Father would presume that the boy was waiting for one of your Lysander aeroplanes to land in the field or to drop someone, or something, from the sky. Even if the boy was doing no such thing, he should have known that being in that field, any field, was not permitted. I wish that he had not ignored my father's curfew.

Interviewer: What do you think the boy was doing in the field, Konstantin?

Informant: (PAUSE) I don't believe he was looking for potatoes. (PAUSE) (...) I think he was waiting for the pigeon. (COUGHING)

Interviewer: Are you alright, Konstantin?

Informant: Yes, I am sorry, I am... er, asthmatiker. (COUGHING/WHEEZING)

Interviewer: Asthmatic?

5

Informant: Yes. I am Asthmatic. (COUGHING/WHEEZING VERY LOUDLY)

Interviewer: Perhaps we ought to summon the doctor?

Informant: No, the doctor is not necessary, Mr Saunders. If I breathe as I am now doing, it will pass. (BREATHING HEAVILY)

Interviewer: Mrs Bloomfield, would you like me to organise the doctor for Konstantin?

Guardian: Don't ask me, Mr Saunders. What do I know about it? Asthmatiker did you say, lovey? Never heard of it. What does it do exactly? All I know is that he hasn't had this particular trouble before, Mr Saunders. Not while he's been stopping with us at any rate. Is it serious this asthmatiker? Is it catching?

Informant: No, Mrs Bloomfield, please do not be alarmed. I will be recovered in a moment.

Interviewer: INAUDIBLE...together with the language barrier of course.

Guardian: Oh, it's the *language barrier,* is it? No of course about it, Mr Saunders. That's a new one on me, this *language barrier* business. I think we all know what's really happening here don't we, Mr Saunders?

Interviewer: INAUDIBLE

Informant: (COUGHING) (SNIFFING) (WHEEZING) (PATTING ON THE BACK?)

Guardian: Bit of fresh air and you'll be as right as rain, I expect, lovey. I expect it was talking about those people hanging from a tree that did it to him, Mr Saunders. Terrible. A terrible thing to see. For a child. For anybody. I wouldn't want to see it, that's for sure. I'm sure I'd do worse than piddle... (INAUDIBLE) really I do. Fresh air will take your mind off it, lovey. That, and a bite to eat I shouldn't wonder.

Interviewer: Er, yes, Mrs Bloomfield, it's probably a good idea to resume after lunch. I'll have someone escort you to the cafeteria.

Guardian: What I'd really like to know is if that poor devil with the pigeon got his soup in the end? I hope he did. I couldn't bear it if he didn't, but I don't spose I'm allowed to ask that, am I, Mr Saunders?
Interviewer: INAUDIBLE.
Informant: (COUGHING)
Interview Suspended: Date: 11/09/44. Time: 11.54 HRS. Interview 1/7.
(Informant: Konstantin von Essen. Interviewer: Saunders. Also present: Guardian: Mrs Bloomfield.)
Location of debrief: Combined Services Detailed Interrogation Unit, Latimer House, nr Amersham, Buckinghamshire.

Apologies, that wasn't the section of transcript I intended you to see, although I don't suppose it matters in the long run. This is the bit you should read if you'd like to know more about the carrier pigeon.

Transcript of Interview. Operation Attar.
Interview Resumed: Date: 11/09/44. Time: 13.11 HRS. Interview 1/7.
(Informant: Konstantin von Essen. Interviewer: Saunders. Also present: Guardian: Mrs Bloomfield.)
Location of debrief: Combined Services Detailed Interrogation Unit, Latimer House, nr Amersham, Buckinghamshire.

Interviewer: What can you tell me about the pigeon, Konstantin?
Informant: The boy's pigeon?
Interviewer: Yes, the boy's pigeon.
Informant: (PAUSE) It was a spy.

2.

Rose Clarke was an avid and comprehensive diarist. For this reason, it shall be necessary to paraphrase much of what I found in her diary though I will endeavour to use Rose's own words where possible. I shall start by saying that Rose was used to seeing pigeons on the Common, but not in the den and not one with a small green canister attached to its right leg.

She had purposely arrived at the den ten minutes later than the agreed meeting time but her best (and only) friend, Dottie Latymer, was absent. This was irritating because now Dottie would be the last to arrive meaning Rose would have to start proceedings and say the longest part of the secret code. Why did the code have to have anything to do with *The Adventures of Robin Hood?* She might not have minded if she'd seen the film. It was beyond comprehension that Dottie was taken to the Regal Cinema every time it was screened. (Rose was never taken to the cinema, nor was she ever given the money to go alone.) If only Mrs Latymer didn't think so much of Errol Flynn, the lead actor, or, at the very least, didn't carry a notebook and pen in her handbag and wasn't a whizz at shorthand. If Mrs Latymer hadn't been a secretary before she married Mr Latymer, she would not have been fast enough to jot down the lines of Dottie's favourite scene, and Dottie would not have been able to declare them the secret code. At twelve, Rose was too old for secret codes, long or short ones. Since Dottie was only just eleven, Rose was too old for Dottie, but there was nothing she could do about that. Dottie was her only friend and she was Dottie's only real friend. Not just at school either. Each child's unpopularity stretched beyond the school gates to the streets of their home town in Surrey. That was the fault of their respective mothers: Mrs Latymer was said to be a Brash American with too much money in her purse and a lazy way with words, and Mrs Clarke was said to be As Mad As A March Hare without the wit, or at least the soap, to wash Rose's clothes now and then. However, neither woman deserved such criticism: whilst Mrs Latymer was American and not short of money, she was nothing but charming on the one occasion that I met her, and if you read between the lines of Rose's neat handwriting, it's plain for all to see that Mrs Clarke was neither mad nor stupid, but simply a melancholic recluse who had not the energy to take a bar of sunlight soap to Rose's school uniform as often as she ought. The reason for the girls' enduring unpopularity amongst their peers was that Dottie was half-Yank, and Rose invariably stank. (It's an unhappy rhyme but I promised to use Rose's words wherever possible.) The point is, no other child wanted to know them.

Rose stood at the den's entrance, which was roughly the same size as the lid to the pig swill bin on Park Road – the bin which reeked of rotting food and made her retch every time she passed it – and recited Dottie's secret code in her head. She counted each of King Richard's words on her fingers: *Arise Robin, Baron of Locksley, Earl of Sherwood and Nottingham, and lord of all the lands and manors appertaining thereto. My first command to you, my lord Earl, is to take in marriage the hand of the Lady Marian. What say you to that, Baron of Locksley?* If she had remembered it right, King Richard's bit, now her bit thanks to Dottie's tardiness, should be forty-seven words long. Dottie, as Robin Hood, had only to respond with a paltry ten words: *May I obey all your commands with equal pleasure, sire!* How could there be any pleasure in obeying commands? Fancy being commanded to marry someone. She thought about her own parents and how miserable they made one another. Had they been commanded to marry against their will? Was that why her father shouted, slammed doors, and broke things? Was that why her mother kept the curtains drawn in the day and spent such a long time sitting in the dark doing nothing, including rarely washing Rose's clothes? In Rose's house, the blackout lasted for months, not just the night. Rose had no intention of ever marrying.

The den itself was really no more than a hollowed-out bramble bush. Mr Latymer's cricket bat, a bat that in its heyday helped to secure many victories for his cricket club at Cambridge University, had proved an excellent excavator for the enterprise. Dottie had swung the bat and Rose had removed the felled branches, employing the tatty sleeve of her cardigan as an impromptu gardening glove to save the palm of her hand from scratches. They did not stop excavating the den until its diameter measured the same as they did, lying down with their legs straight and their toes pointed. A hole in the roof, large enough to let in the rain, was thatched with an offcut of patterned lino that the Latymers' handyman hadn't needed for the family's Anderson shelter. They fashioned a door from a discarded hessian sack they'd found at the back of the greengrocers: it wasn't perfect since it had a purple stain on it, but Rose felt rather comforted by its smell since it reminded her of Wrights coal tar fluid. Two overturned milk crates topped with two grey pillows, pillows that Dottie had acquired from Granny Latymer, made two adequate chairs. A rudimentary cabinet that Dottie's elder brother Edmund had built in woodwork lessons at Eton, a couple of years before, had been salvaged from the bonfire and placed in the centre of the den. (They'd used a wheelbarrow to transport it.) Though items of value had yet to be obtained to dwell inside the cabinet, such as ornaments or curiosities, Dottie had managed to stock it with other treasures such as a small torch, a pair of tweezers (essential for the removal of splinters), an antique Churchwarden pipe with a cracked shank that she'd found in her father's Davenport, two chipped ceramic bowls and an empty milk bottle, and Rose had donated a crocheted doily to adorn its surface as well as a signed copy of A.J.P. Taylor's monograph *The Habsburg Monarchy 1809–1918* (wrapped in an old tea towel to protect it from the damp). There were items they would have liked to have added to the den, such as some sort of flooring so they could remove their shoes without spoiling their socks on the sandy ground, and an eiderdown or blanket so they could keep warm when the wind picked up. But treasures such as these were scarce back then, even for a rich half-Yank. Spare items of this nature had long since been utilised to make air raid shelters more comfortable, or to light-proof the windows for the blackout. Thus, Rose and Dottie did what everybody else around them did: they **Made Do.**

The den's greatest attribute was its situation. Sited amongst a great clutch of Goat Willow, Yellow Gorse, Oak and Silver Birch trees, it was largely invisible to the casual wanderer of the Common. Since its construction, it had only attracted the passing interest of a solitary deer and a dog with worms. (Dottie had stepped in the latter's squirming mess when it had been time to return home. It had got a whiff of Rose's spam sandwich and that was why it had bounded over to the den, flown through the sacking and slobbered all over her hand before Dottie had shooed it out yelling, '*You'll sweat the lard out of that fat carcass of yours before this day is over, my pudgy friend*' (a direct quote from Little John in Robin Hood, I believe).) However, the deer had only paused outside the den to contemplate the early morning air because it hadn't known that Rose was sitting in there marking time that day.

Nobody had.

It had been the half-term holiday, and the morning after Rose's father had returned home on twenty-four hours leave that she'd sought refuge there. As soon as he appeared in the lounge the day before, the mood in the terraced house had changed from sad to dire and the house itself had suddenly felt a thousand times smaller. She'd been sitting cross legged on the floor unravelling an old jumper and re-winding the wool into a new ball. She hadn't heard him come in and so she jumped when she saw him leaning against the door frame glaring at her. She tried to smile, to look pleased to see him, but then he said, 'There's too much of your bloody mother about you: same eyes, same hair, same miserable little face.'

Rose suspected he was waiting for an apology but it was difficult to apologise for her face. She wondered if she could dart past him, go upstairs or outside, but she was worried that he would anticipate the move and block her path, or, if she made it, dash up the stairs after her or out into the street.

'Well, is that it then?' he shouted, throwing his kit bag down. 'Got nothing to say for yourself?'

'Sorry,' she said at last.

'Sorry, what?' he shouted. 'Who do you think you're talking to? Am I nothing in my own house?'

She said nothing. Well, not aloud anyway.

11

He pulled an open bottle of stout from his trouser pocket and, still wearing his boots, slumped onto the orange-coloured day bed that they'd inherited from Rose's great aunt. The antimacassar that Rose had crocheted some months earlier, and had given to her mother as a birthday present, slipped off the back of the day bed and settled in a dusty corner. She watched him rest his Brilliantined head on the now unprotected material with dismay, sure that his thoughtlessness would occasion an oily mark that would be impossible to remove.

'Where's that mother of yours? Sleeping, is she?' He glanced up at the ceiling and rammed the bottle of stout into his mouth. It struck his teeth and made a clink sound that reminded her of the time Dottie's parents had clinked saucers of champagne together to celebrate Edmund's exam results. Dottie and Rose had been allowed a sip from Mrs Latymer's glass and Rose had sneezed at the bubbles. She avoided her father's gaze and concentrated on the ball of wool she was still holding.

'Wake up, you lazy mare,' he shouted to the ceiling. 'I'm hungry.'

Before Mrs Clarke had ceased to function, she laundered the bedding on Mondays, but she was not in the kitchen feeding wet sheets through the mangle, or in the back garden hanging them on the line. She was in bed waiting for day to become night so that she could legitimately go to sleep. But then her footsteps were heard in the room above, then on the landing, and then on the stairs. She appeared in the lounge ashen faced, short of breath, half-dressed. 'I wasn't asleep,' she said. 'If I'd known you were coming home…'

Her words died on her lips as her husband's spiteful eyes roved the length and breadth of her body with an expression that suggested he'd just taken a dessert spoonful of castor oil. 'You're not what they call a sight for sore eyes, are you?' he sneered.

'I've not been well.'

'You never are,' he laughed. 'You're what they call a maringerer, mallinge..rer. You know what you are.'

Rose wondered how many bottles of stout he'd had. He didn't usually slur his words after one. She wanted to laugh at his impairment but she'd have to do it later. She bit the inside of her cheek.

'You can wash that an' all,' he said, nodding at his kit-bag.

12

It wasn't just Mrs Clarke's mind that didn't work very well, her arms were a problem too. She'd had polio as a young girl. It was why she hadn't been conscripted to work in the factories or the Women's Auxiliary Defence Service or **Couldn't Lend A Hand on The Land.** It was why it took her an age to do everything and why she struggled to lift her husband's kit-bag from the floor.

'Christ Almighty,' he scoffed. 'I really did draw the short straw marrying you, didn't I?' Then he shot Rose a filthy look as if she were an even shorter straw. Rose sprang to her feet and dragged the kit bag out of the back room and down the hallway to the kitchen.

'When do you need your washing by?' Mrs Clarke asked, which was her way of asking him, *When are you off again?*

'Tomorrow,' he said, belching loudly. 'After lunch.'

'I'm sorry you're not home longer,' said Mrs Clarke, which I can only assume was code for, *Thank heavens.*

Rose stood in the kitchen staring at the dirty laundry; most of it was caked in mud and smelled of wood smoke. How was her mother supposed to wash, dry and press it all in a day? Wrapped in a dirty pair of his socks were two duck eggs. (Lance Corporal Clarke, as he was officially known, had stolen them from a duck house he'd encountered at the side of the road while on a route march in Lincolnshire the previous day, and before you begin to look more favourably on him, I can tell you that they weren't intended as a gift for his wife and child, but for somebody else living several streets away.) Rose removed the eggs and hid them in the tin of National flour.

'I can manage now, love,' Mrs Clarke said, coming up behind her. 'You go outside while it's still nice out.'

'I can help,' Rose said, angrily wiping a tear from her chin.

'You heard your mother,' Rose's father shouted from the lounge. 'Away you go before I get up off this thing and show you the back of my hand.' He was prevented from issuing any further threats by another round of belches.

A second tear spilled from Rose's eye. This time her mother halted its progress with her thumb. Then she marched her to the front door. 'Don't worry, love, by the time I go back inside, he'll have nodded off I expect. Call on Dottie,' she said, smiling.

Once Rose had reached the doorstep, the front door was shut behind her. She turned to watch the outline of her mother disappear down the hallway before she trudged her own miserable path along Upper Gordon Road. She had a horrible feeling in her stomach and no intention of calling on Dottie. She was in the grip of a thought that, given some encouragement, she might voice. So, she went to the den and marked time until she was sure her father would be back where he belonged: in The Carpenters Arms. And when that time came, she went home, pulled her diary from beneath the mattress of her bed and got rid of that thought. But as I'm not one to reveal the private thoughts of others, I'd rather you read this thought for yourself:

I really hope the Germans kill my father.

Early the next morning, she left the house before her father woke from his drunken stupor and went to the den (that's when she encountered the deer). Then, when she judged that her father's leave was over, she went home, removed the duck eggs from the tin of flour, made an omelette with a scrape of precious butter and shared it with her mother, in her mother's bed, illuminated by a fissure of light from where her mother hadn't drawn the curtains properly.

Now, with Dottie still nowhere to be seen, she made up her mind: she would let the code stand for a few more days because it had required so much effort to learn, but after that, she was going to insist that it was changed to something that suited them both, or better still …no ruddy code at all. She plucked open the door to the den, secured one corner of the sacking by pinning it to the thorns of a branch, and stepped inside.

The pigeon, with the small green canister attached to its left leg, was so tired from its recent flight, not to mention meagre breakfast, that it barely batted an eye.

An Unnarrated Event
The Cartographer

In the Buckinghamshire village of Hughenden, Zurie's little dog, Kikka, hears the dry squeak of a bicycle wheel and the metrical patter of a fine pair of brogues as the bike is pushed through the whitewashed gate and up the garden path to the lean-to at the side of the house. A whistled tune enters the vestibule via a defective letterbox. The tune carries far, but is well out of range of being recognisable to any living creature but Kikka. Leaving a haphazard trail of carrot and potato peelings in her wake, she journeys from where she's been sunbathing on the compost heap in the rear garden, to the sitting room, and from there down the hall to the front door just as Zurie needlessly calls from her studio above, 'Kikka, Kikka, Papa is home. It's Papa. It's Papa.'

Kikka's excitement at the imminent return of her second-best human is conveyed via a series of raspy barks that, to an uninitiated ear, sound like the opening gambit of an outraged spouse; as if the helpmate stopped off at the pub on the way home from work and in so doing, ruined the evening meal. Like all dogs, she prefers routine and is frustrated by delay: Papa doesn't usually remove his trouser clips outside to stow them in a pannier. She snorts at the mat like an inexperienced snuff-taker. Her flat face twitches from left to right and back again as she listens for the habitual brush of Papa's jacket against the holly tree outside the front window, and the stamp of his feet upon the tiled doorstep. It is too long in coming. Her tiddlywink peepers fixate on the door. And the white noise of Zurie's *Where is he, Kikka? Where is he?* travels down the stairs and nettles until Papa appears.

It is not until a good deal later, when Papa is sitting in the armchair facing Zurie's easel and nursing a tumbler of whiskey, that Kikka finally gets what she wants: his lap. With one eye open, she sleeps with her tummy on his thighs and her head between his knees. His tweed trousers serve to dampen her snores. Zurie repositions her husband's head before returning to her easel to paint him.

'Should I be drinking this, or is it just a prop?' he asks, wrecking the pose.

'Drink it up, silly billy,' says Zurie.

He does as he is bid and relaxes into the chair. Kikka slips farther into the valley of thigh and knee. Zurie puts down her paintbrush, steps around the easel and pours her husband a second measure. 'What have I done to deserve this?' he asks surveying the very generous dram.

'You're sitting for me,' she says, repositioning his head.

'You sit for me,' he says.

She returns to her painting. 'True,' she says, 'although not for some time now.'

'Hmm.'

'Do you mind, darling?'

'I love the way you say *darling*.'

'Do you mind, *darling*?' she repeats.

'I shall never grow tired of hearing you say it.'

'You must miss painting?'

'Am I permitted to snooze, do you think?' He sighs heavily and closes his eyes.

'Can you snooze with your eyes open, darling?'

'I don't think so,' he says, opening his eyes.

She peeps around the canvas. 'Kikka can,' she says, flashing her husband a toothy smile.

'She's a dog.'

Zurie feigns disappointment. 'Oh dear, Kikka is cleverer than you.'

'Kikka is cleverer than us all.' He smiles and rubs his eyes.

'Are you very weary, darling?' she asks. 'Don't move your head,' she orders.

'Just a little tired.'

'You've been very busy today?' she says, nodding at his ink stained fingers.

He thinks of the map he's been working on, the number of corrections he's made to it, and the inevitable consequences of his painstaking accuracy for the people that live on his map. 'Yes,' he says simply.

She returns to her painting. 'The work you're doing is…very difficult.'

'Let's talk about your day,' he says. 'Actually, let's talk about *Kikka's* day.' Kikka stirs. He strokes her velvet ears. She purrs like the enemy. 'She smells of the compost heap again. Perhaps we ought to consider fencing it off.'

'Uh-oh, no more sunbathing for you, Kikka,' laughs Zurie.

'You'll never get a sweetheart if you smell of rotting vegetables,' he warns the little dog.

'Don't keep moving your head,' says Zurie.

'Why can't you paint me sleeping?' he says. 'I promise I won't move if you do.'

3.

Eleven miles from Rose and Dottie, Eden House in Virginia Water was home to Lady Darrick-Sinclair. It was also home to her carrier pigeon elite, Ethelred the Unready (Ethel for short...even though it wasn't a hen), service number: NPS.42.13033. You rightly assume that Ethel's loft was The Dorchester Hotel of pigeon lofts: south-facing, elevated position, roof-mounted ventilator, palatial nesting box, removable droppings draw, walls on four sides, straw galore, clipped kisses from Lady Darrick-Sinclair...all that sort of thing. (It had been lauded in The Racing Pigeon as 'Representing the holy grail of avian architecture' and some fanciers had heard it said that George VI was considering commissioning similar for Sandringham.) You are also at liberty to surmise that Ethel indulged in his fair share of black-market pigeon food as well as Lady Darrick-Sinclair's breeding hens. (The former because the Feeding Stuffs National Priority Mixture Order of 1941 only allowed for 7lbs of pigeon food mixture per week to be shared among ten birds, and the latter because carrier pigeons conscripted into the Special Section of the Army Pigeon Service tended to die with alarming regularity on the job.) In terms of Ethel's domestic situation, and by this, I mean his abode, the catering arrangements, and the onsite, ongoing entertainment, he was, on the balance of probabilities, a very contented carrier pigeon. (Had he been otherwise, I'm quite sure he'd have flown the loft to take up residence elsewhere.) But in terms of how he regarded his employment as an Allied agent (and employed he was for he was paid in the region of 4d per mission) I shan't pretend to know: though I may be described as Pigeon-Minded I won't be denounced as Doctor Doolittle. That said, if Ethel were briefly anthropomorphized to, say,

18

give us an insight into his average mission with the Royal Corps of Signals, I'm positive it would read something like this:

I usually receive twenty-four hours advance warning of a mission. To prepare, I'll retire early and rise at dawn. A good breakfast followed by a kiss for luck from Mother usually gets my feathers flapping. Getting into my basket can be a jolly pain, but once in I simply have to wait for Archibald Haines — leader of The Surrey Sprinters pigeon group — to collect me in his van. By the time I'm collected, most of my friends from the neighbouring lofts (fellow group members of The Surrey Sprinters) are already onboard including: Jude the Obscure, William Butler Yeats, Bunty, Scarlet Pimpernel, Albert the Great and The Duchess of Richmond. En route to the local train station we'll have a chinwag about our salary (whether to save or spend), recent race speeds (I'm consistently the fastest of the group), distances covered (I have the greatest stamina of any of my peers), near-misses with Peregrine Falcons (none to speak of) etc., but we never discuss the details of any special training undergone, or up and coming training (in my case, Boomerang) or of the operations we've been involved in because we all know that **Careless Talk Costs Lives**. The motion of the long train ride to Piccadilly invariably sends me to sleep but it means that by the time I arrive in London, I'm well rested and jolly well ready for action. We take the Viscount's Bentley to Wing House *(real name)*, take the lift to the Viscount's office and gather for the operational briefing. Once we are briefed and the Supreme Headquarters Allied Expeditionary Force have told us where to drop in occupied France, we get togged up in our green message canisters and hop into our specially adapted containers. From Wing House we journey to an airfield (mode of transport and route taken unknown: the former because I can't see out of my container, the latter because it's all very hush-hush), board a Lysander aeroplane at RAF Tempsford and parachute into our respective drop zones. From there, my day may end in any one of the following ways:

19

1. My parachute might fail to open with the result that I crash-land and die on impact with the ground.
2. I may survive the landing but roll several times in my container sustaining a fatal head-injury or frayed tail feathers. Either way, I'm done for.
3. As I circle the French sky in order to get my bearings, I may be:
   a. Fired upon by the enemy, shot and killed.
   b. Mistaken for a pest by a farmer, shot and killed.
   c. Seized, killed and eaten by a Peregrine Falcon.
4. I may forget where my bread is buttered and hightail it off to another loft to live with foreign pigeons.
5. I may be eaten by a fox or other hungry animal with sharp teeth.
6. I may be fried with garlic and encased in pastry.
7. I may be exchanged for a reward by a collaborator.
8. I may be captured by the Germans and:
   a. Imprisoned for life.
   b. Sent back home carrying false intelligence.
   c. Be wrung at the neck.
9. I may succumb to heavy fog, torrential rain, gale-force winds and lightening.
10. I may drown in the English Channel.
11. I may die of exhaustion.
12. I may be electrocuted by a live power line.
13. I may be gassed, bombed, or shelled.
14. I may be discovered by a French patriot, lovingly cared for i.e. allowed to stretch my wings at least once a day and fed some of the grain I bring with me, until such time as a message containing noteworthy intelligence has been composed, installed in my message canister, and attached to one of my legs. I will then fly home to my loft and successfully deliver the message to Mother, who in turn will take it to the police station in Ascot, who in turn will hand it to a despatch rider, who in turn will hare it back to London and drop the message on

the desk of a Chief Sneaky Beaky in the War Office. (What remains of the day, I will spend cooing with the hen I most admire, Mary Queen of Scots.)

Needless to say, the final outcome is the favoured outcome, but one time, Mary Queen of Scots had to wait. It was the time I was required to fly above a battle zone and got covered in human blood. Mother had to give me a bath as soon as I got home and it took an age to clean my feathers.

Blood and thunder: what a fascinating insight. Now that Ethel has narrated all that, I promise he'll never speak again. That said, I really don't believe I could have told it better.

4.

Guardian: Whatever do you mean, lovey? How on earth can a pigeon be a spy? (CHUCKLING)
Interviewer: Mrs Bloomfield, with respect...
Guardian: Sorry, Mr Saunders, but I'm no lover of pigeons. Vermin, that's what they are. You should see the mess they've made of our path. Isn't that right, Konstantin? Blooming things. And their doings do something terrible to your lungs. I forget what it's called but whatever it is, it can kill you, Mr Saunders.
Interviewer: Have you misplaced your knitting, Mrs Bloomfield?
Guardian: Oh no, Mr Saunders, it's here, don't you worry about that. I don't go anywhere without my knitting. I'm on the last sleeve of that matinee jacket now. You know the one. For my little grandson George. Though he's not so little now. I started it the day Konstantin was telling us all about the time he met that traitor Lord Haw-Haw in Hamburg. Was it Hamburg, or Berlin? Oh, don't ask me, Mr Saunders, I forget which. In all my years I've never been to a cocktail party and there's Konstantin... What I'd really like to know, lovey, is, did you ever meet that nasty man, Hitler, but I don't spose I'm allowed to ask that, am I?
Interviewer: INAUDIBLE (RUSTLING) Here's your knitting, Mrs Bloomfield. Please don't allow me to

be the cause of George's jacket remaining unfinished.

Guardian: Oh, thank you, Mr Saunders, I've been meaning to finish it, but what with one thing or another...

Informant: It is a very smart jacket, Mrs Bloomfield.

Guardian: Oh, lovey, you always say the sweetest things. I'll knit something for you next. A tank top in Arran, I think.

Interviewer: I'm sure Konstantin will be very grateful, Mrs Bloomfield, but we must press on. Please do answer Mrs Bloomfield's question regarding the pigeon, Konstantin. You said it was a spy.

Informant: (PAUSE) That's what my father called it. It was a British pigeon. The boy was waiting for the British to drop it in the field. He was intending to use the pigeon to send a message back to Britain.

Interviewer: Did you see the pigeon?

Informant: No.

Interviewer: Did you see any message written by the boy?

Informant: No.

Interviewer: Do you know the nature of the information the boy intended to send back to us?

Informant: Only that it was significant.

Interviewer: Who described the information as 'significant'?

Informant: My father.

Interviewer: But he didn't give any further details?

Informant: No.

Interviewer: What did the boy have to say about the information?

Informant: Nothing. He refused to speak.

Interviewer: Throughout the entire interrogation?

Informant: Yes.

Interviewer: How many times was the boy interrogated?

Informant: Every day.
Interviewer: How many days was the boy imprisoned?
Informant: (COUNTING IN GERMAN)
Guardian: Isn't he clever, Mr Saunders?
Interviewer: INAUDIBLE
Informant: Eight.
Interviewer: How long did the interrogations last?
Informant: Sometimes minutes. Sometimes hours.
Interviewer: And in all that time, the boy never spoke about the pigeon?
Informant: He didn't speak at all, Mr Saunders. About anything.
Interviewer: Who interrogated the boy?
Informant: My father.
Interviewer: Always?
Informant: Yes.
Interviewer: At any time during the boy's arrest, detention and execution, did you see any equipment that might belong to the pigeon such as a parachute, a message canister, a travel basket, or a questionnaire?
Informant: No.
Interviewer: Did you see any evidence that the pigeon was ringed?
Informant: No.
Interviewer: How can you be sure that the pigeon found on the boy was an Allied carrier pigeon?
Informant: My father said so.
Guardian: He might have been telling porky pies, lovey. Don't you think, Mr Saunders?
Interviewer: INAUDIBLE.
Informant: I am sorry, Mrs Bloomfield, but I do not understand the meaning of porky pies.
Guardian: Course you don't, lovey, silly me. Lies, lovey, that's what it means. Your father might have been telling you lies.
Informant: (PAUSE) Please may I be excused to visit the lavatory, Mr Saunders?
Interviewer: Of course, Konstantin. Tell Hesketh and he will escort you.

Informant: (LEAVES THE ROOM. QUICK FOOTSTEPS.)
Interviewer: Mrs Bloomfield, I'm afraid I must remind you that you are not required to speak during the interviews. You must neither comment on what is said nor ask any questions. As Konstantin's guardian, your singular role whilst a temporary resident with us is to provide Konstantin with the reassurance that he will come to no harm during the debriefing process. I know you are very fond of Konstantin but could I please ask you to refrain from addressing him during the interviews. I must also remind you that you have signed the Official Secrets Act of 1911 and consequently, whatever is discussed in this room must not be discussed by you thereafter under any circumstances with any person or persons. You are also not permitted to question Konstantin at any time about his past. Is that understood, Mrs Bloomfield? It is imperative that I have your word on this.
Guardian: Oh, blast it. Sorry, Mr Saunders, but it's my tinnitus. It comes and goes without any warning and when it comes, I can't hear a blasted thing except this high-pitched whistling. It's like this... (WHISTLING)
Interviewer: (CLEARS THROAT)
Guardian: (WHISTLES)
Interviewer: (CLEARS THROAT)
Guardian: (WHISTLES) (WHISTLES) (GASPS FOR BREATH) ...That's just how it goes. Just like a kettle that's been left on the stove. It's the war that's doing it. I didn't have it before the war. It's so irritating, Mr Saunders. You have no idea just how much. So, I'm very sorry but I didn't catch a word of what you just said. Could you give it to me again, do you think? I'll try and lip read.

An Unnarrated Event
Blut und Ehre

Once upon a time, Konstantin von Essen could be found, more oft than not, whittling his flagstaff. (Take note, I do not intend for this to be read as a euphemism.) In order to achieve his Deutsches Jungvolk in der Hitler Jugend Proficiency Badge (Gold Class), Konstantin was not only required to demonstrate a clear commitment to National Socialist ideology but also the capability to whittle a flagstaff for the regimental flag because **Victory Was With Their Flags**. Ask yourself the following: Have you ever carried a flag? If you've answered in the affirmative, you will know that Flag Bearing is subject to Flag Etiquette. When it came to The German Young Folk Parade, Konstantin was required to:

1. *Angle his flagstaff over his left shoulder*
2. *Secure his flagstaff at all times in the palm of his left hand*
3. *Keep the palm of his left hand level with his mouth*
4. *Keep his elbow square and level with his left hand*
5. *Keep his right arm free for innumerable Nazi salutes*
6. *Withstand several hours of fanatical flag waving with unremitting enthusiasm*

In light of this, you, I, all those with Girl or Boy Scouting experience, not to mention any self-respecting Oarsman, knows that Konstantin should have opted to whittle something free of ostentation; something that could be tightly grasped for long periods without causing any discomfort to the underside of his hand. But Konstantin was looking for a pat on the back from his father, so he whittled 131 numerically significant swastikas on his flagstaff and got the very thing he was after; as well as a go with his father's Lüger pistol in the back garden. The result of the latter was a decapitated rabbit, an obliterated glass panel on the orangery, a near miss that doesn't bear narrating, a breathless rebuke from his mother, and instruction from his father on how to fire a Lüger with military precision (the latter he enjoyed very much). In relation to the ornate flagstaff, the palm of Konstantin's left hand sustained one of the worst cases of blistering I've ever had the bad luck to read about. Still, what Konstantin lost in skin, he gained in kudos, not to mention standing in his father's eyes, and the weals on his palm swiftly metamorphosed into a calloused badge of courage. And when Konstantin moved into the Château des Beaux Anges and decided that the wooden mantel above the fireplace in his bedroom was ripe for carving, he duly carved the following words of his godfather:

> *The German boy of the future must be slender and supple, swift as a greyhound, tough as leather and hard as Krupp steel.*

Because, by then, he was undoubtedly all of these things and certainly on target to become an **Officer of Tomorrow**.

4.

'May I obey all your commands with equal pleasure, sire!' said Dottie, followed by, 'Holy cow, whaddya got there, sugar?'

Rose didn't mind being called sugar by Dottie, chiefly because she'd been called worse, as her following diary entry attests:

Thursday 4*th* June

Lawrence Laws called me a stench bomb as we were lining up after assembly. It was whispered down the line until it reached me, and as I was second from the end it meant everybody heard it. Miss Butler saw the line twitching this way and that and decided to investigate. She didn't catch what Lawrence had started off and asked me OF ALL PEOPLE to tell her, so I did and then she said, Who is a stench bomb, Rose? So, I had to say, Me, Miss, and then Lawrence laughed his head off because in a roundabout way I was saying that I smell. (GOD, YOU'RE A DOLT, ROSE.) Miss Butler said, Do all try to ignore Lawrence's unceasing stupidity in future, which made Lawrence sneer, but Miss Butler saw it and sent him to get the stinger from Mr Cox for disturbing the peace of the line and pulling stupid faces in her direction. (The stinger is metal and hurts like hell by all accounts, but it couldn't have hurt Lawrence that much because on the way home from school I heard him shouting, Glory, glory Halleluiah, Coxy hit me with the ruler.) And while Lawrence was supposed to be getting a whacking from the stinger, I went off to the toilet to blub! YES, TO BLUB!!! Over Lawrence OF ALL PEOPLE. I could scream. I detest him. I checked my blouse and of course it didn't smell. I washed all my clothes on Sunday. (Even the hankies.) What does he know about cleanliness? He has spots all over his face, and his back for that matter, which shows that he's dirty front and back. HAS HE NEVER HEARD OF SOAP? I know it's rationed, but still. If my back looked like Lawrence's, I wouldn't dare take off my shirt when I play football in the street. It's like looking at a large tray of tripe with powdered egg on top bobbing up and down. And I'm ruddy well expected to keep on eating those two things which isn't easy when you've seen that. And Dottie should know what a stench bomb is. Having to explain it, and then why Lawrence called me it, just made the whole situation ten times worse. I told her that her questions weren't helpful. She said, Well heavens to Betsy, sugar, how was I supposed to know? And then, Anyway, you don't smell, to which I said, I know I don't smell, Dottie.

If Lawrence calls me a stench bomb again, I don't know what I'm going to do. Why does he have to live three doors down?

P.S. A historian called A.J.P. Taylor came to assembly. He presented me with a book entitled, The Habsburg Monarchy 1809–1918. Miss Butler said I got the book because I work hard. The dedication reads: 'This book is presented by A.J.P. Taylor to Rose Clarke in recognition of her continued academic excellence and flair for history'. He's signed the inside of the front cover and Dottie says this makes it valuable. I don't know how she knows this. She doesn't either. Mr Taylor said he expects to see me at Oxford one day, but Oxford is quite far away so I doubt he'll see me there anytime soon. Dottie thinks Mr Taylor's book looks boring. She said, Where are all the pictures, sugar? and she was a bit rough with the pages as she flicked through trying to find them so I took the book off her and told her to change the subject. Guess what she changed it to? I'm not even going to write it. I have already learned one thing about the Habsberg Monarchy: Habsberg is pronounced with a p as if it were written as Hapsberg.

P.P.S. I tried to show Mr Taylor's book to Mother when I got home from school, but she was already asleep.

I'm going to make an educated guess here and suggest that Dottie changed the subject from the tedium of a history book without illustrations to the wonder of Robin Hood in technicolour, but this is conjecture. What can be determined from Rose's diary entry, other than that Rose was unfairly called unpleasant names by an ill-mannered, acne-ridden, reprobate old enough to know better, is that Dottie was unafraid of employing an Americanism or two when she talked. Technically, Dottie was as much American as she was English, but she was born in her parents' townhouse in Cheyne Walk in Chelsea, and, contrary to what her accent and vocabulary implied, had yet to set foot in America, let alone any of the cowboy states. For all her buckaroo affectations, Dottie was as English as Rose, a fact she did her level best to conceal because sounding American was far more interesting than sounding English, even if it did mean that nobody at school, other than Rose, would speak to her because of it.

That Dottie and her mother no longer lived in Chelsea was a temporary measure. Dottie's father was clear on the issue of evacuation from London: **'Children Are Safer In The Country. Leave Them There.'** But Dottie's mother was even clearer: 'Without me, sugar? You have got to be kidding.' So, Mr Latymer rented a detached Edwardian property in Surrey for his wife and daughter (by this time, Edmund was nicely ensconced across the pond studying for a degree in Medicine at Yale University – the academic institution closest to Mrs Latymer's relations). Mr Latymer largely remained in Chelsea but was known to visit the house in Surrey when he had the odd weekend off, and sometimes played cricket on a Sunday afternoon at the nearby Royal Military Academy Ground with some of his old cronies from his Sandhurst days. That said, as MI5's Director of Counter Espionage, Mr Latymer enjoyed about as much time off work as that Former Naval Person, Winston Churchill.

Now, I'm not a betting man but I would cheerfully have put money on the fact that as soon as I mentioned MI5 and Mr Latymer's senior position within that secret service, you became altogether more interested in this story. As for Dottie, she was ignorant of what her father did for a living back then, knowing only the following:

a) His job was important.
b) His oak-panelled office was somewhere in London.
c) He spent more nights sleeping at his office (on a collapsible camp bed which, I can tell you, is hugely superior to a straw palliasse) than he spent at the townhouse.
d) When she wrote to him with her interminable *news* (the Surrey house was deficient in telephone) and wished him to know it sooner rather than later, it was more expeditious to address the letter to his office, not the townhouse.
e) The address of her father's office was simply PO Box 500 which made writing the envelope a *helluva* lot easier than writing the address of the townhouse. (How easy it is to let these Americanisms creep into one's diction.)

Rose's altercation with Lawrence, Dottie's peculiar vernacular, and the war-time situation of the Latymer family is a digression of unacceptable proportions and so I shall remedy this by returning to Dottie's arrival at the den post-haste. In response to Dottie's question regarding the pigeon, Rose said, 'It's a pigeon, Dottie, what else does it look like?'

'Gee whiz,' said Dottie entering the den and promptly kicking over one of their treasures (the empty milk bottle and most ill-gotten of their gains). Rose tutted (not unlike her father, if I'm pressed) but the milk bottle together with the pigeon was unaffected by Dottie's clumsiness. The pigeon was tired. Its flight from Picardy to Surrey had been long, a distance of exactly 226 miles (as the crow flies), and taxing, it had been blown off course and Lady Darrick-Sinclair, not to mention Mary Queen of Scots, were nowhere to be seen.

'Why howdy, little pigeon,' said Dottie, in between puffs on her pipe.
'Quiet,' warned Rose. 'We don't want to scare it.'
'Sorry, sugar,' whispered Dottie.
'It's alright,' said Rose.
'What's that thing on its leg?' asked Dottie, using her pipe as a pointer.
'I don't know.'
'I've never seen a little pigeon with a thing on its leg before.'

'Neither have I.'

'Somebody must have put it there.'

'Yes, Dottie.'

'Are you gonna take a look-see?'

'I don't know. I'm not sure I should. What if its contents are private?'

Dottie laughed because the word 'private' made her think of 'privates' which was Edmund's word for his thingamajig. (Edmund was as English as Mr Latymer.)

Rose frowned at Dottie. 'On the other hand, it might tell us what to do with him.'

'Oh, it's a *him* then, is it?'

'I have no idea if it's a *him* or a *her*, Dottie.'

'You could turn it upside down to find out.'

'Would you like it if I did that to you?'

Dottie shrugged. 'It's what the doc does when you're born. He turns you upside down and he says, "Hey, Mrs Whatever-your-name-is, congratulations you gotta girl, or, you gotta boy" and I don't hear anyone complaining about that. I'm pretty darn sure I didn't.'

'Well that maybe true but it doesn't matter what this pigeon is; it's a pigeon, we know that much and I really don't think we need to know more,' said Rose.

'It sure does matter if we're gonna give it a name, sugar,' ventured Dottie.

'Why would we give it a name?'

'If we're gonna keep it.'

'Why would we keep it?'

'Because it'd be neat. And anyway, it chose to come and live here. It likes us. We can use Edmund's cabinet as a cage.'

'We can't keep it, Dottie. It doesn't belong to us.'

Dottie shrugged. 'Finders keepers losers weepers.' (One of Mr Latymer's favoured idioms.)

'We can't,' said Rose, slowly sitting on her milk crate as if the carrier pigeon were a King Cobra in strike position. 'It's wearing a ring. It means it belongs to somebody. It means it already has a name.'

'Those are numbers, not a name,' said Dottie, peering at Ethel's ring.

'Those numbers can probably be matched to a name,' said Rose.

Dottie sighed and then flumped onto her crate, touching knees with Rose. 'Well, if that's true, maybe, just maybe, its name is in its suitcase.'

'Suitcase?'

'Well, what else you gonna call that thing on its leg, sugar?'

Rose shrugged. 'We might find an address for it there as well, I suppose.'

'Hmm,' said Dottie.

'It would mean we could return it to its owner.'

'Swell,' said Dottie, meaning no such thing of course.

'You hold it and I'll see about getting the suitcase off,' said Rose.

'Will it bite me?'

'Birds don't bite, they peck.'

'Well I know that, but I don't like the sound of that either.'

'Just pick it up, Dottie, we haven't got all day.'

'Darn it, why does it have to be me?'

'Your hands are already dirty, that's why.'

Certainly, it was the case that Dottie could **Plant a Victory Garden** in her fingernails.

'They are?' said Dottie, holding them up to the light at the sacking door, with her pipe clamped firmly between her lips.

'Dirtier than mine, anyway, I expect. Have you never picked up a hedgehog?'

'No, have you?'

'No, but I expect it's the same. Just scoop it up.'

'But I'm busy smoking my pipe.'

'You're busy pretending to smoke your father's pipe. There's never any tobacco in that pipe just as there's never any smoke coming from it. Plus, you don't have any matches and you need matches to light a pipe. Do you honestly think I know nothing about smoking a pipe? You pretend to smoke a pipe, Dottie, and I'm not going to pretend otherwise just so that you can get out of picking up this pigeon.'

'How do you know I never have any tobacco in my pipe?'

'Because I do, and for your information, I also know that your father's pipe is broken and that's likely the reason he doesn't use it anymore,' she said, ignoring the obvious quip: *so, put that in your pipe and smoke it.*

'Broken? Are you kidding me, sugar?'

'Anyone can see the crack, Dottie, unless they're blind or pretending certain things.'

With a theatrical huff, Dottie surrendered to Rose's superior knowledge and after throwing her pipe into one of the chipped bowls, jumped up from her seat. 'Double darn it,' she said, rousing the pigeon from its slumber (Ethel opened an eye). 'I'll pick it up but on one condition.'

Rose sighed. 'Yes?'

'If that suitcase doesn't tell us what this little pigeon is called, or where this little pigeon lives, *I* get to name it and *we* get to keep it.'

Dottie had never been permitted to keep a pet of her own, and the twins (whom we will meet in due course) didn't count even if they did bite worse than any dog she'd ever encountered.

Rose rolled her eyes. 'That's two conditions but I agree to them both, Dottie Latymer, on one condition.'

'Name it.'

'If we were to get into trouble because we kept this pigeon, you take the blame.' The last thing she needed were people coming to the house about this and poking their noses into the things they discovered there.

'We won't get into trouble. Daddy has a very important job. He's a very important man. He would fix it for us if we got into trouble, which we won't, but if we did. You got yourself a deal, sugar.'

Rose nodded and Dottie advanced towards the pigeon wide-eyed and cupping her hands as if she were about to drink from the fount of knowledge.

But I think we'll temporarily leave the girls at this juncture because, without printed instructions at their disposal on how to detach the canister, the removal of Ethel's 'suitcase' was a faff I could well do without narrating.

An Unnarrated Event
Most Secret Sources

As diarists go, Hughie Latymer − MI5's Director of Counter Espionage − could give Samuel Pepys − of the Great-Fire-of-London-Parmesan-cheese-burying fame − or Rose for that matter, a run for their money. Daphne, Latymer's personal secretary, arranges a crisp white sheet of A5 in her typewriter, rests her slender fingers on the keys with a refinement to match that of the classical pianist, Irene Scharrer, and patiently awaits the boss' daily dictation. Latymer sucks on his pipe, and with his free hand writes his initials in the dust that has accumulated in a groove of the wall's wood panel and wonders whether to start the day's entry with talk of C, Frippery, Urchin, John St Michaels, Van de Gucht or ISOS (Decrypted Abwehr hand cipher wireless traffic). With a nod of the head to Daphne, he starts with Frippery.

2 January, 1942

Frippery has sent word that Prickleback is now in receipt of a radio transmitter; a message containing intelligence that relates to Lilliput and promises to keep SLB3 busy for the next few months is imminent. This is superb work by Frippery and I have promised to stand him a gin rickey at the Travellers Club when next we meet.

Unfortunately, Urchin has lived up to his name having been caught with his trousers down by a certain member of the Abwehr whom we know to be based at the Hotel Lutetia in Paris. A subsequent review of Urchin's training has been conducted by Kip McKinney. It transpires that not only was Urchin briefed on the enemy's use of honey traps to solicit intelligence, but that the dullard fell for Fifi in a subsequent training exercise in a hotel in Mayfair. The only reason he was kept on, I understand, was because he did not spill the largest of the beans, as it were. Urchin's incurable weakness for an attractive member of the opposite sex has left McKinney hopping and a number of SOE agents in Urchin's circuit, namely Eunice, Harold, and Beatrix in a tight spot in Saint-Germain-des-Prés. It has been suggested that the Abwehr honey trap is a dead ringer for Betty Grable, but concrete proof of this has yet to be obtained. As a precaution against further arrests by the SS, all agents within the network have been instructed to familiarize themselves with the appearance of Grable.

We have exhausted our investigation into a possible German spy code-named Mopper. We have not identified any charladies with questionable backgrounds cleaning either official establishments or notable domestic houses. Unless further intelligence is received, we shall not waste any further time on this odd little tale.

I met with C. of SIS this morning and he has agreed that Gordon Trott's assessment of Floris Van de Gucht as a belligerent gambler who is liable to grow too big for his breeches in the Belgian Mouvement National Royaliste is probably accurate. C. also warned me that John St-Michaels is a meddling prima donna who was overheard bad-mouthing the department while sloshed on Martinis at the Reform Club. C. finds the noxious fellow rather amusing but assures me that his wings are in the process of being clipped.

In other matters, recent ISOS traffic reveals that the Germans are now in possession of both British and American service uniforms and are planning to infiltrate our countryside wearing them.

5.

The Racial Observer

Hitler Youth member ten-year-old Konstantin von Essen pictured earlier in the day with his godfather, the Führer. Also pictured, Konstantin's father (second left) General Dieter von Essen, the Fuhrer's great friend and brother-in-arms during the First World War

Our Beloved Führer hosts an afternoon of fun and games for his friends and officers of the Supreme Third Reich, followed by a lavish party to mark his 51st birthday

Our most wonderous leader, Adolf Hitler, saviour of the Fatherland, not to mention the most obliging Bavarian gentleman you will ever have the pleasure of meeting, celebrated his 51st birthday today in truly deserving style at his stunning Berghof home. Gifts included priceless works of Old Master art conscientiously sourced by Dr Gurlitt, racially approved Polish antiquities and a Meissen porcelain tea service. Members of the Hitler Youth, The League of German Girls, and specially chosen tots from the triumphant Lebensborn Programme came together to sing the sweetest rendition of Happy Birthday the human ear has surely ever heard. All afternoon, joyful 'Heils' accompanied our Führer as he greeted his guests and watched our finest Aryan children participate in traditional party games. There was birthday cake for all and our Führer personally saw to it that no child went home without a bellyful of the stuff, not to mention cheer. Following the fun and frolics of the afternoon, older guests remained to enjoy a lavish jamboree where vegetarian fayre, low-alcoholic beer and *streuselkuchen* were served without end. Entertainment was provided by the brilliantly funny and most celebrated reporter of truth, Lord Haw-Haw. *Whatever Suits The Party is Right*, and this was a most fitting celebration for our supreme and noble leader.

I'm going to confine myself to making just three points in relation to the *Racial Observer* article: Firstly, I have given it to you in translation because I'm fluent in German but don't know the extent of your foreign language proficiency; secondly, it's an extraordinary example of Nazi propaganda that sickens my stomach to the same degree as I'm sure Hitler's birthday cake did those poor Lebensborn babes; and lastly when it comes to Lord Haw-Haw, I would be most grateful if you would please note the following and treat accordingly: ***This Is Not Big-Hearted Arthur, Nor Is It Old Stinker...Oh, No! It's The Donkey That's Braying From Hamburg. Lord Haw-Haw, Hee-Haw-Haw, Hee-Haw!***

Before we get to the contents of Ethel's 'suitcase', I must address Dottie's description of Ethel's message canister as thus. Though it's inadvertent, I'm afraid Dottie is misleading us all with this noun. I cannot speak for others, but when I think of a suitcase, I think of a vessel designed to contain a fair proportion of not just my own wardrobe, but that of my wife's, when the annual week in Swansea beckons. Ethel's message canister was no larger than the lid of my fountain pen.

Rose held the message canister between thumb and finger. It felt much lighter than she expected. (She wasn't to know it was made of Bakelite.) She glanced at Ethel. I don't know what Ethel did in return, but I imagine that he was mightily relieved that the unnecessary tug-of-war with his leg had ceased. 'Are you sure you want me to do this, Dottie?'

'Heavens to Betsy, sugar, yes, I'm sure,' said Dottie.

Rose took a deep breath, said, 'Here goes,' and began to unscrew the lid.

'A kiss for luck,' said Dottie, who in the time it had taken Rose to detach the canister, had fallen in love with Ethel because he hadn't bitten her once (unlike the twins). Ethel accepted Dottie's kiss in as much as he didn't move a muscle and then went back to snoozing, no doubt warmed by the folds of her cotton utility skirt in which he was, by this time, cocooned.

As Rose worked off the top of the canister, she experienced an unanticipated, not to mention very rare, frisson of excitement: the fine hairs on her arms woke up, her heart made its presence known in her chest, something inside her tummy launched itself at her unmentionables, and her hands trembled as they were wont to do when Miss Butler would announce they were five minutes off the end of an important test, or when her father arrived home on leave. She popped the lid into her pocket and slowly peered into the canister. There, her hazel eyes met...NOTHING. I'm not kidding, I mean jesting. The canister was empty. Not even so much as a, *This Pigeon Belongs To .... Please Return to the Following Address..........* sort of message. Her arm hairs promptly collapsed, her heart resumed normal service, her tummy sprung back to its regular spot, but her hands still trembled out of habit. 'It's empty,' she said, surprised by the depth of her own disappointment.

'Darn it,' said Dottie, with a crafty half-frown. 'We'll have to keep you, Kenneth.'

(Goodbye Ethel, Greetings Kenneth.)

Rose just sighed. She had no opinion on Kenneth as a moniker.

'I'll do all the work,' promised Dottie.

'But you don't know how to look after a pigeon.'

'You mean Kenneth?'

'Hmm.'

'Well, it can't be that hard, sugar.'

'Can't it? What would you know about it? What have you ever had to look after by yourself?'

Dottie pondered the question. There had to be something...and by golly there was: she was responsible for keeping the back lawn mown and the coal scuttle filled, not to mention the twins entertained when Marmee was getting her hair done and Mrs Darby, the charlady (who was supposed to double as the nanny), was nowhere to be found. She opened her mouth to say as much but Rose was on a roll. 'What are we going to feed it for a start?'

Dottie produced a handful of cornflakes from the pocket of Edmund's old Eton bumfreezer — a jacket she'd recently taken to wearing because it made her feel closer to her brother – and said, 'Kenneth can eat these.'

'Cornflakes?'

'Birds eat corn, don't they?'

Rose ignored the question. 'Where did you get those?'

Dottie offered Kenneth a cornflake. Kenneth proved Dottie right by eating it. 'Marmee used our points allocation to get them,' she said. 'They make a great snack.'

'You know it's going to need more than one box of Cornflakes in its lifetime, don't you? Is your mother likely to get them every week?'

Dottie ignored the first question and answered 'Yes' to the second, but in truth she doubted that Cornflakes were going to be a weekly acquisition. Mrs Latymer had needed some serious persuading to spend their precious food points on the cereal: her original intention had been to spend the extra points on a tin of salmon.

(With the degree of wealth at her disposal, I don't blame you for assuming that Mrs Latymer routinely flouted the rationing and additional food points system and simply bought the food her family craved, under the table as it were. But I can assure you that Mrs Latymer did no such thing: she was a true patriot. Besides, tinned salmon in the right hands stretched far which, in this instance, rather rendered the black-market surplus to requirements.)

Rose pointed Kenneth's message container at Dottie and said, 'It's going to want proper pigeon feed.'

Dottie squinted at the canister and said, 'Are you sure there's nothing inside Kenneth's suitcase?'

'What? Yes, I'm certain,' said Rose, taking another look. Then she said, 'Well I thought so... hang on a minute... is that... no... maybe... there does appear to be something.'

'Try using the torch, sugar,' said Dottie.

Rose retrieved the torch from Edmund's cabinet.

What Rose saw on closer inspection was the off-white edges of some rolled paper clinging tightly to the walls of the canister. The paper was so fine, not to mention grubby (from all the re-writes, and the few weeks it had spent secreted beneath a dusty French floorboard), that it was an easy miss in the poor light of the den. Rose felt the earlier frisson of excitement, and all that came with it, return. 'There is something in here,' she confirmed.

Dottie crossed the fingers that were buried in Kenneth's breast and made the only wish she could: *Please don't let it be Kenneth's name and address.*

Rose tried to free the paper but the circumference of the canister was not much bigger than a cigarette, and her fingers were too large for the job. 'Pass the tweezers,' she ordered, like a surgeon.

Dottie leaned over to Edmund's cabinet and with her free hand located the tweezers.

Rose dumped the torch in the milk bottle and moved to the sacking door. With the sacking piled on her head like a raised bridal veil, she inserted the tweezers into the canister, held her breath and with great concentration began to tease out the contents.

Out came two pieces of rice paper.

They were covered front and back in scruffy writing.

'Oh boy,' said Dottie.

'Oh my goodness,' agreed Rose.

I have information for the British. I have two reasons for sending this information. First, I want my father back. Second, I am tired of this war. Château des Beaux Anges near Amiens has been taken over by the Germans. A senior German officer lives at the château and commands the region. Over forty German soldiers also live at the château and hundreds more are billeted in houses and hotels across the town and in nearby farms. Please do not bomb the château directly because there are civilians, including children, in the vicinity. I am one of these children and do not wish to die. I am an ordinary boy and I just want to go home, and to see my mother who is very ill and may not live for much longer. I have seen some important German military documents. I know that the Germans are expecting an invasion soon.

They are strengthening their defences in the Pas-de-Calais region. Please do not invade here as I think you will fail. I will try to find out the best place for your invasion. I overheard the German officer tell his Chief-of-Staff that many German soldiers have been successfully dropped into the British countryside. The soldiers are wearing British service uniforms and have been especially chosen because they speak fluent English. British people should be wary of strangers appearing in their villages, especially at night. Also, there is a radio jammer near to the Notre-Dame d'Amiens and an ammunition dump to the North of the town but I do not have the coordinates for the latter so I have attempted to draw its location. Please forgive the rudimentary nature of the map. I am not very good at drawing and it is not to scale.

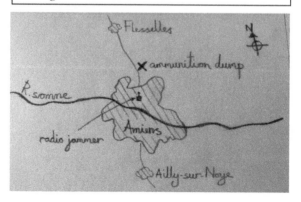

I am placed well to find more information of this nature. Therefore, please send another pigeon as soon as you are able but instruct the aeroplane that it must not drop it in the fields surrounding the château as the soldiers captured one of your agents here in January. She was arrested as soon as she parachuted into the field. Her true name was Bettina Agnes Rutter. She was interrogated at Amiens Prison, before you bombed it, and then guillotined. Anyone found sheltering your agents, and all those that live in that house, are to be interrogated and shot from now on. The children are to be sent to Poland with the Jews. And anybody found in possession of a pigeon is to be hanged or shot on the spot. In either circumstance, there is no trial. Please consider the field located at the following coordinates for the pigeon as the soldiers do not currently patrol here: 49.894066, 2.295753. I will do my best to check this field each morning. I sincerely hope that you will finish this war very soon so that my father may be returned to his family. Yours faithfully, Gilbert Aumont

An Unnarrated Event

The Slug

A man goes into shop. This is not a joke. Not to the man anyway. The shop is more akin to The General Post Office. In fact, it is The General Post Office. He finds himself joining a long queue. Mrs Latymer is also in the queue with Juniper and Jinny. (Like Mrs Latymer, I have no idea at this point in time where Mrs Darby is hiding.) A lady stands between the man and Mrs Latymer and the twins. I think of her as a buffer between the two parties. Mrs Latymer is going to post a birthday present to Edmund in Connecticut (knitted gloves, socks, and wristlets, plus a bottle of Penhaligon's Blenheim Bouquet aftershave). The man wants some stamps. The woman wants the postmistress to get a wriggle on because her shift on the buses starts soon. The postmistress is the friendly type; always happy to stop for a chat.

The bus driver leaves the queue wishing that chit-chat wasn't a thing. The man watches the bus driver step out of the queue immensely glad that there are some people in the world with less patience than him. Juniper and Jinny are camped on the floor. Juniper has a cold; a thick green slug crawls out of her nose and slicks down to her chin. The man's trousers billow in the draught. (In her haste, frustration, impatience…In spite, the bus driver didn't close the door properly.) In the absence of anything else, Juniper's hand (and occasionally Jinny's) has made a good tissue. But here is a trouser leg that seems to be saying, 'Wipe your nose on me.' So, Juniper does. And Jinny rubs it in, or tries to pick if off, depending on your perception of the event. The man surveys the damage and identifies the culprits. He takes the hand of Juniper and smacks it. He takes the hand of Jinny and smacks it. The twins go into shock. 'Man hit me,' cries Juniper. 'Man hid me,' cries Jinny. 'What did you do to my girls?' asks Mrs Latymer. The man tells her, and a few other things beside. (He calls her a war-shy Yank. He calls Juniper and Jinny Yank bastards.) Mrs Latymer tells him what he is, and then slugs him. The man leaves without his stamps. Mrs Latymer posts Edmund's parcel with a bee in her bonnet, a wailing twin on each hip and a very sore hand.

6.

Guardian: How Konstantin speaks such lovely
English I shall never know, Mr Saunders. What did
you call it? Fluent, was it? How Konstantin speaks
fluent is a wonder. I tell him all the time, you
speak better English than my two boys, don't I,
lovey?
Informant: Please, that is not accurate, Mrs
Bloomfield.
Guardian: Oh, listen to him with his *accurate*. See
what I mean, Mr Saunders. My boys wouldn't come up
with a word like that. Posh, that's what you are,
lovey. Who'd of thought we'd have somebody in the
family who speaks so posh. It makes me want to show
him off...to the neighbours and so on, but don't
worry, Mr Saunders, I've been sticking to the story.
Do you know, Mr Saunders, he's got one of those
little what-do-you-call-them? You know what I
mean: it's full of words. Oh, silly me, I can't even
remember what you call it now.
Interviewer: A dictionary?
Guardian: That's the one, Mr Saunders, you got it.
He's got this dictionary in English and, you know,
his own language. In the, you know, in the
(WHISPERS) German. And he reads that dictionary
like a book. Nobody reads books in the family. It's a
marvel, it is. You've always got your nose in that
dictionary of yours, haven't you, lovey? And the
questions! What does this word mean? What does that

word mean? Have I said it properly, Mrs Bloomfield? All day long he asks me!

Informant: I was told I have an aptitude for languages at school. I do not have an aptitude for any other subjects, Mrs Bloomfield.

Guardian: See, Mr Saunders, *aptitude* (CHUCKLING). Where does he get it from, that's what I'd like to know? Though I did have to tell my boys off the other day, didn't I, lovey? Teaching him rude words they were. Very rude words. I won't have that. It's not on. Thought they were being funny. Nothing funny about it, was there, lovey? Don't ask me to say what those dreadful words were, Mr Saunders. I nearly passed out when I heard this young man repeat them, and as for Mr Bloomfield, spilt his tea all down himself. Well, I took the wooden spoon to Davey for it. Chased him into the garden with it, didn't I, lovey? And he laughed. (CHUCKLING) I shouldn't be laughing really. Broke the spoon on him, didn't I, lovey? Had that spoon years as well; it was a wedding present if I recall. That Davey, I don't care if he's one of those Commando whatsits, he's a naughty boy, that's what he is. Not so much Johnny now that little George is here, but Davey... Oh, he'll be the death of me that one. He's a rotter.

Informant: Davey saved my life, Mrs Bloomfield.

Guardian: Oh, yes, I know, lovey, and thank gawd for that. Davey is the apple of my eye really. He's a very brave boy. As are you, lovey, as are you.

Informant: (SCRAPE OF CHAIR) No, Mrs Bloomfield, I am not brave.

Guardian: Oh yes you are, lovey, and I won't hear no different, not from you nor anybody else. No need to start worrying that scar of yours either. Reckons he did that falling out of a tree, Mr Saunders. Not one of ours mind.

Informant: I was not paying enough concentration to the strength of the branches, Mrs Bloomfield. I did fall out of the tree.

Guardian: No offence, lovey, but pull the other one. The trouble is, it's a very angry scar; I'm not convinced it'll fade, but Mr Bloomfield says these things don't matter on boys, even if it is on the face. And it's 'attention', lovey, not 'concentration'. I wasn't paying enough attention. That's what you should say.

Informant: Thank you for correcting me, Mrs Bloomfield. I was not paying enough attention to the strength of the branches.

Guardian: Gordon Bennett. (CHUCKLE) You're welcome, lovey.

Interviewer: I wonder if I might interrupt here, Mrs Bloomfield, since the subject of Konstantin's extraction from France has come up.

Guardian: Oh, yes, Mr Saunders, if it makes you happy.

Interviewer: (INAUDIBLE) (CLEARS THROAT) Konstantin, I'd like to take you back to just prior to the time when Davey arrived at the château and brought you to England, to the very last time you saw your father.

Guardian: Oh, dear, Mr Saunders, this'll upset the apple cart this will. I hope you don't mind me saying this, lovey, but Mr Saunders really ought to know just how upset you've been about your father. (SIGH) I mean, there's barely a night goes by when Konstantin doesn't wake up shouting, Vater, Vater. (PAUSE) That means 'father' in, you know, his own language, Mr Saunders. In the, you know, in the (WHISPERS) German. I don't mean to make you go red in the face, lovey, really, I don't, and I don't want you to worry about the other thing either because with the good weather, it's no trouble getting your sheets dry after your accidents, and I'm sure Mr Saunders understands about that sort of thing, don't you, Mr Saunders? Or, am I'm not allowed to ask that question?

Interviewer: INAUDIBLE

Guardian: Well, the long and short of it is, you don't know what happened to your vater, do you, lovey?

(FIRE DRILL (UNSCHEDULED))

Guardian: Oh, my gawd, we're under attack. All the way out here an all.

Interviewer: You can remove your hands from your head, Mrs Bloomfield, it's just the fire alarm. Somebody must have set it off again. I'm afraid we'll have to suspend the interview. Follow me, please. I will accompany you to our designated meeting point.

Interview Suspended: Date: 13/09/44. Time: 09.31 HRS. Interview 3/7.
(Informant: Konstantin von Essen. Interviewer: Saunders. Also present: Guardian: (Mrs Bloomfield.) Location of debrief: Combined Services Detailed Interrogation Unit, Latimer House, nr Amersham, Buckinghamshire.

7.

Lady Darrick-Sinclair strode across the lawn of Eden House, cheeks flushed, arms ascended, bun unravelling, pigeon poo drying on her weathered gumboots, and the closest she'd been to tears in decades.

As instructed, Archibald Haines had left his battered van tucked out of sight and was waiting for her by the portico, feigning interest in a clutch of snowdrops. 'Still no sign of him, My Lady?' he called, with a surreptitious scratch of his posterior and an involuntary bend of the knees to help relieve the eye-watering itch.

She shook her head, 'No, Haines.'

'I'm very sorry to hear that,' he said, producing a log book from the V of his V-neck jumper.

'It's been well over a week now,' she squawked, joining him on the gravel drive.

'It has,' he agreed, removing a mechanical pencil from behind his ear.

'He was my best,' she said, kicking up a wave of stones in anger.

'He was,' he said, shins pelted by the stones.

'I'm terribly upset, Haines.'

'It's only natural, My Lady.'

'Pigeons of Ethel's calibre are rare,' she said, plucking a stray pigeon-feed oat from her overalls and plugging an aching molar with it.

Archibald frowned, 'They are, My Lady.'

'To think he's been shot down by some bloody Hun makes me want to go over there and shoot a few of them myself.' She patted her hair for the cigarette she'd stashed there first thing that morning, but it had bailed out somewhere over the manicured lawn.

Archibald smiled, interpreting the clumsy search of hair as an attempt to transform herself into the presentable, and in the charitable voice he reserved for women, though not his wife because she detested all forms of charity, said, 'I wish it could be arranged, My Lady.'

'I wouldn't miss and I'd shoot them right where it bloody well hurts too.'

'This I know.'

'The testicles.'

Archibald wondered if he'd misheard, but Lady Darrick-Sinclair seemed to be staring at his crotch and this led him to conclude that he'd heard right. 'Yes, My Lady,' he said, regarding this response as the one that was most likely to steer the conversation past the unsettling subject.

'And only after that, would I shoot them in the head. Hearts are a waste of time. Haven't got them, have they?'

'From what I know, I'd say not, My Lady.'

'So, what now?'

'Ethel will be recorded as Missing-in-Action since his ring hasn't been returned to the National Pigeon Service,' he said, writing as much in his log book. 'If he does reappear, we'll see what's what and go from there.'

'But it's not likely, is it, Haines?'

'No, My Lady, I'm afraid it's not.'

'Poor, poor, Mary Queen of Scots,' she said, allowing a single tear to escape the fiercest of her eyes. 'You know, Haines, I used to bloody hate these pigeons, and now I'm crying over them. The sooner this bloody war is over, and everything gets back to normal, the better.' And with that she turned on her gumboot and returned to the lawn determined to find that bloody smoke if nothing else.

Confidential
Copy 1. Dossier on BOOMERANG

14 February 1944

To: C. SIS
From: MI-14(d) Special Continental Pigeon Service

1. Ethelred the Unready is reported Missing in Action.
2. Earthstar, via BEEKEEPER, reports an increased presence of German Peregrine Falcons in the area.
3. It is assessed that Ethelred probably succumbed to a Peregrine attack.
4. This is a huge setback for Boomerang: failure to fund the programme more widely means that we are now left with no more pigeons capable of boomeranging.
5. Consider securing funds to revive the Boomerang programme forthwith.

8.

File Op Attar: Document No. 165/168
Assessed: Relevance Unknown

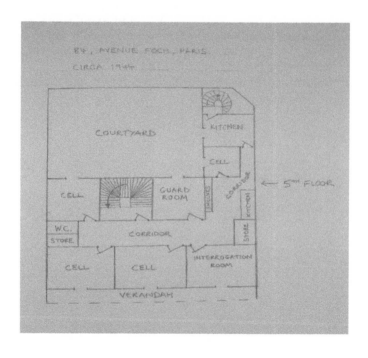

9.

File Op Attar: Document No. 127/168
Assessed: Miscellaneous/Disordered/Incidental

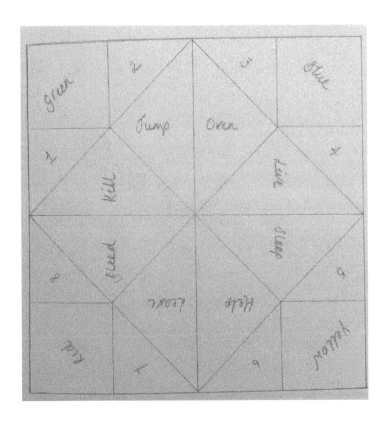

Origami: the Japanese art of folding paper into decorative shapes and figures
Fortune-teller: a person who tells people's fortunes
Jump: push oneself off a surface and into the air by using the muscles in one's legs and feet
Oven: a cremation chamber in a Nazi concentration camp
Live: remain alive
Sleep: a state compared to or resembling sleep, such as death or complete silence or stillness
Help: improve (a situation or problem)
Leave: depart from permanently
Bleed: lose blood from the body as a result of injury and illness
Kill: put an end to or cause the failure or defeat of (something)
Source: Oxford Dictionary of English

Pick a colour.
Red.
R–E–D.
Pick a number.
Two.
One. Two.
Pick another number.
Five.
Sleep.
I wanted Leave. But I settled for Sleep.
Source: Sixth Sense

Don't worry, love, by the time I go back inside, he'll have nodded off I expect Call on Dottie. I smile like an idiot because I am one For listening

For not leaving For living Rose lingers on the door step Go And take me with you She does and she doesn't I close the door on her then open the door wider Something horrible crosses the threshold It runs ahead of me And waits in the lounge On the day bed Oily hair Unshaven face Sour breath Filthy laughter lines Stain Grate Iron Mud Stinking gobbet Do-gooders Church-goers Till death do us part Deaf-eared neighbours Ears shut Curtains shut Off he goes One two miss a few ninety nine one hundred Bruised wrists Mashed breasts Stiff Body Stare at the ceiling Scream inside Heavy weight Suffocate Jesus wept he shouts, it's like f██████ a corpse Tempt fate Second-best Left on the shelf Last chance saloon Mark my words All of that and more Do as you're told Getting old Old Weak Useless Stalked Caught Sacrificed Curtains shut Ears shut Shut off Off I go Somewhere else Holkham beach Bucket of seawater Nine orange starfish Sun-bleached hair Sunburned skin Sand in the eye Carefree Careless Careworn Scare Scar Stop Cigarettes all round Say thank you Ungrateful b███ Thank you Thank you Thank you Green Seven Eight Bleed: Cut Bleed Relief
Source: Brookwood Hospital

Pick a colour.
Yellow.
Y–E–L–L–O–W.
Pick a number.
Six.
One. Two. Three. Four. Five. Six.
Pick another number.
Six.
Help.
Who will help me?
Source: Sixth Sense

10.

I must admit, the fortune-teller was a new one on me. *Good Lord,* I thought, *what the devil is this and how on earth am I supposed to assess it?* If you return to the document above you can see that I was somewhat at a loss, hence the assessment: miscellaneous/disordered/incidental (I was also tempted to write, *Have absolutely no idea how this arrived here or the reason for its inclusion,* but decided in the end that it must have some relevance to the file so permitted it to remain. As for the handful of hair tucked inside it, I'm afraid I'm at a loss to offer any sort of assessment.).

Last evening Joyce, that is my wife, said, 'Oh yes, dear, we all used to make those as little girls.'

Without giving away the character of this one – Joyce understands that I can't talk about my work in the War Office – and the somewhat puzzling nature of the fortunes, which quite frankly one ought to view as misfortunes really, I asked Joyce to give me an example of the fortunes she had once written. 'Oh, goodness,' she said. 'Let me have a think, dear.' She thought for a while and then laughed, 'I do remember one fortune, but it didn't come true I'm afraid.'

'What was it?'

'I'm not certain you want to know, dear.'

'I certainly do.'

'I'm not certain I wish to tell it.'

'Oh, come on, darling, be a sport.'

'If you insist, dear.'

'I'm afraid I must, Joyce.'

'Very well then. The fortune was that I would marry the most splendid man in all of England.'

'What? You stinker,' I laughed, nudging her in the ribs.

'I've just remembered another,' she said, with the wicked gleam in her eye that I've come to adore.

'I'm not sure I want to hear any more of your fortunes, Joyce,' I said reaching for a cigarette.

'Very well, dear, although this one did come true.'

'Oh, go on then, let's have it.'

'This one promised that I would marry the most splendid man in all of the world and would be happier than I ever imagined possible,' she said, brushing my foot with her own.

'That was a very long fortune to write in such a limited space,' I said, lighting up.

'I had very small writing,' she claimed, taking the cigarette from me.

'You have an answer for everything,' I said, pulling her towards me so that her ████████rested on my chest.

She blew smoke over my shoulder. 'How's this for an answer to the question, how much do I love my husband?' she said, pushing me away

███████████████████████

'It's a perfectly reasonable answer,' I said, taking my cigarette from her and placing it in the ashtray.

'But do you have the energy for such an answer?'

'Am I not the most splendid man in all of the world? Of course I have the energy for an answer of this nature.'

Her scented hair dri████████████████████████████████
█████████████████████████████████...

How easy it is to get carried away with one's good fortune. But for all the fun, usefully, Joyce gave me a tutorial on how one should go about questioning the paper fortune-teller in order to obtain one's fortune. I confess to having a brief dalliance with the one on file. The fortune I received was…Oh, I forget now, it might have started off with *Kill* and ended with *Live* (I wouldn't have put it past me to have opted for more than one fortune in an effort to secure one that was palatable, not to mention legal). But my coming upon this fortune-teller when I did (together with the hand-drawn plan of the fifth floor of the Gestapo's Parisian Headquarters) is evidence that while I was out of the office last week (with a truncated influenza that had me on my back for several days), somebody must have taken this file from my desk, dropped it, then thrust the documents back without any due consideration for their chronology or indeed their magnitude. So, whilst I was going to show you the transcript in which Konstantin recounts how he chanced upon Ethel as he travelled back to the château following the hanging of the three boys, I find myself reading about Rose and Dottie's pursuit of pigeon feed for Kenneth in the attic of Dottie's house. Joyce has laced my flask of Camp coffee with brandy to soothe away the last vestiges of my ailments so a quick dose of medicine and off to the attic we go.

But first, like Dottie and Rose, we must somehow get past the twins, Juniper and Jinny Monroe, or as Dottie had nicknamed them, Ferret and Badger (which sounds like a fantastic name for a Public House to me).

Juniper and Jinny were seventeen months of age and from West Dulwich. When Mrs Latymer took the decision to evacuate herself and Dottie to Surrey, she also took the decision to take two evacuees with her. '**Women Are Wanted For Evacuation Service**,' she told Dottie, 'and **Caring For Evacuees Is A National Service**,' she added, when Dottie, presciently (as it turns out), suggested that it wasn't one of her better ideas. When the twins arrived, Mrs Latymer said, 'Twin babies, how darling,' and immediately set about hiring Mrs Darby as a charlady-come-nanny. There was nothing wrong with Mrs Darby, or her work per se except that she was petrified of the twins and avoided them at all costs. Consequently, it was fair to say that Mrs Darby was more charlady-than-nanny. 'Give me a mucky toilet to clean any day of the week,' she said, when people asked after the girls (whom, in short order, had achieved the status of a local cause célèbre). From what I can gather, Juniper and Jinny were the sort of toddlers who drew the eye with their golden curls, dolly faces and pudgy limbs, and many felt compelled to stop and pet them, but it was wholeheartedly unadvisable unless you were Mr Latymer. The twins, for no obvious reason, adored him. In fact, if Mr Latymer had been the girls' nanny instead of being MI5's Director of Counter Espionage, nobody would have had cause to fear Mrs Latymer's little evacuees. 'Absolute charmers' was how he described them to his personal secretary, Daphne. I'm sorry to report, it was a misguided assessment.

At the front gate of the house, Dottie wanted to discuss countersurveillance measures. 'If I hide behind the bush over there,' she said, pointing at a flowering forsythia on the other side of the gate, 'I can see into the morning room. This is where Ferret and Badger watch out the window for me. All the live long day, as it happens.' She ducked down and ran to the forsythia like a British Commando. 'If I look just about here,' she continued, talking to a small gap between the blooms, 'I can…usually…just…about…see them without them… seeing…me.' She held her breath and surveilled the sitting room window with an attention to detail that would have impressed the Special Operations Executive. There appeared to be some movement inside but the sheen on the windows made it difficult to determine the size, shape and number of bodies involved. Darn it, why did Mrs Darby have to go and clean the windows today? Why did she like cleaning so much?

Rose looked at her watch. It was nearly tea-time. She was going to be late bringing tea up to her mother. Not that tea was going to consist of much: bread and dripping. Not that her mother would care: she'd stopped eating. Well, she didn't eat much, anyway. Well, she didn't care about tea, anyway.

'I think we're gonna have to chance it, sugar. When I give the word, we run for it. In through the front door and straight up the stairs without stopping. Don't even stop for my mother.'

'That would be impolite,' said Rose.

'Well, if you insist on stopping to say howdy, get over the chicken wire first, then you're safe.'

'What chicken wire?'

'Mrs Darby put chicken wire across the foot of the stairs to stop Ferret and Badger helping themselves to the bedrooms whenever they feel like it. They scribbled all over my bedroom walls with my green colouring pencil. They didn't even care. They can't even draw.' (Dottie was an excellent artist.)

'Terrible,' said Rose, with an eyeroll.

'Sure was. They didn't even have to clean it off; I did.'

Rose said nothing, so Dottie returned to the task at hand: Operation Twin Evasion. 'Ready?' she said.

Rose sighed, then nodded.

'Run for it, sugar,' shouted Dottie, abandoning stealth and launching herself at the garden path.

Rose stepped in front of the gate and watched Dottie go splat on the gravel. Then she watched Juniper toddle to the window and point at Dottie. 'Juniper's pointing at you,' she said.

'Darn it,' said Dottie, sitting up.

'You've torn a hole in your skirt,' noticed Rose.

'That's the least of my troubles,' said Dottie, picking a stone out of her knee; she used her skirt to mop the blood that trickled down her shin. 'We'll never get past those two now.'

Rose offered her a hand. Dottie took it. Rose pulled her up, wrenching her shoulder in the process, and watched her hobble to the front door. Juniper and Jinny were guarding the other side.

'Dottie,' squealed Juniper.

'Doddie,' echoed Jinny.

Both girls employed a gesture that was designed to be misconstrued as friendly: they threw open their wingspans as wide as possible.

'Don't fall for it,' warned Dottie. 'Do not even think about picking them up.'

'I wasn't going to. Hello, Juniper. Hello, Jinny,' said Rose, massaging her shoulder.

The twins scowled. Remembering that you should never look a mad dog in the eye, let alone two, Rose looked elsewhere. She looked in the direction of the kitchen hoping to see Mrs Darby.

'Not now, Ferret. Not now, Badger,' said Dottie, adopting a sidestepping motion as she headed to the stairs. 'Tell them the same, Rose,' she whispered.

'I'm not calling them by those silly names,' said Rose flatly, although she did adopt the sidestep.

But it was a pointless exercise because without further ado, Juniper let loose.

'Ouch,' shrieked Dottie, as Juniper seized her ankle.

Rose froze.

'Marmee,' Dottie shouted. 'Marmee, Juniper's biting me again.'

'Is that you, Dottie?' called Mrs Latymer from somewhere too far away for Rose's liking.

Then Jinny wrapped herself around Dottie's bad leg like a too tight compression bandage. 'Darn it, Badger's joining in now. Marmee, help. Marmee, the twins are attacking me again. They're killing me. HELP...ME.'

Slowly and carefully so as not to draw attention to her actions, Rose stepped over the chicken wire and landed on the third stair. Now that she had reached the safety zone, Dottie's predicament was funny. She began to laugh. She laughed so hard she had to hang on to the baluster.

'This isn't funny,' complained Dottie. 'Why don't you try being me for a minute, huh?'

Rose went back to being herself and immediately stopped laughing.

'Marmee,' screamed Dottie.

At last, Mrs Latymer appeared.

As you may have imagined, Mrs Latymer was a glamorous woman. Indeed, so at variance was she with any other woman Rose had ever seen that she was frequently compelled to marvel at the woman in her diary.

Saturday 15th February

Mrs Latymer never, ever, wears a housecoat or a cardie. When I'm older, I'm going to be just like her. Things I will need to do to be like Mrs Latymer:

1. Favour red lipstick
2. Paint my nails red
3. Smoke menthol cigarettes
4. Use a cigarette holder
5. Wear Fur
6. Never wear Slippers
7. Wear high-heeled shoes in the house
8. Walk on tiled floors
9. Wear a party dress in the day
   a) Grow my hair long
   b) Have it set more than once a week at the hairdressers
10. Smell nice
11. Grow tall.
12. Never get in a flap.

'Juniper and Jinny Monroe, what in the Sam Hill do you think you are doing to poor ole Dottie?' said Mrs Latymer with well-rehearsed horror.

Juniper (the chief instigator) employed, with miraculous rapidity it has to be noted, an ever-increasing wail as her defensive response to Mrs Latymer's rebuke, while Jinny (the accomplice) covered Dottie's shoe in drool and pointed at it as if it had nothing whatsoever to do with her salivary glands.

'Only animals bite,' said Mrs Latymer, 'and animals, as we all know, belong outside where they can do no harm to the furniture, or human flesh,' she added, taking a hand of each twin. Jinny did not like to be tethered thus and so joined the wailing club. 'Mrs Darby, are you there? Why, hello, Rose.'

'Hello, Mrs Latymer.'

'How is your mother?'

For the record, Mrs Latymer had yet to meet Mrs Clarke. (Same went for Dottie because Rose kept her on the doorstep, without exception.)

'Mudda,' wailed Jinny.

'Very good, Jinny,' said Mrs Latymer. 'Although not strictly true.'

'My mother is very well, thank you, Mrs Latymer.'

'I'm very glad to hear it, honey. Please give her my regards, won't you?'

'I will, thank you, Mrs Latymer.'

'Mrs Darby.'

'Yes, Mrs Latymer, what can I do you for?' Mrs Darby appeared in the hallway armed with her version of the sleeve gun: a loo brush. However, this resourceful move was somewhat undermined by the trepidatious character of her face. Therefore, as a **Method of Irregular Warfare**, the wielding of the loo brush did little to **Undermine the enemy's morale and that of his collaborators** (as per the aims of the Special Operations Executive). 'Look at my shoe,' whined Dottie. Her sock was fast becoming a secondary casualty of Jinny's impressive excretion.

Mrs Latymer glanced at it. 'I think we can agree that your shoe has been subjected to a lot worse, sweet cheeks.' (I can only presume she was referring to the dog mess incident at the den.)

'Mrs Darby, would you be so kind as to take the girls into the garden please. Girls, if you don't figure out this biting business any time soon, I'm gonna have to ask the handyman to build you both a kennel. Now what do you say to that?'

The twins said nothing, largely because they lacked the vocabulary. Mrs Darby also said nothing even though the handyman had died the previous year when an ill-constructed medieval wall fell on top of him.

'Would you like to live in the garden, Juniper?'

Juniper nodded through her tears.

'How about you, Jinny?'

Jinny nodded through her tears.

'It can be arranged, believe me,' said Mrs Latymer.

Rose wasn't sure if Mrs Latymer was serious — perhaps this was how they dealt with naughty children in America — but at least it was spring and the nights were getting warmer.

Mrs Latymer released the girls and Mrs Darby shooed them away from the scene of their feral crimes into the immaculate rear garden with the promise that the little blighters could bite the trees therein till the cows came home.

'Phew,' said Dottie. 'That was close.'

Without a ladder to assist them, getting into the attic involved a bit of derring-do and a hint of gymnastic ability as Dottie and Rose climbed, balanced and heaved their way up to, and then through, the narrow hatch. Rose had never been in an attic before. She anticipated treasures. Stuff they could use in the den. She was disappointed. The attic harboured just one wooden box. And that box was full of bosoms. Here I must interpolate: the bosoms were made of pigeon feed. Essentially what Dottie and Rose held in their hands were pouches fashioned from silk that had been filled with pigeon feed and then neatly sewn closed. The bosoms (there were several sets) varied in cup size (and yes, I am feeling rather awkward about narrating this).

'This pair are Edmund's favourites,' said Dottie, holding the largest pair aloft like prizes.

Rose screwed up her face. Dottie stuffed them down her blouse. 'Look at me,' she said, wiggling and jiggling them.

Rose refused.

'Edmund says the landlady must have had small bosoms and probably needed bigger ones. To fit a dress or something. Edmund says that if I end up with small bosoms, I'm gonna have to do the same.'

So far, Rose had no bosoms. Like her mother. Although her mother's bosoms looked like drained waterskins (the water receptacle favoured by Robin Hood and his merry men way back when). And in case you are wondering how Rose came to be in possession of such intimate knowledge about her mother, it was now her job to keep her mother clean, as well as the clothes. But Edmund be damned. Even if her bosoms didn't grow another millimetre, Rose was not going to bother with false ones. The entire endeavour was a waste of silk, for one thing.

'The tricky thing about using pigeon feed as a bosom,' went on Dottie, 'is that the little bits of wheat can be a bit sharp. Have a feel,' she said, removing a bosom from her blouse.

Rose declined the invitation.

'They poke through the silk and dig right into your nip…'

'Don't say it, Dottie Latymer. Don't you dare say any more about it. Let's collect the pigeon feed and go.'

The Need Is Great, The Time Is Short, Urgency Must Be The Watch Word.

'Alright, sugar, keep your bosoms on,' laughed Dottie.

Rose rolled her eyes and slumped against the eaves.

'Do you think Kenneth's gonna need every bosom?'

'Please, Dottie, just get on with it. I have to go home soon.'

Dottie whipped off her skirt and turned it into a haversack, careful to ensure the newly created hole (the one she made when she fell over) was at the gathered end. Without a skirt, she looked even more peculiar in the bumfreezer, but one can't fault the innovation. Next, and I can't help but think the twins may have proved useful here, she set about undoing the stitching of each bosom with her teeth. Once each bosom had been released of its filling, Kenneth's daily bread amounted to quite a decent hoard.

11.

Attention

Any person or persons engaged in any act of sabotage against *Allemagne* will receive *la peine de mort.*

Any person or persons found in possession of *une pigeon voyageur ou non domestique pigeon* will receive *la peine de mort.*

Any person or persons found removing this poster from whence it was placed will receive *la peine de mort.*

Par ordre deGeneralfeldmarschall von Essen

12.

Interviewer: So, just to ensure I've understood all that you've said correctly, Konstantin, following the deaths of the three French boys, you say a photograph was taken of them still hanging from the tree?

Informant: (PAUSE) Yes, Mr Saunders.

Interviewer: By whom?

Informant: By my father's official photographer.

Interviewer: What is his name?

Informant: Her name is Madame Blandine Brugière.

Interviewer: She is French?

Informant: Yes.

Interviewer: Was Madame Brugière forced to act as your father's official photographer against her will?

Informant: No.

Interviewer: So, she is a collaborator?

Informant: Yes.

Interviewer: Is she still alive?

Informant: I'm afraid I do not know the answer to this question.

Interviewer: Was she still alive when you were rescued?

Informant: I am sorry, Mr Saunders, but I do not know about this. I did not see her at this time.

Interviewer: We'll come back to Madame Brugière shortly. But for now, on whose instruction did Madame Brugière take this photograph?

Informant: (PAUSE) My father's instruction.

Interviewer: For what reason did your father make this request?

Informant: (COUGH) He wanted to use the photograph to make a... poster.

Interviewer: A poster?

Informant: Have I selected the correct word? A poster? A picture...with words.

Interviewer: Yes, Konstantin, a poster is the correct word for what you describe. This poster, was it made for the purpose of propaganda? Do you understand the word *propaganda?*

Informant: Yes, Mr Saunders, but the poster was made to serve as a warning.

Interviewer: Go on.

Informant: My father wanted to warn the French people in his...er...his...er, Zuständigkeit. Er..his...

Interviewer: Jurisdiction?

Informant (cont): (PAUSE) Yes, Mr Saunders, his *jurisdiction.* That is the correct translation.

Guardian: Well, well, well, you're a dark horse, Mr Saunders. You never let on you spoke, you know, Konstantin's language. (PAUSE) (WHISPERS) German.

Interviewer: (CLEARS THROAT) It was just a lucky guess, Mrs Bloomfield, nothing more.

Guardian: Is that so? Well in that case, well done you! I wouldn't have guessed that word, Mr Saunders, not for all the tea in China. (CHUCKLE)

Interviewer: Thank you, Mrs Bloomfield. Do continue, Konstantin.

Informant: My father wished to warn the people in his *jurisdiction* that it was forbidden to engage in acts of sabotage against Germany, and also to be in possession of a pigeon.

Interviewer: Just to be clear on this, Konstantin, any pigeon?

Informant: Yes, Mr Saunders.

Interviewer: Even undomesticated pigeons? That is, pigeons that are not trained to carry messages?

Informant: Yes, Mr Saunders.

Interviewer: And where were these posters put up?

Informant: Everywhere.

Interviewer: And the punishment for anyone found taking down these posters was also death?

Guardian: That can't be right, lovey?

Informant: (PAUSE) (COUGH) (LABOURED BREATHING)

Guardian: Oh gawd, here he goes again with this asmatiker business. It's got something to do with this room, Mr Saunders, I'm telling you now. It only ever happens when we're stuck in here, doesn't it, lovey? Maybe he's allergic, you know, to something in this room?

Informant: I will take a sip of water, Mrs Bloomfield.

Guardian: You get it down you, lovey, don't be shy. That's the way. How about one of these? (RUSTLE OF PAPER)

Informant: (PAUSE) Thank you, Mrs Bloomfield.

Guardian (cont): That's it, lovey, suck on that. You can't beat a lemon sherbet in my book. I might as well have one as well; I don't much like being in here myself. Gives me a dry mouth an all. No point offering you one, Mr Saunders, I can tell.

Interviewer: Well, I...

(SUCKING OF SWEETS?)

Interviewer (cont): (CLEARS THROAT) (PAUSE) Perhaps...

(SUCKING OF SWEETS. VERY LOUD)

Interviewer (cont): Perhaps we ought to pause for a cup of tea. Would you like some tea, Mrs Bloomfield?

Guardian: Bless you for asking, Mr Saunders; I wouldn't usually like to interrupt your interview, but a cup of tea would go down a treat at the present time.

Interviewer: Of course. Hesketh?

(DOOR OPENS, HESKETH WALKS INTO THE INTERVIEW ROOM)

Hesketh: Sir?

Interviewer: Tea for Mrs Bloomfield please.

Guardian: Excuse my grumbling tummy, Mr Saunders. Must be the lemon sherbet that's set if off.

Interviewer: And the addition of some biscuits perhaps, Mrs Bloomfield?

Guardian: Oh, go on then, Mr Saunders, if you insist.

Interviewer: It seems I must. Biscuits too, Hesketh. Whatever you can lay your hands on, but do please spare us the carrot cookies.

Hesketh: Yes, sir. Right away, sir.

Guardian: (CHUCKLE) Don't you like carrots, Mr Saunders?

Interviewer: INAUDIBLE

Guardian: Ever so good for your eyes. It's the only vegetable Mr Bloomfield will eat. Apart from a potato. Nothing wrong with his eyesight. Not like me.

(DOOR SHUTS, HESKETH LEAVES THE INTERVIEW ROOM)

Guardian: I'm as a blind as a...

Interviewer (cont): Where were we?

Guardian: Oh, don't ask me, Mr Saunders. Asking me a question like that is a waste of your time. Especially when I'm knitting. See, I have to concentrate when I'm matching up the cast-on and cast-off edges. I can't concentrate on what you're saying as well when I'm doing that. It's all very well that poster saying, *Remember Pearl Harbor, Purl Harder* but knitting doesn't come easy to all us ladies that knit, Mr Saunders, I can promise you that. It's a skill and it takes a lot of practice and a lot of concentrating on, especially when you're doing a knitted turban. Does your wife knit? Perhaps you're not married? I wouldn't know. Are you?

Interviewer: INAUDIBLE

Guardian: (TUTS) Yes, well...

Interviewer: Ah, I remember where we were, Mrs Bloomfield, please don't trouble yourself. As far as you know, Konstantin, did anybody take down one of these posters.

Informant: (PAUSE) I'm afraid I do not know the answer to this question, Mr Saunders.

Guardian: It's alright, lovey, you can't be expected to know everything; isn't that right, Mr Saunders?

Interviewer: INAUDIBLE

Guardian: Hmm. (PAUSE) Nobody knows everything, lovey. And even if they do, you can take it from me that nobody *likes* a know-it-all, do they, Mr Saunders?

Interviewer: INAUDIBLE

Guardian: (TUTS) If you say so, Mr Saunders.

Informant: I must apologise...

Guardian: (LONG SIGH) It's probably not that important, lovey, so I shouldn't fret if I were you.

Interviewer: Perhaps we should press on. Konstantin, what happened to the bodies of the boys?

Guardian: (MUMBLED) Dear oh dear he's like a dog with a bone, this one.

Informant: (CLEARS THROAT) (CHAIR SCRAPES) Nothing happened to them, Mr Saunders, they remained in the tree.

Interviewer: On your father's instruction?

Informant: Yes.

Interviewer: For how long?

Informant: For seventeen days.

Guardian: Oh, my sainted aunts.

Interviewer: As a warning to others presumably?

Informant: Yes, that is correct.

Interviewer: And you do not know the identities of any of these boys?

Guardian: Konstantin already said he didn't know the names of the boys when you asked him the last time, Mr Saunders. Don't you remember? I don't know, you're just like Mr Bloomfield you are; he's got a memory like a sieve an all. Can see for miles, but can't remember a thing.

Interviewer: I'm very sorry if this is difficult for you, Konstantin, but we must gather as much information as possible. You do understand?

Informant: Yes, Mr Saunders.

Interviewer: Let's talk about another time.

Guardian (MUMBLED): Thank Gawd for that.

Interviewer: In your own words, Konstantin...(PAUSE) Please tell me what happened immediately after the boys were hanged.

Guardian: Oh, I do wish you wouldn't keep saying that, Mr Saunders, really I do. Those poor boys. Those poor, poor, boys. Oh, I could weep. (BLOWS NOSE)

(SILENCE)

Interviewer: In your own words, Konstantin...immediately after (CLEARS THROAT) afterwards.

Informant: You would like me to tell you about how I came to find Kenneth?

Interviewer: If you found Kenneth immediately after the boys were ... then, yes.

Guardian: Oh, I do like the name Kenneth; although Kenny sounds better to my mind.

Informant: Yes, Mrs Bloomfield, I also think Kenny is a good name, but it is not my place to shorten Kenneth's name to Kenny.

Guardian: (CHUCKLE) Oh, you are a funny boy, lovey. Not your place. Whose place is it then?

Interviewer: That information is classified I'm afraid, Mrs Bloomfield.

Guardian: Is it now? (TUTS REPEATEDLY) Well I think Konstantin has every right to call that pigeon whatever he likes, all he's done for this country.

Informant: Please do not be alarmed, Mrs Bloomfield. I am quite content with the name Kenneth.

Guardian: All this fuss over a bloomin pigeon. By the way, Mr Saunders, I think your Hesketh must have gone all the way to India for the tea. (PAUSE) Don't you think, Mr Saunders?

Interviewer: INAUDIBLE

Guardian: Let's hope I don't die of thirst in the meantime, then, if that's all you've got to say on the matter.

Interviewer: (DEEP BREATH) I believe you found *Kenneth* as you made your way back to Château des Beaux Anges.

Informant: Yes, Mr Saunders. Dusk was descending when I found him. This was because I had spent the afternoon sitting behind the tree from which I witnessed... INAUDIBLE I was concerned that if I did not return to the château soon, my father would send someone to look for me. I did not wish to anger my father... (PAUSE) I did not want to meet one of his men at that time. I just wanted to go back to my room for a while. I was... INAUDIBLE Kenneth was laying in an assembly of nettles next to the small track that I was walking upon. He was not moving. To begin with, I thought he was dead. I saw the message container (PAUSE) glued? Glued to his leg. At first, I did not know his nationality. I decided to retrieve his message container. When I picked him up, he felt warm. I knew then that I had been mistaken about his dying. I turned him over and saw that he was injured. His chest was torn. The wound was large. It must have been caused by a falcon. My father sometimes employed a falconer to send Peregrines sky...borne to kill your pigeons. Kenneth was most fortunate; a pigeon does not usually escape such an attack with his life. He was weak when I found him. He did not move in my hands. I placed him inside my vest and buttoned my jacket so that he would not be seen by my father, or his men. I expected Kenneth to die before I got back to my room. I was relieved when I discovered that this did not happen. I cleaned Kenneth's wound, then sewed it up. My mother taught me to sew as it was a requirement of the (PAUSE) Hitler Youth. She is... (VOICE WAVERS) very good at this type of activity. (PAUSE) But I had not sewn a wound before. I had to sew twenty-two stiches in Kenneth. I was not sure that it would be successful because his skin was very narrow. Thin. Like paper. I was very pleased that it was successful. Then Kenneth required food. I took food from the falconer. Without his permission. After five weeks, Kenneth was recovered. He had only a faint scar. I waited to a time when I knew the falconer was not with his birds. Then I took Kenneth back to the place where I found him. I released him into the sky and watched him fly away.

Interviewer: This was a very dangerous thing to do, Konstantin.

Informant: (CLEARS THROAT) Yes.

Interviewer: Had you been discovered you may also have been sentenced to death.

Informant: (NO ANSWER)

Interviewer: (PAUSE) Where did you hide Kenneth while he was recovering?

Informant: Mostly inside my jacket. I am greatly ashamed to say that I took a... I am sorry, but I do not know what you call them? May I consult my dictionary, or perhaps you will be able to translate from the German?

Interviewer: Oh, no, Konstantin, it is highly unlikely that I will be able to do that, given that I don't speak German. Please proceed with the assistance of your dictionary.

Informant: Thank you, Mr Saunders. My mother calls them a Büstenhalter. (PAGES FLICKED) Büstenhalter... Büstenhalter... Ah, here it is: Büstenhalter...A brassiere. Do you know this word, Mr Saunders?

Interviewer: (CLEARS THROAT) I am familiar with the word, yes, Konstantin.

Informant: Women's underwear to hold the...

Interviewer: Yes, I believe so.

Informant: Have I said it correctly?

Interviewer: (PAUSE) As far as I know, your pronunciation is flawless, Konstantin.

Informant: Thank you, Mr Saunders. I will remember this word from now on. I took a brassiere from Madame Brugière. It was drying on the washing line. I did not go into her room to take it. She had many such brassieres on this line. Fortunately, just one of the... (PAGES FLICKED) cups... yes, one of the cups of the brassiere was large enough for Kenneth to sleep inside. I wore it across my body er...like a sling, over my vest but beneath my shirt and jacket. This enabled Kenneth to remain a secret. To remain safe. At night, I made a secret of him on a ledge in the chimney breast in my bedroom. The chimney was not in use. Once my father retired for the night, I permitted Kenneth to fly around my room to grow his strength. During this time, I built Kenneth a cage. Once he was well, I took Kenneth into the forest and kept him in the cage until I was ready to send him back to Britain with my message.

Interviewer: Was Kenneth carrying a message when you found him?

Informant: Yes, Mr Saunders, but it was not a message I could read.

Interviewer: Why not?

Informant: Because it was a cryptogram that I could not decode.

Interviewer: Cryptogram. That is an impressive word, Konstantin.

Informant: (LONG PAUSE) Thank you, Mr Saunders.

Interviewer: How do you know this word?

(PAUSE)

Informant: (DROPS A BOOK) (PICKS UP BOOK) I'm afraid I cannot say how I know this word. I just know it.

Interviewer: What did this cryptogram look like?

Informant: It consisted of many letters and numbers. Jumbled up. Letters, then numbers, then letters. I did not understand it.

Interviewer: How many pieces of paper contained this cipher. I take it you know the meaning of the word 'cipher'?

Informant: (PAUSE) Just one side of one piece of paper. Four other pieces of paper did not have anything written on them.
Interviewer: What did you do with this message?
Informant: I ate it.
Interviewer: You ate it?
Informant: Yes, Mr Saunders, because the paper was made from rice.
Interviewer: How did you know that?
Informant: I have seen rice paper before.
Interviewer: You have seen intercepted messages before?
Informant: No, Mr Saunders, I have seen rice paper before. And I have eaten it before. My mother (PAUSE) (VOICE WAVERS) uses rice paper to make Lebkuchen at Christmas. I like to peel the rice paper from the bottom of the biscuit and eat it last.
Interviewer: Why did you not give this message to your father?
Informant: Because...
Guardian: (VERY LOUD SNORING)
Informant (cont): Mrs Bloomfield has fallen asleep, Mr Saunders.
Interviewer: So she has, Konstantin; she must not have had a good night's sleep. It did occur to me earlier that Mrs Bloomfield might have got out of her bed the wrong side this morning.
Informant: I am very sorry but I do not understand your observation about Mrs Bloomfield exiting her bed.
Interviewer: Please don't trouble yourself, Konstantin.
Informant: Shouldn't we wake her, Mr Saunders?
Interviewer: Wake her? Certainly not; wake not the sleeping lion, that's what they advise. Now, where were we?

An Unnarrated Event
Ethel's Revenge

Lady Darrick-Sinclair sits at her dressing table, and considers writing a letter to her husband, Brigadier Sinclair. But as with Ethel, she doesn't know where in the world he is, and it matters. The difference between knowing where he is and what he is doing and not knowing this information plays out as follows: far away from home husband waits in a waterlogged trench with his men, trench is shelled by the bloody Hun, great chunks of her husband take to the sky and land in the trees. Also, she doesn't want to tell him about Ethel: the favoured child. Having written the D of Darling, she gives up on the letter, snaps up her diary and begins work on a flip-book cartoon. In the bottom right hand corner of the first page, she draws a small silhouette of Ethel. The cartoon on the next page is a slight variation of the same and so it continues until Ethel has had enough of standing around doing nothing and decides to **Back The Great Attack**: off he flies to Hitler, lands on Hitler's head and does, what many consider to be lucky, all over Hitler's balding pate. Hence forward, whenever Lady Darrick-Sinclair feels the loss of Ethel, Ethel is permitted to defecate on Hitler as many times as Lady Darrick-Sinclair pleases.

13.

Mrs Clarke's boudoir was a drab affair. No embellishments. No knick-knacks. No photographs. Not even of Lance Corporal Clarke and Mrs Clarke on their wedding day. Or of Rose as a baby. No cosmetics on the dressing table. No dressing table. The walls were papered brown in the twenties and now looked like dirty great squares of contorted fly paper. The two single beds were each missing an eiderdown and clean sheets, and the curtains were flagging. A plastic carpet runner ran over the wooden floorboards at the foot of the bed, though why it was there, instead of being on an actual carpet, Rose couldn't say. The blood-stained floorboards she did know about. She hadn't been able to scrub the blood away; it sort of leached into the varnish and remained, stubborn, vivid in the daylight, like a salmon patch birthmark. Like the one Rose had on her forehead that was invigorated by anger or distress. None of it was discussed. Mrs Clarke had recently stopped talking. Not deliberately of course. The tunnels that were supposed to carry the words from her brain to her mouth had collapsed. Her tongue had grown heavy with inaction. The words remained trapped in her brain. Space there was limited. They crashed and bumped into one another. They made her head ache. She tried to free them another way. But the method made a mess of the floor. It was best not to think of any new words. Prevention rather than cure. If she could help it.

Rose took her diary into her parents' bedroom and clambered into her mother's bed. Mrs Clarke was lying on her side, hugging the edge, face to the curtains, back to Rose. The soft mattress bobbed up and down like a boat. She closed her eyes and held her breath. The bobbing stopped. She breathed out. Rose pulled the blanket over her mother's shoulders because she'd seen enough of the bones in her back. They made her think of strays. Of dogs that preyed on rubbish left in the streets. Of dogs that were kicked by people that didn't think themselves vicious, or cruel, or uncharitable. A new bone had appeared on the top of Mrs Clarke's shoulder, between baths it seemed; it looked like a switch that might turn something off or turn something on. But on, or off? Rose didn't know the answer. She stroked her mother's hair; the next gesture in the incremental role reversal that had been kick-started a few years before by Mr Clarke and his hobnailed boot.

'I'm going to keep you company,' said Rose. 'Is that alright, Mother?'

Mrs Clarke hadn't thought of suffocation as an option for the fortune teller but it occurred to her now that this was something she could do, here, quietly, without a fuss; she held on to her breath. It seemed a simple thing.

'I have some writing to do,' said Rose. 'But I'll be quiet. I won't disturb you, I promise.'

The breath died, but Mrs Clarke didn't. The greed with which her lungs drew in the room's stale air was a betrayal that disgusted her.

Rose had so much to tell her diary. Indeed, it was plausible that this might be the longest diary entry she had ever written. She'd found a pigeon. A pigeon carrying a letter from a French boy named Gilbert Aumont. A letter that had come all the way from France. She'd never been outside of Surrey. France was a faraway land, a dangerous country where people were murdered by the Germans in places with exotic names: Amiens; Château des Beaux Anges; Pas-de-Calais and Notre-Dame d'Amiens. As she prepared the tea, she'd tested these names on her tongue. Rolled them around her mouth like a boiled sweet. She made them sound like they belonged in England: *Pasty-Caliss*. But she'd felt desperately sorry for that lady agent Bettina Agnes Rutter, especially after she and Dottie had read the word 'guillotine.' 'The Germans chopped her head off?' spluttered Dottie, when Rose, who had been reading Gilbert's message aloud, reached that event.

'Yes,' said Rose.

'Like Henry the Eighth did to Anne Boleyn?'

'Yes, except I think he used an axe rather than a guillotine, but I don't suppose it matters. I don't think Henry did the chopping himself.'

'But I mean, chopping off somebody's head just for parachuting into a field?'

'Yes.'

'But it's not even their field. It's a French field. It belongs to the French, not the Germans.' (Now and again, Dottie could be quite astute.)

'I know, Dottie.'

'Jeepers. You know what, I really don't like the sound of this General Fed Marshall guy.'

'No,' agreed Rose, 'but can I finish reading now?'

'Sure,' said Dottie, 'go ahead.'

'*Anyone found sheltering your agents, and all those that live in that house…*'

'Do you think Gilbert's making this stuff up?'

'Why would he make it up? Why would he send us a pigeon with a suitcase and a made-up story inside?' asked Rose.

Dottie shrugged.

'No more interruptions,' warned Rose, 'or I won't read anymore.'

(Dottie was more than capable of reading Gilbert's note for herself, and this was a fact Dottie had considered telling Rose, but she preferred to get on with smoking her pipe.)

They didn't understand half of what Gilbert had written. Why were the children going with the Jews to Poland? What was happening in Poland? Who was going to look after these children and these Jews once they got there? And to be hanged or shot on the spot for holding a pigeon. 'What sort of hokum is that?' said Dottie. 'We'd both be dead by now. I sure am glad we're not in France.'

'But Gilbert is,' said Rose.

'I wonder what he looks like,' said Dottie.

Rose wondered what was wrong with his mother. *I am an ordinary boy and I just want to go home, and to see my mother who is very ill and may not live for much longer.* 'What does it matter what he looks like?'

'He might have told us a little more about himself, is all. Like how old he is for a start?'

Rose shrugged.

'And where he lives? You know, his real home, not this *Chateoo* place. Why doesn't he live with his mother?'

'Juniper and Jinny don't live with their mother.'

'Worse luck.'

'Maybe he doesn't live with his mother because she's very ill, too ill to have her son around,' said Rose, and then wondered if that might happen to her. How ill did a mother have to be before the child was taken away? And if Gilbert wasn't with his mother, and Mr Aumont was away somewhere else in France fighting the Germans, who was looking after Mrs Aumont? She wondered if she would describe her own mother as *very ill* in a note to a stranger. Was her mother to be considered very ill? She didn't have a cough, or a temperature. She never complained of being in any pain. She didn't take any medicine. The doctor never called round to see her.

'But most of all, Gilbert could have at least told us Kenneth's name, instead of all this boring stuff about an ammunition dump and a radio jammer.'

'You've given him a name.'

'Yes, but Gilbert's probably given him a name too. Kenneth probably has two names. It's gonna confuse the hell outta him.'

'I don't think he'll notice.'

'Are you serious? Imagine having two names.'

'I have two names: Rose and Clarke. I'm not confused.'

'You know what I mean,' she said, batting the comment away with the bowl of her pipe.

'I also have a middle name: Loveday. Still not confused. I wouldn't be surprised if you have more than three names.'

Dottie had more names than the average aristocrat so she decided to drop it and get on with using the long stem of her pipe as a back scratcher – something that proved to be very effective. 'I like the bit about the invasion though; it'll be real good if Gilbert can find the best place for that, won't it? I'll bet it'll make everyone so happy.'

'Hmm,' said Rose, frowning.

'Gilbert's daddy will return home. Hey, your daddy will return home.'

'I have to go,' said Rose.

'Already?'

'I told you ages ago that I had to go soon.'

'If we can do what Gilbert asks and get this war over with, do you think Gilbert will let me keep Kenneth?'

'I don't know,' said Rose. 'I'm going.'

And that's the problem, wrote Rose in her diary, I don't want this war to finish very soon because I don't want Father to come home. 'I don't know what to do about it, Mother,' she sighed.

Mrs Clarke's pale eye lids fluttered open and shut like the wings of a butterfly; she'd been reaching for sleep, it had been within her grasp, but now two words were holding it back: *About what?* She spun the words into a rhythm about-what about-what about-what until they soothed and lulled the grey matter like the bounce and sway of a long train ride.

Rose wrote on.

And what are we supposed to do with Gilbert's note? This is also a problem that Dottie has not given one iota of thought. (All she's worried about is what we should write back. She hasn't once thought about how we would get a letter to Gilbert without his address. She never thinks things through. That's her problem.) If we take Gilbert's note to the police station, we'll have to say how we found it and then we'll get into trouble for opening a suitcase that doesn't belong to us. They might say we stole it? I don't care what Dottie says, Mr Latymer won't be able to fix that. He can't tell the police what to do. Nobody can. Then the police will say that it's all my fault because I'm the oldest and should have known better. And I bet Dottie won't say a word about it. I bet she'll be quiet for once in her life-time and let me take all the blame. Then the police will come here, round to the house, to speak to Mother (I won't be able to tell them that they can't come in) and then what? They'll take me away, that's what, and put me in a home for criminal delinquents. And who will look after Mother? And what will the delinquents be like to me? I guarantee that they will be absolutely HORRID. Much worse than that ruddy Lawrence.

Problem number 1,050 (out of a possible million problems): Gilbert has asked us to send him another pigeon, but we don't have another pigeon. We only have the one we've got and he's tired. And even if he wasn't, we don't have an aeroplane so how are we going to drop him in that field Gilbert wrote about? And even if we did have an aeroplane, which is a ridiculous idea, it's not as if we know the way to France or know how to pick out one field in the whole of France. They must have thousands of fields. The truth is, we can't send him another pigeon, so he can't send us any more information, so we might as well throw Gilbert's note away and forget about it. I really am very sorry that we can't help finish the war for Gilbert and his father, but we just can't. We're not being deliberately mean about it. All things considered, it's for the best. I will tell Dottie all this tomorrow when I take the note from her.

P.S. I'll let her keep the pigeon as a consolation prize.

P.P.S. Until the pigeon feed runs out and then it will have to go.

When it came to Dottie and the pigeon, Rose was very clear: she was going to **Stand Firm!**

14.

A .-	J .---	S ...	1 .----
B -...	K -.-	T -	2 ..---
C -.-.	L .-..	U ..-	3 ...--
D -..	M --	V ...-	4 ....-
E .	N -.	W .--	5 .....
F ..-.	O ---	X -..-	6 -....
G --.	P .--.	Y -.--	7 --...
H	Q --.-	Z --..	8 ---..
I ..	R .-.		9 ----.
			0 -----

Fullstop .-.-.-
Comma --..--
Query ..--..

Message on: Operation Attar.
Message Status: Highly Confidential
Message Transmitted: 25 July 1944, 15.35 hrs
From: 1st Special Service Brigade
For: MI5/Director of Counter Espionage
Message As follows:

```
- .- .-. --. . - / ... . -.-. ..- .-.
. -.. / .-.-.- / -... --- -.-- /.. -./
.--. --- --- .-. / .... . .- .-.. - ....
/ .-.-.- / ..-. .- - .... . .-./-. ---
- / ..-. --- ..- -. -../ .-.-.- / - .-.
.- ...- . .-.. .-.. .. -. --. / - ---
/ -... .-.. .. --. .... - -.-- /.-- ..
- .... / -... .-.. --- --- -- ..-. .. .
.-.. -.. / .-.-.- / ...- / ..-. --- .-. / ...-
.. -.-. - --- .-. -.-- / .-.-.- message
end
```

15.

Dottie had a future in forgery. No doubt in my mind. She forged A.J.P Taylor's unique hand with aplomb when she addressed the envelope to Mr Latymer at his PO Box address. Or, if not in forgery, then a future in design, certainly: the insignia she drew on the back of the envelope comprising a rose surrounded by a circle of dots (drawn in lead pencil because she forgot to bring her colouring pencils to the den) was simply charming, not to mention clever: a cryptographic signature that only she and Rose would ever be able to recognise. Historically, Dottie had been unfairly judged by many to be the match that was unlikely to light the oven, but her approach to ensuring Gilbert's note reached an important person, a person she trusted would know where to send the note on, was nothing short of ingenious. She'd taken the initiative and was rather pleased about that. Recognising that Kenneth was bound to be ravenous after the long journey from France she had, after Rose had left the attic and gone home, hot-footed it to the den to feed him an egg-cupful of bosom. When she arrived, Kenneth was where she and Rose had left him a few hours before: tucked up in Edmund's cabinet on a bed of sand, bay leaves, gorse, stems of wild garlic and handfuls of elderflowers. Kenneth was unusually fragrant and very pleased to see her. When she threw the cabinet door wide (it had been left ajar to allow for adequate ventilation) his eyes didn't just open in alarm as one might expect, they winked at her, a gesture that had nothing to do with the fact that she was accidentally shining the torch in his eyes. She plucked him from the cabinet, perched on her crate, and settled him in her lap (she was now wearing an antique pair of itchy gold, raspberry and turquoise pantaloons from the dressing-up box, via Casablanca). She reattached the suitcase to his leg because she thought he might be feeling naked without it, kissed him, stroked him, hand-fed him his supper, kissed him some more, then soothed him with a rendition of *On Top of Old Smokey*. It was as she was belting out the lines: *Not one girl in a hundred a poor boy can trust/They'll hug you and kiss you and tell you more lies/Than cross lines on a railroad or stars in the skies*, that the idea of anonymously sending Gilbert's note to her father came to her: Dottie was a girl in a hundred poor Gilbert could trust. As well as unfettered access to Rose's inscribed copy of A.J.P Taylor's monograph to assist with the forgery/masking of the sender's identity, she had her very own supply of postage stamps too.

'Finders keepers losers weepers,' dictated Latymer to Daphne.

Usually, Daphne didn't interrupt Latymer's dictations because they always came at the end of a very long day and she just wanted to get home and be free of an irritating suspender belt that, had it not been war-time, would have been slung out months before; and she didn't interrupt him on this occasion, not with words at any rate, but rather with the raising of a quizzical eyebrow. Latymer just winked at her and leaned back in his chair. Daphne's fingers returned to their posts.

```
                                    9 March, 1944
Finders keepers losers weepers. If we are to take
Gilbert Aumont's message at face value, I am inclined
to believe that Aumont has a very good reason for making
contact with us in MI5, rather than with our colleagues
in SIS. Perhaps, like us, he is somehow alive to SIS'
disdain for the use of pigeons as a means of gathering
intelligence. Whatever the reason, I am loathe to pass
Aumont's message on even though this decision may cause
quite a stink if SIS come to hear of it. That said, and
only if we must, it is better to share this message
with SIS once it has been assessed as genuine since I
am quite sure that jumping the gun is likely to do more
harm than good in this case. The overriding problem
with this message is, of course, the exact journey it
```

has taken to arrive on my desk. It raises a number of questions, principal among them a) how did Aumont's message travel from France to Britain? Aumont implies that he has used a pigeon to carry the message, but if this is the case it rather begs the question, where is the pigeon now? To bring the message to Britain under its own steam, the pigeon would have to be one of ours, but messages received via pigeon are 1. Traceable and 2. Certainly do not come to me in their raw form. I saw Binksy in MI-14(d) and queried Aumont's pigeon. We briefly discussed Operation COLUMBA and it is his deep feeling that something is seriously awry here: Binksy suspects that the Germans have captured one of our pigeons and have sent it back to us with false information. I am mindful that the pigeon apprehended by the Admiralty back in 1940 with the message concerning the Beach Hotel and the barmaid's pink drawers was not German as we first suspected. However, the military detail in this message, together with Aumont's claim that he is well placed to obtain more information of this nature bears all the hallmarks of a German attempt to deceive by pigeon. As a civilian French boy, how could Aumont possibly know the real name of an SOE agent, or have access to significant German military documents? Furthermore, a scenario in which Aumont would be in a position to overhear senior German officers discussing plans for an espionage operation in England, is difficult to imagine. In relation to the pigeon, Binksy will make enquiries with the National Pigeon Service and Air Ministry post-haste. B) why is the sender not also the originator? The address on the envelope is clearly written in a different hand to that of the message, and in my opinion the hand of an adult. C) how is Aumont acquainted with the sender? On the face of it, Aumont appears to be in contact with somebody in Britain. D) what, if anything, should be inferred from the attractive rose and dot motif hand-drawn on the seal of the envelope? I would also very much like to know how my name and address have come to be known by the sender. To this end, it would help a great deal if the General Post Office took more care when applying postal marks to correspondence: the one on the envelope is smudged and at best I can only suggest that it has been posted from a place that begins with the letter C, or possibly the letter O. Furthermore, by Aumont's own admission he is not just a boy but an ordinary one at that, yet if this is the case, how is he able to correspond in such excellent English? This message is clearly not the work of an ordinary boy. Whilst nothing would give me greater pleasure than to be told that Aumont's message is authentic, it seems more and more likely that the legitimacy of this message should be doubted. It also strikes me that this could, of course, be no more than an elaborate hoax by somebody in SIS, notionally John St-Michaels, to undermine the credibility of my department. This sort of exploit seems right up his street. To establish whether Aumont is real, I have tasked Stan Paroclett in B2 to make enquiries with Earthstar's spymaster, since Earthstar is currently operational in the Amiens region, as well as the evasion line in Europe. In relation to the military intelligence contained in the message, RAF Special Duties Section in tandem with SOE will seek by all means necessary to a) establish the identity of the German Commander installed at the Château des Beaux Anges, assuming such a place exists; b) confirm that the Germans are strengthening their defences in the Pas-de-Calais region; c) confirm the presence of a radio jammer in the vicinity of the Notre-Dame d'Amiens and the ammunition dump to the north of the city; d) make enquiries in relation to Bettina Agnes Rutter, specifically, whether she is an SOE agent, and if so, whether, as Aumont claims, she has been captured by the Germans and executed in Amiens Prison; e) the precise location of the given coordinates. Of course, if the message is deemed to have come from a bona fide agent in France, then I hope we may receive more messages of this calibre since the intelligence proffered in this instance, particularly in relation to the enemy's strengthening of defences in the Pas-de-Calais region, is precisely what we are after and may offer an exceptional opportunity to hoodwink the Germans on a monumental scale. Consequently, establishing a regular channel of communication with Aumont has the potential to be a real game-changer in the war against Germany. However, without knowing the sender's identity, this may prove impossible. In terms of meeting Aumont's request and getting another pigeon to him in the field specified, Wing Commander Delaney of 161 Squadron informs me that whilst accurately dropping pigeons in a pinpoint location is possible, it is not guaranteed. Often, it is only possible to drop a pigeon in the general vicinity. Should this message be deemed genuine, I shall show it to Churchill for he relishes intelligence of this flavour and has a particular fondness for hand-drawn maps. As insurance against a possible missed opportunity, I shall also arrange for the daily BBC broadcast to France to include a message for Aumont. In the interim, I have code-named this enquiry Operation ATTAR.

In other matters, this morning's meeting with Hibbert of Special Branch proved rather humdrum; I suspect Hibbert was a touch worse for wear since his tie was well stained with, if I were to hazard a guess, egg yolk, and his general appearance very down at heel. I wouldn't be at all surprised if he came to our meeting direct from an all-night bender.

Also, the letters found stuffed inside the ceramic head of the Pierrot doll had no real intelligence value although they did reveal that the authoress has enjoyed a number of assignations with a well-known Hollywood screenwriter widely suspected of having Communist sympathies. The FBI have been informed of this but are not likely to take any action at this time.

I am seeing Guy Burgess and Anthony Blunt tomorrow to discuss the en clair telegram from the managing director of the Williams Jones and Brown group regarding his intention to show Vickers round the factory.

Franklin Aleshire was condemned to death this afternoon for treachery and will be executed next month at Pentonville.

The ticking off Dottie received from Rose for sending Gilbert's note to her father, albeit anonymously, far exceeded anything I am capable of imagining, let alone narrating. Rose was not interested in the rose and dot design, or the quality of the A.J.P Taylor handwriting forgery, or the fact that in sending Gilbert's note on, Dottie was singlehandedly doing both their bit for the war effort. And by God did Rose want her book back. That Dottie took it without her permission was unforgivable. It almost deserved a slap. But not quite. Fortunately. Dottie was spoiled. She had lots of things. She just had to ask for something and her parents got it for her. Take the cornflakes for example. And the postage stamps. What did Rose have? Nothing worth having, that was for sure. Except the book. (And the diary, but that was a secret.) The book was her history prize. And Dottie took it. Without her permission. And then posted Gilbert's note without checking first. Now they could expect a visit from the police. Well not Dottie, but Rose because she was bound to be forced to take the blame because she was older and her father didn't have a very important job and he wasn't a very important man. (He was just a horrible one.) They might be helping to shorten the war, but it wasn't going to help Rose. (It was only going to bring her father back home sooner rather than later and that was only going to make her mother immediately, and perhaps fatally, worse.) Rose was on the verge of hysteria. Dottie had never seen the like of it before, in anybody, except perhaps in Edmund that time when he discovered her trying on a pair of his Y-fronts (an import from America); an event that was made worse by the fact that she proceeded to poke a straightened finger through the hole in the crotch before asking what in the heck the hole was in aid of. Dottie considered squeezing out a few tears as an expression of her regret for taking the initiative, but in the end, she couldn't rally them. Besides, she didn't regret posting Gilbert's note to her father. Gilbert's daddy was in danger. Rose's daddy was probably in danger. She didn't want the daddies of her friends to die. And what's more, she didn't want the nation's evacuees to go on being kept from living with their real parents, especially those that hailed from West Dulwich. Rose stormed off to the den and warned Dottie not to follow. So, Dottie followed a safe distance behind (about ten paces if your legs are short).

Rose barrelled through the sacking door. Edmund's cabinet was wide open. There was pigeon mess on the pillow that topped her crate, but none on Dottie's pillow, she reflected sourly. She glanced inside the cabinet to shoot Kenneth a filthy look.

'Where's my baby bird?' cooed Dottie, bringing up the rear. 'Marmee's missed you.'

Rose stood aside. 'If you are referring to the pigeon, I'm afraid he's gone.'

Dottie shoved Rose further out of the way. Rose knocked over the milk bottle because Dottie had left it in the middle of the den. She tutted savagely then swapped her soiled pillow for Dottie's.

'Say it isn't true, sugar,' wailed Dottie, her head in the cabinet.

'As you can see, it's true,' said Rose, sitting on her crate.

'Oh, no,' said Dottie, turning to Rose. 'I loved Kenneth and now he's gone and left me.'

'You barely knew him,' snapped Rose, as she plucked a hair from her forearm with the tweezers.

'It doesn't matter how long you know someone for, you can still love 'em.'

Rose was extremely doubtful about this and continued plucking. 'So, the pigeon is a *someone* now?'

Dottie's eyes narrowed. 'You did this, didn't you?'

'Pardon?'

'You heard me, sugar. You got rid of Kenneth. You shooed him away?'

'I did no such thing, Dottie Latymer,' said Rose, accidentally stabbing herself with the tweezers. 'I haven't been here since the time I first found him. When I came in here just now, the door to the cabinet was wide, and I mean wide, open. Did you forget to push the door to, Dottie? After all, *you* were the last one to see him.'

It was as if the tears Dottie had tried to rally earlier had finally heard the call to arms. They flew out of her eyes with a speed that must have strained the ducts. 'No,' she said. 'No.' And then she thought about it and conceded that she might have done. 'Oh, Kenneth,' she lamented into her palms. 'What in the heck have I done?' She collapsed onto her crate, entirely unfazed by the soiled pillow. What did pigeon poo matter now? If anything, it was a memento.

Rose began to feel a teensy bit sorry for her. She patted her shoulder and said, 'There, there. It's probably for the best, Dottie. I think we might have got into a lot of trouble if we'd kept him. The police would have taken him from you in the end anyway. He's probably just flown back to his owner and that will make him happy. You want him to be happy, don't you?'

Dottie faked a nod.

'The best thing we can do,' continued Rose, 'is to forget all about the pigeon…and Gilbert, and get back to normal, don't you think?'

Dottie shrugged.

'I'll have my book back,' (she stopped herself from adding a *thank-you-very-much*) 'and you can clean the droppings from Edmund's cabinet, and it will all be like it never happened.'

'I loved him,' confessed Dottie.

'Never mind that,' said Rose, with a final pat. 'Smoke your pipe instead.'

16.

"Ici Londres! Les Français parlent aux Français.
S'il vous plaît avant de commençer écoutez-bien ces messages
personnels"
Jean-Pierre fait l'élevage porcin maintenant.
Donnez un baiser à chaque orteil/pied l'un après
l'autre. Les gaz retenus demandent d'être lâchés. Le
professeur coupera la pomme en quatre. Le sommeil
est plus doux dans le pré. On répète le soleil est plus
doux dans le pré. Je vais embrasser l'ours et toi tu
embrasseras le lion. Gilbert, nous souhaitons réunir
la famille Aumont. Ta soeur préfère la baguette avec
du beurre. Le Boulanger met des boules
Quies/bouchons d'oreille pour dormir. Ramassez les
noisettes maintenant dans des chaussettes rouges et
des gants verts. Le chaton joue avec la ficelle. Sauter
à la corde tenant l'horizon ferment à gauche/ sur
votre gauche est amusant. Joan à envied de jouer du
violoncelle aussi bien du violon. Il faut pétrir le pain
et le donner à manger aux chèvres. Permettez/ Offrez
à votre grand-père une grande tranche de cake. Le
tracteur a besoin d'un mécanicien. La trompette de
l'herbe joue trois chansons tristes.

"This is London! The French speak to the French.
Before we begin, please listen to some personal messages."
Jean-Pierre breeds pigs now. Kiss each toe in quick
succession. Trapped wind demands freedom. The
professor will quarter the apple. Sleep is sweeter in

the meadow. We say twice, sleep is sweeter in the meadow. I will kiss the bear and you will kiss the lion. Gilbert, please be advised, we wish to reunite the Aumont family. Your sister prefers her baguette buttered. The baker wears ear plugs at night. Harvest the hazelnuts now in red socks and green gloves. The kitten plays with the string. Skipping with the horizon firmly on your left is fun. Joan is keen to play the cello as well as the violin. Knead the bread and feed to the goats. Permit your grandfather a large slice of fruit cake. The tractor has need of a mechanic. The grass trumpet plays three sad songs."

An Unnarrated Event
Commando Comedian Stinker Schoolteacher

Davey rests on a shovel. He's on leave but he can't relax. He might die tomorrow, or the next day, or the day after that, and he's not going to waste his last day at home sleeping. The vegetable patch requires some attention. And teaching Konstantin the meaning of certain words and phrases has so far been worth doing. 'No, you great aris, that's not how you say it. Say it like you really mean it,' Davey insists.

'I will try, but I do not know the word aris. Please tell me what it means, Davey.'

'What am I, your bleeding schoolteacher?'

Konstantin smiles. 'If you are, you are not a very good one.'

'Listen to you; not so shy now. I think I prefer the little ▓ I found in France. Wouldn't say boo to a goose that one.'

Konstantin treats his shoes to a grave stare and repatriates the earth on his trowel with the earth he stands upon.

Davey laughs. '▓ me, I'm joshing…'

Konstantin raises his head and frowns.

'I'm just joking. Joshing. Joking. It's all the same.'

'What are you two doing out there,' calls Mrs Bloomfield from the backdoor.

'Well I don't know about him,' says Davey, nodding at Konstantin, 'but I'm about to have a smoke.'

Mrs Bloomfield is suspicious. 'What have you *been* doing?'

'*Cultivating Every Available Piece Of Land*,' he says, grinning and gesturing at the soil.

'Up to no good more like it. Has he been teaching you more rude words, lovey?'

Konstantin thinks about this, but since he doesn't know the meaning of aris he can't say no with the conviction Mrs Bloomfield will require if he's to be believed.

95

Davey answers for him, 'I was just about to teach him some cockney.'

'Gawdalbloomingmighty whatever for? We live in Kent, Davey.'

'We didn't always live in Kent, Mum.'

'What does he need to know cockney for?'

'For when he goes to the East End?'

'The East End?'

Davey does an impressive wink formation and says, 'To see the relatives.'

'Oh, yes, that,' says Mrs Bloomfield, with a clumsy wink then a frown. 'Well, nothing rude I hope,' she adds.

Davey just laughs.

'I knew it,' says Mrs Bloomfield.

'No, Mrs Bloomfield,' says Konstantin. 'Do not be alarmed…'

'Give the Mrs Bloomfield a rest, cuz. She's supposed to be your aunt,' ventriloquizes Davey.

'Do not be alarmed…Aunt,' says Konstantin.

'Jesus,' mutters Davey. 'We need to work on that accent of yours: straight out of Berlin.'

'I do not come from Berlin,' whispers Konstantin.

'Where do you come from?' asks Davey.

'*Do not be alarmed?*' scoffs Mrs Bloomfield. 'I'm sorry, lovey, but that'll be the day.

'Potsdam,' whispers Konstantin.

'Wrong answer,' says Davey, 'you come from Cumbria.'

'I told you, Davey, I won't have it. You're ruining that good boy,' says Mrs Bloomfield.

Davey reaches into his pocket for a tin of tobacco. 'See what you've done: you've got me into trouble now.'

'I am very sorry,' says Konstantin. 'I didn't mean to…'

Davey playfully punches Konstantin's arm, 'I'm joking, you daft sod.'

Konstantin attempts a smile. 'I come from Cumbria.'

'Lucky bugger,' says Davey.

'But I have many relations residing in London,' finishes Konstantin.

'Are you sh▬▬▬ me?' says Davey.

Mrs Bloomfield waits for Davey's apology. Davey doesn't know the meaning of this word. He says, 'I think the old man just called you.'

'Did he? I never heard him.'

'That's because you're Mutt and Jeff.'

'I'm not deaf, son, it's my tinnitus. What does he want?'

'I did not hear Mr Bloomfield calling for your mother,' confesses Konstantin to Davey, 'and I do not have a problem with my hearing.'

'Keep that to yourself,' advises Davey. 'There he goes again, Mum. Must be urgent.'

Mrs Bloomfield sighs, 'I better see to him.' She retreats into the kitchen shouting, 'What do you want now, Eric? Why do you always wait till I've gone downstairs and then start...'

'Aris,' says Davey. 'It means arse, cuz.'

'Arse,' nods Konstantin, and then, 'I am very sorry, Davey, but I do not know the meaning of arse... And perhaps you would also kindly tell me why I would be expected to say aris and not arse?'

17.

National Centre for Chemistry
Berlin W.35, Date 7.5.41

Sigismundstraße 5

Dr. Möller/Fischer

Confirmation
-.-
The company: Temmler-Werke, Berlin-Johannisthal
Re: Methylamphetamin. Under the trademark: Pervitin
From: The Commissioner

The pharmaceutical product, Pervitin, is certified in
accordance with the assignment given to it for war-time
use:
To lessen fatigue
To promote self-confidence
To sharpen the senses
To boost performance
To enhance motivation in combat

The decree of the Reich Ministry of Economics II Chem: 19
692/41 dated 11.4.1941 has declared that Pervitin is
decisive for the war, and is in agreement with the Supreme
Command of the Wehrmacht and the Ministry of Armaments
and Ammunition. The Minister of Labour, as well as the
chairmen of the examination commissions, have been
informed.

This measure is by the decree of the Chairman of the Reich Defence Council, Minister President Reichsmarschall Göring, and is issued in response to the urgent productivity demands of the Wehrmacht.

According to the decree of the Reich Ministry of Economics S 1/1098/41 dated 22.3.1941, the securing of the war-critical production of Pervitin is essential. Misuse of this confirmation by submitting to deliveries for products not mentioned above will be severely penalized by the Reichsmarschall.

18.

Only very recently did Joyce inform me that when I tell a story, I'm inept at painting the entire picture. I told her somebody had dropped this file when I was at death's door with influenza, and had hastily rearranged the documents without a care for their original order, but she must have forgotten. She also criticized my narrative structure, a criticism I thought grossly unfair given the circumstances I have just, once again, narrated. Naturally, Joyce understands that, in order to comply with the Official Secrets Act of 1911, it is not permissible to include every detail, as it were. However, if I were to tell Joyce that Dottie Latymer spent the war years in rented accommodation with her mother and the twin *enfants terribles* in Surrey, I can assure you that she would ask for a description of the house, its architectural origin, an inventory of the furnishings contained within, and probably the sum of the monthly rental tariff. And, if I were also to tell Joyce that a French boy was hanged from a tree during the war simply for picking up a pigeon he stumbled upon as he scoured a field for potatoes, she would want to know such details as the species of the tree (having already been warned that I could not give her the particulars of the murdered boy).

Heretofore, for me, a tree was a tree, a house was a house, and the monthly rental tariff of another's temporary lodgings was none of my concern. (Only in regard to the furnishings would I be likely to take an interest, but this would purely be on account of my pre-war study of furniture design.) But in relation to the latter occurrence and to satisfy Joyce's hypothetical desire to know the species of tree involved, I noted that the boy was hanged by *Generalfeldmarschall* Dieter von Essen that dim February afternoon of 1944 from a Norwegian Maple tree. Given that Norwegian Maple are hardly ten a penny in the borough of London in which my wife and I reside, Joyce, undoubtedly, would be impressed that I had not only been able to identify the species of tree (for I am no arborist), but that I had done so from a grainy image on a dog-eared poster. I'm not suggesting that Joyce may take credit for my powers of observation for, had we never married, I would still have noted that the boy had been hanged from a tree rather than from the rafters, a balustrade or a purpose-built scaffold, but I do take this particular example of specificity to be evidence that my powers of description may at last be evolving; this is a development for which Joyce may take credit (although I have not conceded as much to her). Suffice it to say that a tree is no longer just a tree but may well be a Norwegian Maple and what's more, as far as the specimen in this story goes, one with leaves that are clearly afflicted by Tar Spot: an unsightly bacterium that spreads through the foliage and causes young green leaves to turn brown and prematurely drop to the ground above which they once flourished.

And so it follows that the picture I am about to paint of Konstantin's life in France will, I hope, be somewhat striking in terms of its descriptive entirety; something that could not have been guaranteed prior to Joyce's unsolicited but candid denunciation of my storytelling.

By the time *Generalfeldmarschall* Dieter von Essen requistioned the Château des Beaux Anges to serve as his command centre for Operations in the North Zone, it was nearing five hundred years of age. It had long been considered the prettiest château in the region, with its slender turrets, precipitous roofs and ornamental spires. It passed through generations of the same family until it didn't, eventually falling into the hands of a wealthy Jewish industrialist whose name can now be found in the Death Books of Auschwitz.

Before the outer walls were bedizened with the usual Nazi flags and the personal Standard of the *Generalfeldmarschall*, the façade of this historic building boasted intricately carved renaissance window frames and stone dragon gargoyles that gaped open-mouthed, seemingly at the incongruous symbols of Catholic iconography they lunged beside. Many of the mullioned windows were embellished with stained glass. The glass produced kaleidoscopic rainbows of light on the panelled walls and monochromatic tiled floors. The rooms themselves had been renovated by the celebrated interior designer André Groult in the Art Deco style. They contained an eclectic mix of furniture collected over the years from various periods and decorative movements.

A spring-fed pond of considerable depth lay on the western side of the property. It had been used for swimming. It had also served as an ill-considered hiding place for a priceless collection of Imperial Chinese ceramics. To the east lay an undulating flower meadow. To the rear, a substantial ancient woodland of Norwegian Maple, Ash, Sycamore, Alder and Cherry.

Under the occupation of the *Generalfeldmarschall*, the cellar had been emptied of red wine and vintage champagne and converted into a gaol and interrogation hub. (Konstantin successfully purloined a case of the champagne and stashed it under his Louis XIV, gilded four-poster, silk-canopied bed; a bed, I wish to add, that was never intended to facilitate the slumber of a fourteen-year-old boy with a touch of athlete's foot and newly developing nocturnal enuresis.)

One of the very first things the *Generalfeldmarschall* did upon arriving at the château was to drink the plundered red wine and champagne, and to supervise the hanging of his favourite painting above his bed. This was a painting he brought to France from Germany but had originally looted in Munich from a Jewish couple fleeing the country. As his most prized possession, the still life painting of some spring flowers in a vase, went everywhere with him; a surprising fact given that the variety of flower was said to be a favourite of his wife.

The formal gardens at the front of the château had been flattened to accommodate a plethora of Wehrmacht military vehicles. Also parked here was the sleek Citroën Traction Avant that the *Generalfeldmarschall* had acquired via dubious means and the aid of his Lüger from the Departmental Councillor of Amiens. The stable block, with its wide canopy, fourteen bays and two-storey central pavilion, was turned into offices and additional bunk-bed accommodation for the *Generalfeldmarschall's* men. As if broken, the beak of the zinc rooster weathervane that stood on the roof (above the clock and stone entablature) took no account of the actual wind direction, but instead persistently signalled that some force was coming from the northwest. And this is where I must leave the description of the château, since such a rigorous consideration of its architectural structures, historical trivia and enemy repurposing has put me behind with the redaction of this file. And yet I can almost hear Joyce pleading with me to describe how the place smelled, but really all I can suggest is that, once it was occupied by the enemy, the château and its immediate surroundings no longer whiffed of jasmine, rose, and bergamot.

In quick time, Konstantin learned to do the following in France:
1. Avoid his Father.
2. Keep shtum.

Because in France, his father was different to the way Konstantin had known him in Potsdam. He was:
1. Short-tempered.
2. Fixated with vermin.

'Whatever vermin is crawling on my back, get it off,' he shouted at Konstantin, the first time his obsession reared its ugly head.

'But there's nothing on your back, Father.'

'*Gott sei verdammt,* are you questioning my senses, son?'

'No, Father.'

'Then get the *kleine schweine hund* off. *Schnell! Schnell!*'

Konstantin brushed the invisible vermin from his father's back wondering which species of vermin he was supposed to be eradicating.

'What in hell's name are you doing, son?'

'I'm doing what you asked, Father.'

'*Halt deinen Mund,*' he said, shrugging Konstantin off. 'Why is it, if I want something doing properly these days, even a little thing like this, I must do it myself? Tell me, Konstantin, when did you become so incompetent?' He fought with the buttons of his tunic, losening one to the point that it would require repair, and wrested the damn thing from his back. The diamond-studded Knight's Cross medal that he'd been awarded in 1941 for bravery and leadership during the first weeks of

Operation Barbarossa, and which he wore suspended from his collar, was discharged not unlike a bird fired from a clay pigeon trap; it soared through the air, hit a wall and skated across the varnished wooden floor, finally coming to rest in a place that was not observed by either father or son. *One Battle, One Will, One Goal: Victory At Any Cost!*

His father approached the hearth and, holding the tunic above the fire, shook the vermin off as Joyce does the sand from our towels when we've spent the day on Pobbles Bay Beach: with a ferocity entirely at odds with the task. (Indeed, Joyce does not so much shake our towels as beat them with a sandal. And before the beachgoers among you rush to Joyce's defence, I'm not suggesting that damp sand does not adhere to Terrycloth, but the degree and duration of the violence employed can only sensibly be described as over-the-top.) Only when the flames reared and spat at the frenzied activity taking place above them, and some of the carmine waffenfarbe piping from an epaulette began to unravell, was the *Generalfeldmarschall* placated. The half-dozen or so rats that he'd felt scurrying the length and breadth of his back lay contorting in the fire, some still screaming from the pain of the searing heat: *Into Dust With All Enemies Of Greater Germany.* He wiped the perspiration of combat from his face and the back of his neck, recombed his recently barbered blond hair, and shuddered back into his tunic. His hands wouldn't work and he fumbled with the buttons, making the loose one worse; he gave up on the button nearest the collar, and forgot all about his Knight's Cross medal. Then he pulled an orange and blue tube of Pervitin from his trouser pocket. He raised the tube to his mouth, and onto his furry tongue tapped out four pills, double the prescribed dose. He chased them down with several draughts of Calvados. 'Get out,' he quitely ordered Konstantin, at around the same time as a few more nerve cells perished in his brain.

And away went Konstantin to his stockpile of illicit booze. The champers went down a treat, and then came back up with the speed of a V−2 rocket because downing an entire bottle in a few minutes wasn't customary for him. Sadly, the silk drapes that hung from the top frame of the four-poster bed took a direct hit. Even worse, the *Deutsches Jungvolk in der Hitler Jugend* had not taught its young conscript how to remove vomit from any fabric, let alone a delicate one, with the result that, for the first time in his military career, Konstantin failed to exhibit the following *Essential Characteristic Of The Hitler Youth:* **To Be Clean.**

It was a waste of an excellent vintage.

It was a disaster for the drapes of the priceless bed.

It was the start of a slippery slope.

The very next day, **The Front Spoke To The Homeland.** In his usual scuffy hand, Konstantin penned a letter to his mother at the sanatorium. I cannot give the letter to you in full as it was redacted prior to its inclusion in the file; not by me, nor by anybody in the War Office, I hasten to add. I can only surmise that the *Generalfeldmarschall* took exception to some of what Konstantin wrote, perhaps from a, **Shame On You, Chatterer! The Enemy Is Listening. Silence Is Your Duty** point of view. Then again, I have to acknowledge that the redactor had a very steady hand, as the lines used to conceal Konstantin's words are far straighter than any line even I can draw. And let me tell you this: following the Pervitin overdose, the *Generalfeldmarschall* was in no fit state to hold a pen, let alone draw lines, unswerving or otherwise. Another explanation, as implausible as the first, is that an orderly at the sanitorium felt some of Konstantin's words might cause Frau von Essen distress and, by extension, impede her recovery from the consumption with which she was afflicted. That the orderly owned a pen I can well believe, but why an orderly would have a ruler to hand is beyond me. So, if on the balance of probabilities you, like me, find neither of these explanations satisfactory, then I encourage you to consider what is said by Konstantin in his letter, rather than what has been erased from the record, and by whom. For a consideration of the latter will only give rise to feelings of frustration and suspicion that will not be assuaged and serve no useful purpose here.

Liebe Mutter,

Thank you for being the kindest mutter in all the world; I think you are probably too good to me and spoil me far too much. Vater certainly thinks so. I am very grateful for the marzipan and pocket money you sent. We have a small, but decently stocked Kiosque in the nearby town, and with your generosity I have been able to use the francs to buy some sophisticated literature for my bed-time reading. (You will be pleased to know that I shared the marzipan with my many French friends.)

▬▬▬▬▬▬▬▬▬▬▬▬▬▬▬▬▬▬▬▬▬▬▬▬▬▬▬▬▬▬
▬▬▬▬▬▬▬▬▬▬▬▬▬▬▬▬▬▬▬▬▬▬▬▬▬▬▬▬▬▬
▬▬▬▬▬▬▬▬▬▬▬▬▬▬▬▬▬▬▬▬▬▬▬▬▬▬▬▬▬▬

Vater is keeping very well and we are having the most wonderful time in France. Our only wish is that you could be with us to share in the merriment. Do not worry about us; though the war goes on and Vater is kept very busy by his administrative duties, we do not suffer much hostility here, and we are especially safe, with so many brave and masterful soldiers at the château to keep us so. Vater is confident that the war will soon be over and we shall return victorious to glorious Potsdam, and to you. I hope this makes you as happy as it makes us.

Last night, Vater and I relaxed before the fire with a mug of kakao and spent the entire evening reminiscing about our fishing trips on the Havel river. Do you remember them, liebe Mutter? Vater would permit me to bait the hook and sometimes he would lift me onto his shoulders if it was necessary to wade into the river to land the catch. We laughed when we recalled the time Vater cast off and his wedding ring flew into the river and disappeared beneath the reeds. You hitched up your skirt and I rolled up my trousers and we helped Vater to look for it. But it was you that found it! Vater said he couldn't believe it when your hand emerged from the water triumphant! Last night he told me that he misses you very much.

▬▬▬▬▬▬▬▬▬▬▬▬▬▬▬▬▬▬▬▬▬▬▬▬▬▬▬▬▬▬
▬▬▬▬▬▬▬▬▬▬▬▬▬▬▬▬▬▬▬▬▬▬▬▬▬▬▬▬▬▬
▬▬▬▬▬▬▬▬▬▬▬▬▬▬▬▬▬▬▬▬▬▬▬▬▬▬▬▬▬▬

▆▆▆▆▆▆▆▆▆▆▆▆▆▆▆▆▆▆▆▆▆▆▆▆▆▆ and so, when Vater tells me that the doctors think your health is beginning to improve, I think I am the happiest boy in all of Germany and of France, and probably the world.

I must close now, for Vater and I have plans tomorrow that begin very early in the morning. Vater asks that I send his love to you.

Von Ihrem liebenden sohn,
Konstantin.
P.S. Please send more marzipan, if you can. Enough for me and my many friends.

Though I am as much in the dark as you in relation to what is behind the redacted text in this letter, what I have ascertained is that a number of the unredacted statements may be challenged and subsequently rendered suspect. For example, *'sophisticated literature for [...] bed-time reading'* was Konstantin's code for a four-page, twice monthly comic entitled, *Le Journal De Mickey*: a comic that told stories about *Mickey Mouse* and his friends, *Goofy*, *Pinocchio*, *Le Petit Indien*, and *La Famille Vole-Au-Vent* et al. Enquiries into *Le Journal De Mickey* have since revealed that Konstantin's claim that he bought the comic from a *'Kiosque in the nearby town'* is spurious at best, since the publication was not available to purchase in Occupied France. Furthermore, evidence also suggests that the kiosque, described as *'decently stocked,'* folded well before Konstantin and his father set foot in the region.

Fundamentally, I have no idea how Konstantin came by *Le Journal De Mickey*, but I can tell you that due to his godfather's Smut and Trash laws of 1933 – laws that ensured only literature that espoused Nazi ideology dominated the shelves of German libraries and book shops – he'd been deprived of a rollicking good read for the majority of his life. Small wonder then that he was captivated by the playful escapades of the cartoon characters he encountered in the Disney comic strip, and was prepared to go to extreme lengths to acquire it. That said, even in France it was still necessary to read the comic surreptitiously; a feat he achieved by reading the prohibited material in bed, with the silk drapes drawn tightly around the mattress, lest his father burst into his sanctuary unbidden, and discover the abject filth he was reading. (A feat that, incidentally, was made nigh on impossible once the drapes had been subjected to the contents of his stomach, such was the degree of shrinkage and rigidity they sustained.) We also know from the *get-the-rats-off-my-back* farce that Konstantin's father was taking hefty doses of Pervitin. Controversially, Joyce maintains that the best lie is rooted in truth. Konstantin's claim that his father was *'kept very busy'* was true, but it was not his *'administrative duties'* that kept him so, but rather his methamphetamine misuse, amongst other things. Pervitin drove the *Generalfeldmarschall* day and night, keeping him from a decent kip.

It's all very well pulling the odd all-nighter. Many of us did it during the war (and I can assure you that Joyce and I pulled a few during the early months of our marriage), but pulling countless all-nighters takes the biscuit. It also erodes Konstantin's claim that his father was *'keeping well'*; *'[was] happy'*; and, following the ugly hallucinatory episode after which he launched another load of Pervitin down his gullet, *'[had] relaxed before the fire'*. As for the *'mug of Kakao'* and the *'many French friends'*, all I can do is commend Konstantin on his talent for invention and embellishment and hope that some of it rubs off on me. In relation to the remaining statements in Konstantin's letter, I regret that I have not yet reached a point in the file whereby I can safely doubt what he writes. But I do find it improbable that Konstantin was *'very grateful for the marzipan'* his mother sent him since I've yet to meet an individual who can abide the stuff.

Thus far, this file has been short on facts and heavy on personal testimony. Indeed, I've been required to read and sift through an inordinate amount of memoir minutiae to get to the crux of the story. Consequently, I don't blame you for anticipating more of the same from Konstantin. How effortless it is to imagine Konstantin plagiarising the words of Rose in a leather-bound diary decorated with the Siegrune, albeit with one obvious modification, *I really hope the British kill my father.* But even though he now resided in France, he was still a German stripling in the Hitler Youth (Section Leader, albeit on secondment and with no fellow striplings to command) and still wore the uniform (black shorts, tan shirt, and black neckerchief with woggle). Also by this time he paid a good deal of lip service to the propaganda dished out by Hitler Youth HQ such as this little gold nugget: **Hitler Youth And BDM Girls Are Not Only Obedient And Faithful Comrades, But Above All Silent. Talkativeness Shows A Need For Attention, Whereas Modesty Is Silent. The War Demands Silent Fulfilment Of Duty.** Aside from seeing the tedious repetition of the word 'silent' here, you can also see why Konstantin chose not to wax lyrical in a diary, as such. And I say 'as such' because it transpires that Konstantin *did* produce a record of his daily life in France with his father.

It was unorthodox.

It was short on words.

It was a joy to scrutinize.

It was pure Smut and Trash.

It also cast doubt on Konstantin's claim that his father *'missed [Konstantin's mother] very much.'*

Postscript: As you may have deduced from the flavour of some of the comments I let slip earlier in this chapter, Joyce and I quarrelled last evening about this file. Joyce suggested that I cannot take criticism. I disagreed. I introduced the concept of constructive criticism. We discussed the merits of this form of evaluation. Joyce scoffed at the distinction between the two. She said my telling of the file was circumlocutory, circumnavigatory, and concentric in style, and accused me of being quite inept at painting the entire picture. I asked her if she'd been reading all the C words in the dictionary. She told me that I displayed the symptoms of having swallowed the dictionary and that, if I were a dog, she would take me to a veterinarian for its surgical removal; the idea brought a broad smile to her beautiful lips. (And here I couldn't help but imagine Dottie interjecting with a quote from her beloved Robin Hood that went, *What a pity her manners don't match her looks.*)

I ignored the dog jibe and reminded Joyce that I was not responsible for dropping this file, nor did I deliberately contract influenza. She implied that my influenza bore all the hallmarks of a common cold and nothing more, and had I recognised the difference, I'd have been present at the office, albeit with a streaming nose, to prevent the calamity that befell the file. She also insisted that there was no such thing as *truncated influenza*. I said it was a legitimate strain of the infection. She laughed a laugh that I had not heard before and had no impact on the features of her face.

I addressed her assault on my descriptive prowess. I urged her to recall the degree of detail imparted when I described Rose and Dottie's den. She insinuated that my description gave no account of how the den smelled. I reminded her that the den was a hollowed-out bramble bush constructed by two children, as opposed to a permananet erection constructed by a building firm and, as such, open to the elements and subject to a vast array of transient smells. She said if that were really the case, I should have captured a smell from a singular moment in time or, failing that, narrated a smell that would not be considered out of place in the den in order to validate the description. It was obvious she wanted me to say that in the den a discerning nose would detect a top note of bergamot and a middle note of jasmine, as with her favourite perfume, *Soir de Paris*. I also wondered if perhaps some elements of the file ought to be left to the imagination. She shook her head (as she shakes a sandy towel before the sandal is brought to bear). I took a moment to consider Joyce's three Cs, then admitted that during one previously narrated moment, the den smelled strongly of dog excrement and spam. She gave this spare truth a tremendous clap and then we made up in the usual way. It was just like old times. Without necessarily meaning to, we pulled an all-nighter.

19.

Guardian: I don't mean to sound rude, Mr Saunders, really I don't, but I don't think much of your interrowhatsit room.

Interviewer: Interview room, Mrs Bloomfield?

Guardian: Oops, begging your pardon, Mr Saunders. (CHUCKLE) Is that what you call it? An interview room? Smells like some poor devil died in here. I've been trying to think what the smell could be, but for the life of me, I can't come up with anything. As for the way you've got it set up in here, well, it's ever so plain, isn't it? You'd have thought somebody would have put a curtain up at the window. That funny looking glass makes me feel like I'm sitting in a public lavatory. It's very unsettling.

Interviewer: It's simply designed to afford us some privacy, Mrs Bloomfield.

Guardian: Is that right? As you know, Mr Saunders, I'm not one to complain, but, well, a curtain at the window, a picture on the wall, a rug on the floor, doesn't have to be fancy mind, but they'd be a nice touch. Espcially since you keep us so long in here. I know it's the war and all that, and things are scarce and all that, but you can make a curtain from any old piece of material. You can knock up a curtain in minutes, if you've a mind to. It's like being in our Anderson shelter with all this...plainess. It wouldn't hurt to put a few more electrics in, either. It's like being stuck in a permanent blackout. It's no good for the eyes. And another thing, we don't have fancy chairs at home either, but at least they're comfortable. I can sit on them for hours and not get this pain in my backsi...

Interviewer: (CLEARS THROAT)

Guardian: And goodness me, what on earth were they thinking when they picked the colour for these walls? Can you at least answer me that, Mr Saunders?

Interviewer: INAUDIBLE

Guardian: I know I've never been one for green, but some greens are worse than others, don't you think? And this green, gawdalbloomingmighty, I've never seen the like of it before. You can blame a lot on the war, Mr Saunders, but you can't blame the war for everything and this green... I think I'd have left the bricks unpainted if it'd been down to me.

Informant: I am not alarmed by the green, Mrs Bloomfield.

Guardian: Oh, he's ever so polite this one. Too polite sometimes, if you ask me. If I told him I was going to saw his arm off, he'd probably thank me for it, wouldn't you, lovey?

Informant: I...

Guardian: But do you know what, when we've been sitting in here all day answering question after question after question...Mr Saunders, you do ask a lot of questions if you don't mind me saying so...but...erm...where did I get to? (CHUCKLE) Don't look so worried, lovey, I know what I was going to say: when we've been sitting in here all day listening to you rattle on, I'm left with no appetite whatsover for my tea. I tell you why, shall I? I think its because this green reminds me of pea soup. (CHUCKLE) You have no idea how much I'm against pea soup, Mr Saunders. I'd rather eat that terrible bloater fish paste than eat that other muck and that's saying something because I'm no lover of fish. Doesn't agree with me. Never has. Ask

Mr Bloomfield if you don't believe me. And as for
the pong: I promise you now, there's not a nose in
Kent wrinkles faster than mine when it comes to
fish. That's any fish, mind. And it doesn't matter
what you do to it. You can fry it, grill it, bake it.
Makes no difference to me. Just one mouthful is
enough to make me sick for hours and hours. I
wonder if that's what this room smells of? Fish.
Something got me thinking about it and you can't
say that it didn't, Mr Saunders.

Interviewer: I'm terribly aggrieved to hear that
you find fish so disagreeable, Mrs Bloomfield.

Guardian: That's very kind of you to say, Mr
Saunders. It does make life difficult at times, but I
don't complain. But, erm, that pea soup, that's
something else that is. (SIGH) No point asking if
you like it, is there, lovey? You'd say you do, even
if you don't.

Informant: I...

Guardian: Well you won't get it at our house, lovey,
that's a promise.

Informant: Thank you, Mrs Bloomfield.

Guardian: I don't believe in making children eat
things they don't like.

Informant: Thank you, Mrs Bloomfield.

Interviewer: I'm afraid I had no say in how the huts
here were furnished or decorated, Mrs Bloomfield.

Guardian: (SIGH) More's the pity, Mr Saunders.

Interviewer: I rather suspect practicality won
over appearance.

Guardian: Or comfort.

Informant: I do not mind the room, Mrs Bloomfield.

Guardian: (TUTS) Well you would say that, lovey. I
expect you'd be happy in a pigsty. And you wouldn't
be alone in that. The state of Davey's room at home.
It's naughty really. And him being one of those
Commando whatsits as well. You'd think they'd have
taught him a thing or two about looking after
things.

Interviewer: Wonderful. Now that we've agreed on that... I have a question for Konstantin.

Guardian: Tell us something new, Mr Saunders. (CHUCKLE)

Interviewer: Who is Gilbert Aumont?

Informant: (SILENCE)

Guardian: Gilbert who? Did you catch that, lovey?

Informant: (SILENCE)

Interviewer: Aumont. Who is Gilbert Aumont?

Informant: (SILENCE)

Guardian: Don't you know, lovey?

Interviewer: Mrs Bloomfield, please.

Guardian: (LOUD SNIFF) I suppose that's your way of telling me to get on with my knitting, Mr Saunders? (CHAIR SCRAPE) (BAG RUSTLING) Why you can't just come out with it, I shall never know. All this going around the houses all the time. (KNITTING NEEDLES CLICKING) Ask anyone, they'll tell you, I can take a hint you know.

Interviewer: INAUDIBLE

Guardian: Blooming roll on.

Informant: (CLEARS THROAT)

Guardian: You best get on with answering Mr Saunders, lovey, else we'll be kept in here all day again, and we'll turn into moles, what with these second-rate electrics.

Informant: (PAUSE) I am very sorry, Mrs Bloomfield, but I don't think I understand the meaning of Mr Saunders' question. It is for this reason that I cannot answer it. Also, I am not sure I know what a mole is. It is possible that it is a *maulwurf*, but I cannot be certain. Please may I check my dictionary?

Guardian: Forget the mole, lovey. Put your dictionary away for once. See, Mr Saunders, I was only trying to help you out. Don't forget, I know you've been struggling with that *language barrier* trouble as you call it. Whereas Konstantin and me, we've come to understand each other. Now, I don't pretend to know his language, and half the time he doesn't pretend to know mine, but we know what the other one's on about, if you get my meaning?

Interviewer: Apologies, Konstantin, let me see if I can put it another way. In each of the messages you sent to Polly and Oliver via Kenneth, you signed off as Gilbert Aumont. Is that correct?

Informant: Yes, Mr Saunders, that is correct.

Interviewer: Please could you say more about Gilbert Aumont.

Informant: (PAUSE) No, no, no...I, I, I...

Guardian: Spit it out, lovey.

Informant: I am very sorry, but I cannot say more because it is just a name that I thought of.

Interviewer: Do you mean, a name you made up?

Informant: (PAUSE) Yes.

Interviewer: Gilbert Aumont was merely a pseudonym?

Informant: I'm very sorry but I do not...

Interviewer: Understand... yes, of course not, apologies, Konstantin. Gilbert Aumont was merely a name you made up so that you didn't have to write your name on the messages. Is that correct?

Informant: Yes.

Interviewer: Presumably because if the pigeon were shot down and your message recovered by, for example, your father's men, you could not be identified as the true author of the message?

Informant: Yes.

Guardian: Very clever, lovey.

Interviewer: So, just to be clear: Gilbert Aumont was not a real boy?

Informant: (PAUSE) No.

Interviewer: He was merely a figment of your imagination?

Informant: (PAUSE) I do not know the meaning of your word *figment*, not without checking my dictionary, but I think you are asking me again if I imagined the name. If I am correct, then I can say to you again, yes, I imagined the name, Mr Saunders.

Interviewer: The name just came to you off the top of your head?

Informant: (SILENCE) (COUGH) (LABOURED BREATHING)

Interviewer: The name just appeared in your imagination, just like that? (CLICKS FINGERS)

Guardian: Gordon Bennet, Mr Saunders, how many times are you going to ask him the same question? I keep telling you, Konstantin is a very clever boy. Of course it's no trouble for an imagination like his to think up a name. Even a French one. If you wanted him to think up a name from North of the River he'd do it, and faster than you could click those fingers of yours again, I'm quite sure of that.

Interviewer: I wonder why, of all the names you could have imagined, Konstantin, you imagined the name Gilbert Aumont?

Guardian: Well what name would you have imagined, Mr Saunders?

Interviewer: INAUDIBLE

Guardian: Hang on a minute, so what you're saying is, there's no right or wrong answer? Is that actually what you're saying, Mr Saunders? Because if you ask me, it's not playing fair to ask Konstantin trick questions. Not in my book, anyway. (SIGH)

Informant: (WHEEZE) Please do not be alarmed (WHEEZE) Mrs Bloomfield. (WHEEZE)

Guardian: That's easy for you to say, lovey, but now I've gone wrong on this balaclava helmet and I'll have to knit these three rows again. Whose fault is that, I wonder?

Interviewer: (SILENCE)

Informant: (SILENCE) (COUGH)

Guardian: Would anyone like to answer me?

Interviewer: (SILENCE)

Informant: (SILENCE) (WHEEZE)

Guardian: I thought as much.

20.

'Of course this boy is to be believed,' roared Churchill, 'for to dismiss the prodigious message he has bestowed upon us simply because we cannot conceive it as the work of an ordinary boy, is to underestimate the power and fury of a youthful mind, the power and fury of a youthful spirit, a mind and spirit that our mutual enemy, so cruel and vindictive in character, seeks to supress and obliterate. This is an enemy that deliberately keeps a boy from his treasured father, a father from his only son, and a family from their hearth and home. The magnitude of fury this hideous act inspires shall never be miscalculated by us. Those who doubt the provenance of this message shall look to the boyhood exiles imposed upon them at boarding schools the length and breadth of this island for the reassurances they crave. They shall recall their fear of the headmaster's birch and how they flinched at the sight of the sixth-formers to whom they were enslaved as fags. They shall remember the terror of losing the protection of those whom they cherished or held most dear, be it their fathers, their mothers or indeed, their nannies. And they shall ask themselves this: Was I never the architect of a deed engineered with the sole intent to resolve the miserable existence to which I was shackled, a deed spurred by a longing for home so great, and so profuse as to be tangible?

'This message is not the work of an ordinary boy, but these are not ordinary times. If we insist on doing only what is ordinary in extraordinary times, failure will stalk us and victory will elude us. We should not doubt, then, the words of this extraordinary boy, but shall marvel at his valiant act of sabotage, at the use he has made of the pigeon and the pen, and the blow he has cast upon our enemy in the name of justice and freedom. And we shall do all that we can to give this boy back his father. And in so doing, we shall send out the message that we will work with ordinary men, and with ordinary women, with ordinary girls and with ordinary boys, no matter their nationality, to finish for good, the wicked tyranny of Nazism.'

Latymer waited, then nodded, then cleared his throat. Then he said, 'I was on the verge of pointing out that the intelligence contained in Aumont's message has, save for a few details, now been corroborated and, consequently, Aumont has been deemed a genuine, not to mention, valuable informant. To be clear, sir, Aumont's claims are, in the main, no longer doubted by us, and we hope that Aumont will see fit to write to…'

'Very good,' barked Churchill, 'and next time, Latymer, finish your bloody sentence before you allow me to speak. Now let me have a better look at the boy's map.'

21.

To a trained ear, it was evident that Dottie's American accent had flown the coop along with Kenneth. In company with the accent went the vernacular peculiarities: the *sugars*, the *hecks*, the *holy cows*, the *gee whizzes*, the *huhs*, the *hecks*, the *swells*, the *howdys*, the *heavens to Betsys*, the *darn its*, the *double darn its*, and also the ungrammatical contractions: the *gottas*, the *gonnas*, and the *whaddyas*. Now, she sounded like her father, only a good number of octaves higher. It culminated in the dawning of a new possibility: forthwith, she could aspire to be a broadcast journalist for the BBC. She was no longer bullied at school for sounding like a Yank, but for sounding like a Toff: the slurs had changed but the malice remained. (Another unhappy rhyme, but as this file evinces: truth is stranger than fiction.)

She'd lost more than her pigeon, she'd somehow lost herself; not unlike when Edmund left for America. Ferret and Badger spied a weak animal in the pack and went after it for all they were worth, viciously ambushing her in the drawing room as she lay on the chaise longue contemplating Kenneth's whereabouts. Ferret savaged her nose, while Badger bled her ankle like an eighteenth-century leech. Dottie didn't even call for help. And it wasn't an isolated incident. The loss of Kenneth left her in such bad humour that she even suspended all trips to the den. The sight of Edmund's cabinet was too painful to bear. It was no longer Edmund's cabinet but Kenneth's loft and it could never revert to type. Not in a million years. Then there was the newly installed bucket of emptied bosoms, bosoms that would now never nourish Kenneth again. And not to forget Kenneth's poo on her cushion: the realisation that there would be no further tokens of such good fortune from Kenneth's quarter, induced spasmodic bouts of hysteria in Dottie that made Ferret and Badger all the more rabid.

What Dottie had initially regarded as potentially comforting mementoes of her dear departed friend (albeit, there was no conclusive evidence to suggest that Kenneth was now delivering the words of God in Eternal Heaven rather than the words of Gilbert from Northern France), she now regarded as instruments of emotional torture. In addition, there was a noticeable change in her behaviour at school, although nobody in fact took much notice (including Rose because she was consumed by her own troubles). But I can tell you that Dottie was no longer interested in the playground, and that was a colossal problem for the girls that skipped. The favoured skipping rhyme sounded silly with a Surrey accent (it was the only time Dottie's American accent was not treated with disdain):

> Salome was a dancer
> She danced the hootchie-cootch,
> She shook her shimmy shoulder
> And she showed a bit too much.
> Stop! said King Herod,
> You can't do that here.
> Salome said, Baloney!
> And kicked the chandelier.

Without Dottie, they had to settle for:

> When the war is over Hitler will be dead,
> He hopes to go to heaven with a crown upon his head.
> But the Lord said No! You'll have to go below,
> There's only room for Churchill, so cheery-cheery-oh.

It was a reasonable substitute. However, none of the lines held quite the same magic as *Salome said Baloney!* Furthermore, Dottie's teacher, Mrs Treacher (fear not, this isn't the beginning of another skipping rope rhyme), was left rather puzzled by Dottie's response to the set essay title, 'My Friends and Why I Like Them'. This was because Dottie's essay was not about Rose. It was about a boy named Kenneth. Kenneth was not a boy that Mrs Treacher knew. Also, some of Dottie's reasons for liking Kenneth seemed a little cockeyed.

My Friends and Why I Like Them
by Dorothea H. M. I. G. Latymer

My friend is called Keneth. Keneth is not his real name, and I don't know if he has a last name. I don't know where he lives either, or where he comes from. He is very small and probly younger than me, but he might be older than me for all I know. Even though I only met him the other day, I really like Keneth because he lets me kiss him as much as I want, sits in my lap without wrigling and he likes my singing. He isnt always very tidy but I don't mind because I'm not always tidy either. He owns a very special suitcase, that is smaller than you can imagine, and likes to travel to far away places that I have never visited such as France. I really like the colour of his eyes becase they are as dark as the blackout but I do not like the blackout but I do like the colour of his eyes and when he is really pleased to see me, he winks them at me. (Although some people think he is just blinking at me but I don't listen to them because they don't know Keneth like I do.) Also, he likes Cornflaks as much as me. What I like the most about Keneth though is that he never gets cross with me, he never calls me meen names, he never bites me, he doesn't mind that I am halve-American and he doesn't accuse me of showing up late to the war. In conclusion, I wish I had more friends like Keneth and I wish that he hadn't gone home early, especialy without saying goodby.

Mrs Treacher did all that she could to address her puzzlement over Kenneth in her feedback:

Dottie, you have written a very interesting response to the essay title, although it does read a little like a True Riddle (see me if you don't know what this is). Who is Kenneth? Whilst I quite like the mystery surrounding Kenneth's identity, what I had asked for was an essay about your real friends, not your imaginary ones. Why did you not write about Rose Clarke in Miss Butler's class? I deliberately did not stipulate that you had to write about a child, or children, from your class for your benefit. I liked your simile: more of these please! In terms of your essay structure, whilst I can see that you have attempted to include an introduction and conclusion, both are a little on the short side to be of any real merit. Also, please try to write more overall next time, and check your work for errors of spelling, grammar and punctuation before you hand it in for marking. Reasonable effort, but could do better.

I'm glad Dottie mentioned the cornflakes in her essay because it reminds me that, since the loss of Kenneth, she'd also lost her appetite for that hard-won cereal, and it is this, if nothing else, that should convince you of Dottie's misery and that it was absolute. Speaking of misery, I must now turn to Rose, but before I do, I urge you to remember that misery, like most things, is relative.

Granted it was the first time Rose had found her mother half hanging out of her bedroom window dressed in nothing more than her sweat drenched shift, but given the preceeding few days, this new display of odd behaviour neither surprised nor shocked her. Unnoticed, she watched the scene from the doorway instead of instantly sprinting to the window to recover her mother as one might expect. Why? I cannot say for certain, but it's plausible that Rose was trying to ascertain the precise object of the observed exercise before deciding upon the correct course of counter-action. You see, it was raining, and it was the type of rain that instantly refreshes fevered skin.

I'm quite sure that we've all been on a long hike in woodland on a sultry morning and brushed past a Killarney fern that had yet to lose the dew from its fronds to evaporation: how welcome was that unexpected caress of cool moisture on the exposed and pyretic skin of the calf? (That Rose's mother was not actually suffering from a fever is neither here nor there for, by this time, she behaved as if she were permanently beset.) Even though her arms didn't work very well, she seemed to be reaching for the rain, cupping her hands as if to fill them with water, as if her sole intent were to fetch enough to bathe her wan face. Her lips moved but no words escaped. She talked in silence but it was not in any language I know, and the intended recipient of the nonsense she was spouting was not plain. In the bright light of the day it was also evident that her hair was beginning to thin, to recede at the temples and to disappear entirely from the crown, as if she were a middle-aged man.

Rose had found the many displaced strands of her hair on her pillowslip, they stood out as thin auburn welts against a faded cotton that had long since died a horrible death in a weekly boil wash of a bygone age. Initially, Rose diagnosed scurvy. It was a condition she had learned about in a school history lesson. Centuries ago, it had affected sailors. The cure back then had been limes, a regular ingestion of vitamin C. With no limes to hand, Rose prescribed a daily dose of orange juice and fed it to her mother from a tablespoon as if it really were medicine. And this went on until such time as the medicine didn't go down well and emerged from her mother's mouth like a geyser, spraying the bedroom wall. For Mrs Clarke, sustenance was the nemesis, and orange juice stung her sore mouth. The peeling brown wallpaper turned sticky once more, but on the wrong side which was unhelpful to say the very least. (Rose swigged what remained of the orange juice directly from the bottle because there was nobody to prevent her from doing so, and because it had been drummed into her that *Food Is A Weapon, Don't Waste It!*)

So there was Rose's mother: thin, shabby, balding, sweating, jibber-jabbering away, and leaning out of her bedroom window simply collecting rain water in her hands. Or not. This is a scene that is entirely open to interpretation. It could be argued that the degree to which Rose's mother was leaning out of the window put her firmly at the angle of a ship's figurehead. Indeed, with her slip in disarray, and little evidence of any underwear thereunder, Rose's mother easily resembled one of Neptune's wooden angels. Was this what she imagined herself to be? Perhaps she was conversing with mermaids. Perhaps she was sailing towards the Norfolk coast and Holkham beach. Perhaps she imagined

124

herself to be leaning over the North Sea and not a concrete yard that entertained neither flowerbed nor bush to break her fall. Pehaps I am getting carried away. Nonetheless, Rose began to see a fatal accident in the making and took the action that one expected all along.

I'm not sure it could be successfully argued by any reader of this file that the continued deterioration of Mrs Clarke's wits was entirely unanticipated. However, I think we can agree that the speed with which the deterioraton advanced was eyewatering. Furthermore, I think I have the document that may have precipitated it. It was only as Rose wrestled her mother to the bedroom floor that she noticed the letter from her father discarded beneath her mother's bed. Dated two days before Mrs Clarke saw fit to throw herself at the ground, it read in full:

I'VE GOT A WEEK'S LEAVE BEFORE THEY SHIP US OUT TO ITALY. I'LL BE HOME ON THURSDAY. SEE TO IT THAT THERE'S SOME SODDING FOOD IN THE CUPBOARD THIS TIME. AND GET SOME OF THAT GOLDEN SHRED. I'M SODDING STARVING.

There was no date, no salutation, no polite enquiry after the health of his wife and child, and no sign-off. There was just shouted menace. Though there was marmalade left on the ration book, Mrs Clarke was in no fit state to visit the shops to stock the cupboard with that or any other foodstuff, or to withstand seven long days of her husband's distinct attention. Rose clutched her mother's head to her chest while a sickening dread clutched both their hearts.

But it's not all bad news. A good story never is, so Joyce argues. But I would argue that a file is a different matter. Anyhow, Kenneth was back in the den. I know I claimed that Dottie had suspended all trips to the den and so should not have been reunited with him, but thanks to Ferret and Badger's prolonged and ungovernable campaign of harassment, the den, in Dottie's mind, was, in quick time, transformed from something of a mausoleum into an absolute safe haven. She found him snatching forty winks atop his loft/Edmund's cabinet and not a moment too soon for Kenneth had arrived back in Blighty hungry. Had there been no bosom on offer when he awoke, I expect he'd have promptly cleared off back to the *nom de plume* in France where both food and affection were aplenty. Dottie's reaction to Kenneth's reappearance went something like this: *Oh my golly/ Oh gee whizz/ Howdy, baby bird/ Oh, sugar, where in the Sam Hill did you get to, huh?/ Holy cow, I've been goin outta ma mind with worry/ Heavens to Betsy, Kenneth, how could you just take off like that?/ It's sure been darn hard this past week without you/ It sure is swell to have you back/ Are you hungry?/ Let's celebrate with some bosom, huh?/ Would you like that, honey?/ I'll bet my bottom dollar that you would/ Eat up, sweetie pie/ Come on now, don't be shy/ It will liven your gizzard/ Well, this is what we Normans like - good food, good company, and a beautiful [bird] to flatter me.*

As you probably deduced, the last line was an amended quote from Robin Hood, but that's beside the point. The principal point I wish to make here is that, like Kenneth, Dottie was back. A double helping of bosom was served in one of the den's chipped ceramic bowls and some rainwater was decanted from the den's milk bottle and offered in the other chipped bowl. Following a long cuddle, many kisses, and her favourite chorus of Big Rock Candy Mountain, Dottie opened Kenneth's suitcase. Gilbert Aumont had sent another message on what appeared to be tracing paper of a type I regularly used back in my furniture design days. To be quite honest, in terms of content, the message, or letter, as Dottie regarded it, was deemed by her to be as disappointing as the first:

Thank you for the pigeon. I was greatly surprised to discover that it is possible to send the same pigeon back to me. I do not know how you have achieved this excellent skill but I am glad to see this pigeon again. I am writing this message on water closet paper and hope that this is agreeable? If this is a problem for the message, please may you be so kindest to return the pigeon with more rice papers.

I am alarmed by the worsening situation here. The German officer takes too much narcotics and is no longer a happy man. His men drink too much wine and caused problems in the town with the local people. A soldier was drowned in the river because he physically offended a local woman. Many French men were killed in retaliation.

I have copied a list of co-ordinates for the situation of many stores of weapons:

48.933772, 2.475189, 43.114707, 5.876305, 48.56309, 2.267007, 44.872193, -0.540046, 47.912954, 1.987529, 47.467038, 6.082852, 43.375004, -1.781588, 45.683262, 4.802274. I have also seen a letter concerning the marrying of an English artist to a Belgian woman. The woman pretends that she is Belgian but she is really a German spy. I do not know her real name, but her code-name is Mops. Mops is the German word for a breed of dog but I do not know how to translate it properly because Mops is not in my dictionary. It is a small dog with a squashed face and curly tail. I also know that the artist has spent much money fixing the spy's teeth. Somehow, the spy is giving the Germans lots of good information about your Royal Air Force, and this might make the war go on longer than it should. I think you should look for a woman who has recently married an artist, has a foreign accent, and has good teeth. Also, this woman might have a Mops in the garden. I have seen other important documents on the officer's desk.

However, I do not understand most of them so cannot relate them to you. It is for this reason that I request a Minox camera. I will photograph these documents and send the film back to you with the pigeon. Please drop the camera in the field I told you about in my last message. Also, if you have it, some secret ink as it may be useful in the future. After many considerations, I have also decided that the best place for your invasion is Normandy. This is because the German troops are moving away from Normandy so please start planning to invade here as soon as possible before the Germans change their minds. This is a dangerous place and I feel very afraid for my father and myself. I am most desperate to go home. I will keep looking for useful information to help you end this war.

Yours faithfully, Gilbert Aumont

P.S. Your recent attack on the château from the air did not kill any German soldiers. However, it did kill one woman and two of her five children, additionally a horse and a foal that did not belong to the horse. I would be most grateful if you please do not attack the château again as you may kill more children and you may kill me.

Thank you. G. A.

P.P.S. Please do not broadcast my name on the BBC as the officer listens to the personal messages. I am fortunate that he was at a party in Paris when you acknowledged receipt of my first message. He may be at home next time. Please address me as Ordinary Boy since this is what I am. Thank you. G. A.

Though Dottie didn't rate Gilbert's letters, she nonetheless regarded him as a new penfriend and immediately began thinking about the letter she must write back. (A letter that, for now, she thought best to keep from Rose: **Keep Mum, She's Not So Dumb**.) However, the problem with using Kenneth as a postman was that his suitcase was too small to accommodate her high quality stationery, particularly given that she intended to write a reply of some length. Furthermore, in a bid to **Save Waste Paper, Don't Waste Paper,** ménages across Britain were using squares of old newspaper to wipe the aris and mop the other; so unlike Gilbert, Dottie could not use loo paper as an alternative source of stationery for the task. She pondered the dilemma over a handful of cornflakes, and somehow got to thinking about Rose's father, Mr Clarke (which must have been deeply unpleasant). She remembered that Mr Clarke smoked rollies. He'd been rolling a cigarette that time she'd called for Rose and he'd told her to *piss off.* (This ungaurded edict led to a rather awkward conversation between Dottie and her mother that went like this:

> **Dottie:** Marmee, earlier today, Rose's father told me to 'p██ off'. What in the heck does this 'p██s' mean?
> **Mrs Latymer:** Can't say as I know, honey.
> **Dottie:** I sure wish I knew.
> **Mrs Latymer:** Thank the Lord that neither of us knows.
> **Dottie:** But I'm afraid I didn't do it.
> **Mrs Latymer:** Do what, honey?
> **Dottie:** P██s *off.*
> **Mrs Latymer:** Honey, I think it's better if we don't repeat that word.
> **Dottie:** Gee, Marmee, what if it was important?
> **Mrs Latymer:** I'm quite sure it wasn't.
> **Dottie:** I wouldn't want Mr Clarke to be cross with me. He might stop me seeing Rose.
> **Mrs Latymer:** Well let's see. After Mr Clarke said what he did, what did you do?
> **Dottie:** I said thank you and then left because I remembered that I was supposed to meet Rose some place else.
> **Mrs Latymer:** In that case, honey, worry no more, I'm quite certain you did as Mr Clarke asked.)

How Dottie let Mrs Latymer's somewhat hollow assurance go unchallenged, I don't know. What I do know is that Dottie never did get to the bottom of the meaning of that word since Rose, who was similarly interrogated, followed Mrs Latymer's lead and feigned ignorance too (in accordance with item number eleven in the list she wrote in her diary and titled: *Things I will need to do to be like Mrs Latymer*).

So Mr Clarke used Rizla rolling papers. It's fair to say that Dottie didn't know an awful lot about such things but she did know that Rizla rolling papers were extremely thin and very happy to be rolled up. In this respect, they could have been made for Kenneth's suitcase. Dottie placed Kenneth in Edmund's cabinet – taking care to fasten the cabinet door – went home, crept past the family pets (as she had latterly come to label Juniper and Jinny), collected some money from her money box, and hot-footed it to Witts' Stores for some papers. 'For my Daddy,' she told Mrs Witts. Mrs Witts didn't bat an eye even though she knew that Mr Latymer smoked a pipe because the only things that ruffled Mrs Witts' feathers were bad language, unstockinged legs, and Shetland ponies.

Now, I ought to mention that in 1942, Rizla revoluntionized their rolling papers by adding arabic gum to the long edge. This was a fantastic development because it meant that by the time Dottie was in need of Rizlas she didn't also need either glue or Sellotape, both of which may have rendered her letter too large for Kenneth's suitcase. (Hurrah for Rizla. I say twice, Hurrah for Rizla.) Dottie returned to the den and set to work licking and sticking her packet of papers until such time as she had two narrow and very long sheets of wonky writing paper. Her mouth tasted of glue but by jove it was worth it. Next, she removed her pipe from her bumfreezer pocket and took a puff because, in her experience, a good puff on the pipe aided the thinking process immeasurably. 'Now for the letter,' she told Kenneth, and taking up a pencil began to write in her very best, not to mention smallest hand on both sides of her Rizla stationery, pipe hanging from the side of her mouth like a fanambulist's pole.

Howdy Ordinary Boy,

My name is Oliver and the other person writing this letter to you is called Polly, although she isn't here` right now as she is looking after her mother I expect. Polly doesn't actually know that I am writing to you because she would worry that we'll get into trouble for keeping Keneth if anybody finds out because Keneth is not ours and we shouldn't really keep him. That's what Polly thinks. Is Keneth yours, or does he belong to your father? Keneth is what we have called the pigeon. But maybe you have a whole other name for him? Perhaps you could tell us what this is, unless it's a secret, or unless you prefer Keneth and we can keep calling him this, which I really like and think Keneth likes too. Well, I think I should start by telling you some stuff about us. I have only just turned eleven and Polly is twelve but sometimes she acts like she is much older, but don't tell her I said that as she would get cross with me about it. I have a big brother who is swell, and my parents have got two evacuees who are not. I agree with you about ending the war soon because I want the evacuees to go home before they wind up killing me by pinching me to death and stuff like that. Also, I miss Daddy probly as much as you miss yours and would like to go back to live in London where we can be together all the time just like we used to be. I would also like to see my brother again, which won't happen until the war is over as it's to dangerous for him to cross the Atlantic.

Polly hasn't got any brothers or sisters, but she does have a history book that she got from A.J.P. Taylor, but it's very boring and I don't expect you'd like it. But don't tell her I said that, will you? because she can be very moody sometimes. So, you know you said that you are not very good at drawing, well I am, and I think you are good at drawing to. I liked the map you drew in your first letter of the radio jamer and the other thing I can't remember the name of, although I think you could have used more colours. Why didn't you draw any trees or fields? If you had, you could have coloured them green or brown. Don't you have any colouring pencils? I asked for an artist's box for my last birthday and I was lucky enough to get one, and it's full of paints and pencils except for the black pencil because that was ruined by the evacuees when they scribbled on my bedroom wall without my permission. Have you ever thought about asking for an artist's box for your birthday? It sure is good that you know so much about invasions and coordinates and want to help to end the war. I know nothing about stuff like that, but I do know a lot about animals and I think that Mops you were on about is what we call a pug. Is she an artist as well, or just marred to one? I'd like to be an artist when I'm older. What would you like to be? Why did her teeth need to be fixed? What happened to them I wonder? Gee, whatever it was, I bet it hurt. By the way, what is wrong with your mother and where do you really live? Some of the stuff you wrote in your last letter sure was sad. Is it right that the Germans chopped that lady agent's head off? You know its what Henry the 8th did to some of his wives, right? Did you see the Germans do it? Also, I'm not very happy about what you said happens to people who hold pigeons in France. I'd be dead right now, if I were there. Even though I've never met him, I think the General Fed Marshall man stinks and he better not try to come here, that's for sure. Another question I have that I hope you'll be able to answer is why are the children and the Jewish people being sent to Poland? What happens to them when they get there? Will you get sent there to? Have you been to Poland? Is it swell? You are probly wondering what happened to your last letter. I sent it to a very important man in London who I know will know what to do with it so don't worry. I will send your second letter to him as well. You are probly wondering how I know this man but I don't think I'm allowed to say, but he has a very important job. And also don't worry because he doesn't know that it was me that sent your letter to him because I didn't write the envelope in my own handwriting so Polly and I won't get into trouble for finding the pigeon and reading your letter, even though she keeps saying we will. WE WON'T.

MY DAD WON'T LET US. I hope you get that camera you've asked for. I sure would like one of those. Maybe I'll ask for one for my next birthday even though I have to wait almost a year. Is secret ink real, or have you made that up? If you haven't, I'd like some

of that too. Could you tell me what you look like? I am quite short compared to other boys my age and have crazy curly hair that won't lay down properly and that I have to put a lot of spit on to get it to do what I want,

especially on Sundays. I have green eyes with bits of yellow in them, which I think is quite unusual. I have dimples and freckles which I don't particuly like and I am not completely British which is sometimes a problem for me

at school. Polly says I have big teeth but they are straight at least. My voice hasn't broken yet. How about yours? I have big feet and hairy arms which my brother says is very unattractive.

So I am really glad to have you as a pen friend as I haven't had one before. So please write back soon, and answer my questions if you don't mind. It's starting to get dark now so I have to go home. I will post your letter to that man I told you about, on my way to

school tomorrow. (I don't like school, do you?) I'll tell you what Polly looks like next time I write (if she lets me). I don't think she is going to be very happy that I have written this letter to you but it's too late now. I will try some French now.

Oh River,
Oliver.
P.S. I'm glad you didn't get killed in that attack on the chateoo. P.P.S. Thanks for the tip about the German soldiers wearing

British uniforms. I will tell Mummy to be carful and to start locking our doors at night in case they come into our house, though they can have the evacuees if they want.
P.P.P.S. Sorry I can't send you any rice paper but it's because I don't have any.

Is it actually made of rice? I think your water closet paper is swell but if you don't like using it, you can always just go and buy some Rizla papers like me.

I won't mind if you copy my idea. You can probably get them from a nearby shop.
P.P.P.P.S. Bust a gut.

Before Dottie had a rethink about the point of an alias, her first draft read: 'These are not our real names, but I wish I was a boy and was called Oliver. Being a girl stinks because there are a heck of a lot of things girls are not supposed to do and I think this is unfair on a girl like me as I particuly like climing, playing football, and fixing things like the chain on my bicycle for example, which I can do better than any boy I know, and don't give a hoot when I get grease on my hands. As for Polly, she really likes being a girl, but doesn't like Keneth much and that's a darn shame.'

There is no doubt in my mind that if Joyce were to read Dottie's letter she'd say, 'Oh dear, this letter purports to be from a boy, but is patently written by a girl.' One only hopes that Gilbert is not as astute as Joyce. I for one thought Dottie's attempt to throw Gilbert off the scent with all that boy twaddle was commendable, and I don't know about you, but I find myself applauding the attempt and very much looking forward to reading Dottie's next letter (if Rose permits the writing of such a thing).

An Unnarrated Event
Come and Get It

It's a sticky August day in 1941 and a dense cloud of black flies loiter above the flat roof of the Wolf's Lair, Hitler's bunker in Poland's Masurian Woods. The air outside is as impenetrable as the bunker's concrete walls, but inside the air is cool, if not a little stale. Nevertheless, Hitler is hot, and he's bothered too: he has the trots, and is now late for a meeting with Dieter von Essen and Joseph Goebbels in which policy, strategy and the recent Battle of Raseiniai are to be discussed. Slumped on a chair in his bedroom, sweat runs down his clammy face in channels. The collar of his shirt acts as a dam. The belt on his trousers, though loosely buckled, throttles his bloated stomach. The drips from his nose make for his tie and give it a sheen that is lost in the gloom. The veins on his hands are compressed by the weight of the skin above them. If his life depended on being able to keep the bounce from his legs, he'd be shot. The tap, tap, tap of his polished boots upon the polished floor are an insult. He wonders how much pressure the eyes will endure before they'll burst in the sockets. This sounds like an experiment worth pursuing.

His ears ring louder than the Maria Gloriosa bell. His heart marches with total incompetence. The size and number of blood spots on his body are enough to inspire envy in a decomposing corpse. His moustache has lost its majesty and lies above his lip like a sample of cheap carpet snubbed by the salesman. There are fissures in his back passage that deserve a geographical name. His bones quietly crumble like undiscovered fossils. His fingernails are thick and furrowed. If the network of needle marks on his forearms were copied and printed on canvas, a stirring piece of degenerate art would result. He delivers his words in rasps. His breath is toxic, a torrid gas that will extinguish Eva Braun. The corners of his mouth are not held down by gravity alone, and the pain in his head chuffing well hurts.

Dr Morell, his personal doctor, bursts into Hitler's sleeping quarters with all the finesse of an elephant seal being chased by a polar bear. It's an awkward display that endures well beyond what is palatable. Hitler looks abroad, to the flag above his bed. His neck cracks. It's worrying as a good orator needs a strong neck to lob menacing words and hate into a horde of thousands. As if apprehending this, Dr Morell stands over him and grasps his neck, holding it in his corpulent hands, turning it from side to side, making it sound like a metronome.

'My dear doctor, I'm stiff all over,' complains Hitler. 'I feel like a leader twice my age.'

Morell takes Hitler's temperature. 'Don't worry, Mein Führer, I have something for that.'

'I also have a splitting headache.'

Morell studies Hitler's bloodshot eyes. 'Mein Führer, I have something for that, too.'

'And one minute I'm crapping like a goat, the next like a man with dysentery.'

Morell prods his abdomen. 'Naturally, Mein Führer, I also have something for that.'

'For which?'

'For both. For all.'

'What about for the blood and the mucus that comes with it? And for the sores in my rectum?'

Morell glances at his medical bag, a dispensary so cosmic it travels the labyrinthine corridors of the Wolf's Lair by trolley. 'Mein Führer, I have something for all of those things.'

'I drink, but cannot quench my thirst.'

Morell pinches the skin on the back of Hitler's hand. 'Yes, Mein Führer, that, too.'

'And I can't get rid of this awful taste.'

Morell takes a pen torch from the overtaxed breast pocket of his tunic. This is the tunic he designed for himself when it was clear Hugo Boss wasn't up to the task; and which Frau Morell fashioned from material not woven to contain a dirty great sack of potatoes. 'Mein Führer, I definitely have something for that,' he says, before holding his breath and pulling Hitler's chin down to reveal the sewer that is his mouth.

'Look at my legs. They move when I haven't given them permission. People might think I have the shaking palsy.'

Morell stills Hitler's thighs with the weight of his hands. 'Inconceivable, Mein Führer, but anyway, I have something for that.'

'My heart races one minute and stops the next. Now and then it feels as if it might storm my ribcage and breach the wall of my chest.'

Morell checks Hitler's pulse. 'Mein Führer, it wouldn't dare, but I have something for that.'

'As for my skin, each square inch smarts like Zyklon B.'

135

Morell rolls back a sleeve of Hitler's shirt and lightly strokes what lies beneath. 'Rest assured, Mein Führer, I have something for that.'

'My dear doctor, I feel altogether wretched.'

'My dear Führer, do not concern yourself with this, for I also have something for that.'

Hitler loses patience. 'Whatever you have, doctor, be quick about getting it to me. The delay is unacceptable.'

Morell bobs over to the trolley with the speed of his spirit animal in the mating season, opens the goody bag, and begins the lengthy process of filling Hitler's stomach, veins and *sitzfleisch* with the requisite chemicals: Acidol-Pepsin, Adrenalin, Antiphlogistine, Argentum nitricum, Belladonna Obstinol, Benerva forte, Betabion, Bismogenol, Brom-Nervacit, Brovaloton-Bad, Cafaspin, Calcium Sandoz, Calomel, Cantan, Cardiazol, Cardiazol-Ephedrin, Chineurin, Cocaine, Codeine, Coramin, Cortiron, Digilanid Sandoz, Dolantin, Enterofagos, Enzynorm, Esdesan, Eubasin, Euflat, Eukodal, Eupaverin, Franzbranntwein, Gallestol, Glucose, Glyconomr, Gycovarin, Hammavit, Harmin, Homburg 680, Homoseran, Intelan, Jod-Jodkali-Glycerin, Kalzan, Karlsbader Sprudelsalz, Kissinger-Pills, Kösters Antigas-Pills, Leber Hamma, Leo-Pills, Lugolsche Lösung, Luizym, Luminal, Mitilax, Mutaflor, Nateina, Neo-Pycocyanase, Nitroglycerin, Obstinol, Omnadin, Optalidon, Orchikrin, Penicillin-Hamma, Perubalsam, Pervitin, Profundol, Progynon, Prostakrin, Prostophanta, Pyrenol, Quadro-Nox, Relaxol, Rizinus-Oil, Sango-Stop, Scophedal, Septojod, Spasmopurin, Strophantin, Strophantose, Sympatol, Targesin, Tempidorm-Suppositories, Testoviron, Thrombo-Vetren, Tibatin, Tonophosphan, Tonsillopan, Trocken-Koli-Hamma, Tussamag, Ultraseptyl, Vitamultin, and last but not least, Yatren.

'Just a little something to make you feel better,' says Morell, wiping a needle with the hankie he's recently used on his nose.

Hitler smiles, claps his hands and jumps to his feet with the athleticism of Jesse Owens. 'My dear doctor, I feel better already. In fact, I am cured.'

Goebbels and von Essen wait for the boss in the dimly lit conference room of Building 6. It's well past the scheduled meeting time and both know it's unprecedented for the boss to be late, just as they both also know this is a fact best ignored. Goebbels is threatening to fill the time by reading von Essen one of his recent editorials on the invasion of the Soviet Union. 'It's really no trouble,' he says. 'I have it here, and, if I do say so myself, it's rather good. I think you'd describe it as, very on point,' he adds, removing a neatly folded piece of paper from the inner pocket of his navy pinstripe jacket.

von Essen turns to the tray in the middle of the conference table. It contains thin slices of freshly baked gingerbread, but the things beside the gingerbread are a mystery. He reaches across the table and grabs one. It looks like a sweet, but it's a sweet he doesn't recognise, wrapped in silver paper.

Goebbels checks for signs that von Essen is preparing to listen to his article but the signs aren't good: von Essen is unwrapping his sweet with a degree of interest that rankles. To von Essen, the sweet looks like an antacid, but one stamped with an abbreviation he doesn't recognise: 'SRK'. Goebbels ignores von Essen's blatant apathy and begins, *'Hundreds of thousands of young German soldiers have been crossing our eastern border and marching through the famed "workers" and "peasants" paradise. Had National Socialism not been victorious, many of them would...'*

'What is this?' says von Essen.

Goebbels squints at the sweet to signal its irrelevance. 'Vitamultin,' he says, dismissively.

'Vitamultin?'

'Yes...*many of them would today be members of the League of Red Fighters, readers of the Red Flag, and singers of adoring hymns...'*

'I've never heard of it.'

'Well, that's what it is. ...*and singers of adoring hymns to the "workers Fatherland". At the end of their meeting they would have praised "wise Stalin"...'*

137

'What is it exactly?'

Goebbels sighs like a condemned man and says, 'Since I'm not involved in the manufacture of Vitamultin, I can't answer your question but the boss swears by it...*they would have praised "wise Stalin"*...'

'Where does it come from?'

Defeated at last, Goebbels throws his article at the substantial table. 'Doctor Morell developed it, and those ones,' he says, nodding at Dieter's hand, 'he developed especially for us.'

'Especially for us? Especially for whom?'

'The *Sonderanfertigung Reichskanzlei*. It's a special product for the Reich Chancellery. The SS have their own version, as well as the boss, of course, but Morell has the manufacturer wrap his in gold paper.'

'What does it do?' asks von Essen, assessing the Vitamultin as if it were a cyanide pill.

Goebbels shrugs. 'It's a tonic of some type. Supposed to be good for night vision among other things.'

'Have you tried it?'

'Yes.'

'Any good?'

'In what regard? Do I see better at night?'

'Does it taste good?'

'I would describe it as relatively flavoursome.'

von Essen flicks the tip of his tongue at the one he holds. He detects rosehip but other things too, things he can't identify, even though he considers himself to have a sophisticated palate. He pops the entire thing in his mouth.

Goebbels takes the opportunity to resurrect his reading and reclaims his article, '..."*wise Stalin*"...'

At that moment, the door to the conference room swings open. Hitler enters, closely followed by Morell, who, in the manner of a child wishing to be forgotten by his parents so he may stay up past his bedtime, promptly disappears into the darkest corner of the room where he can no longer be seen, nor his heavy breathing heard. Goebbels and von Essen jump to their feet for the salute. von Essen pushes the Vitamultin to the side of his cheek; it's like storing a lump of chalk. Goebbels tries to make his salute reach further than von Essen's, a hopeless ambition given the height of his adversary. von Essen smirks behind his raised arm. *'Heil Hitler,'* they chime.

Hitler waves his hand at them. 'Did I just hear you call Stalin wise?' he asks Goebbels.

'Oh, no, Mein Führer, no, no, most certainly not. Dieter wished to hear my recently published critique of Stalin in which I strongly expressed my perennial belief that National Socialism is, in perpetuity, immune to the disease of bolshevism.'

Hitler takes his seat and signals to the two men to do the same. 'What did you make of Joseph's article, Dieter?' he asks.

von Essen makes a show of giving the question some serious consideration before replying, 'I thought it was very, erm, how shall I put it, *on point*, Mein Führer.'

'Dear, Dieter, I believe it is, given that we are now just days away from taking Leningrad.'

von Essen doesn't mask his frown. 'Well, Mein Führer, I...'

'Is that not so, Dieter?'

'Well, I for one regard that as an incredibly accurate assessment, Mein Führer,' says Goebbels.

'In that case, no more talk of the war for today,' says Hitler. 'I want news of Gerda, and of Konstantin, my clever godson. Tell me, Dieter, isn't it time your dear lady wife gave you more children? The future of Germany depends on women such as Gerda producing good Aryan stock. Nothing would give me greater pleasure than to one day personally award her with the Mother's Cross for doing so.'

von Essen thinks about the nine miscarriages Gerda has suffered and how they both regard Konstantin's existence as a miracle. He opens his mouth to respond to Hitler's query, but Goebbels' need to do so is far greater. 'With all due respect, Mein Führer, Gerda has a long way to go before she's eligible for that accolade,' he splutters, thinking of the six children his own wife has given Germany, as well as the one she produced during her first marriage, and how the production of all these children for the Fatherland has resulted only in the issuing to Magda of a Second-Class Silver Mother's Cross.

'There's time yet,' says Hitler, patting Dieter's arm. 'Gerda's still relatively young.'

'I'm afraid she's been a little under the weather of late, Mein Führer,' admits von Essen.

'With what?' demands Goebbels.

'With fatigue,' says von Essen, trying to keep the irritation from his voice.

'Fatigue?' scoffs Goebbels. 'Oh, come on, Dieter, we all know that in women fatigue is merely a euphemism for frigidity. You ought to try her on some Hildebrand Chocolates. They perk Magda up no end. Granted, I have to buy three boxes a week, but I regard it as a good investment. Not only do they get Magda in the mood, but they also help her get the housework done, and in a fraction of the time. It's a small price to pay, and she insists they're tasty in spite of what they put in them. You might also remind your wife that *The Mission of Women Is To Be Beautiful And To Bring Children Into The World.*'

Dieter's SRK escapes his cheek and provides a welcome, if not deliberate, distraction.

'Well, Dieter, Joseph,' says Hitler, yawning at each man in turn, 'it's been a very successful meeting, but I think we've said all we need to say for one day, and I'm afraid I'm so tired I can barely think straight.'

'Of course, Mein Führer,' frowns von Essen, and, as a subtle act of charity towards an old friend adds, 'I know the feeling only too well.'

'Oh, me too, Mein Führer, me too,' bursts out Goebbels like a thrombotic haemorrhoid.

And out rolls Morell from the shadows to say, 'My dearest gentlemen, I have just the thing for that.'

22.

The War Office,
Whitehall
London
SW1

1 Farringdon Terrace,
Hackney
London
E9
7 December 1944

The Dickin Medal

Dear Mrs Dickin,

As requested in your last letter, below is further information regarding the flights made by the Allied carrier pigeons most recently nominated for the Dickin Medal. I understand that you have already received their Service Numbers, the suggested wording for each dedication, and which of the medals are posthumously awarded (originally five, but regretably now six as Scarlett Pimpernell succumbed to his injuries on the 4th of the month). Please do let me know at your earliest convenience if this is not the case, and also if I can be of any further assistance.

PIGEON	DISTANCE	TIME
'Royal Blue'	120 Miles	4 Hours, 10 Minutes
'GI Joe'	20 Miles	20 Minutes
'Jude the Obscure'	117 Miles	2 Hours, 8 Minutes
'Scotch Lass'	200 Miles	UNRECORDED
'William Butler Yeats'	224 Miles	4 Hours, 23 Minutes

'Albert the Great'	316 Miles	7 Hours, 40 Minutes
'Monarch of the Glen'	260 Miles	4 Hours, 25 Minutes
'Billy'	250 Miles	27 Hours, 40 Minutes
'Bunty'	91 Miles	UNRECORDED
'Kenley Lass'	300 Miles	6 Hours
'Paddy'	230 Miles	4 Hours, 50 Minutes
'Dutch Coast'	288 Miles	7 Hours, 30 Minutes
'Ethelred the Unready'	218 Miles	3 Hours, 27 Minutes
	218 Miles	3 Hours, 29 Minutes
	218 Miles	3 Hours, 17 Minutes
	218 Miles	3 Hours, 42 Minutes
	218 Miles	3 Hours, 28 Minutes
	218 Miles	3 Hours, 30 Minutes
	218 Miles	UNRECORDED
	226 Miles	UNRECORDED
	226 Miles	UNRECORDED
	226 Miles	UNRECORDED
	226 Miles	UNRECORDED
	226 Miles	UNRECORDED
	226 Miles	UNRECORDED

MIA

'Pinkie Halligan'	20 Miles	5 Hours
'Duchess of Richmond'	73 Miles	25 Hours, 2 Minutes
'Gustav'	150 Miles	5 Hours, 16 Minutes
'Scarlett Pimpernell'	179 Miles	9 Hours, 23 Minutes

With great appreciation,
Joe Binks
(Special Continental Pigeon Service)

142

Minutes of Meeting: August 30th, 1943
14.01 hours. Room 254, War Office.

Present: Brigadier Curtis, Deputy Director of Military Intelligence.
Air Chief Marshall Tyrell
'CD.' SOE
Clifton Hobbs MI5
Captain Blackbourne, Army Pigeon Service
Joe Binks MI14 (d)
Professor George Courteney MI14 (d)
Willoughby Moore MI14 (d)
Selwyn Stewart MI14 (d)

Absent: Hughie Latymer, Director of Counter Espionage MI5
Hamish Davidson MI14 (d)
Louie Honeyset, National Pigeon Supply Officer

Others present: Secretary: Winnifred Spearing

Proceedings:
-   Meeting called to order at 14:01 hours. By Brigadier Curtis.
-   (Last quarter) meeting minutes were amended and approved.

Report:
-   Recent off the cuff comments made by SIS to Moore demonstrate that the department continues to doubt the value of pigeon operations, preferring to use 'human agents' over the 'feathered variety' in spite of the fact that the intelligence gathered by pigeon is always received and disseminated much faster than the intelligence gathered by their human counterparts. SIS's claim that intelligence received by pigeon is small when compared with the loss of pigeon life, no longer holds true.
-   Following a comprehensive review of Columba messages received to date, Brigadier Curtis asserts that Columba has

consistently proven its worth as a valuable Intelligence resource.

- Binks expressed his intention to do all that is necessary to see off any attempt by SIS to terminate the operation.

- 'CD.' believes that the backing Columba enjoys from the wider intelligence community, not to mention GHQ Home Forces, means that its future is secure, particulary given that SOE agents favour the pigeon over the radio transmitter as a safer means of communicating with their handlers.

- Following consultation with Archibald Haines, Leader of The Surrey Sprinters pigeon group, it is confirmed that Ethelred the Unready (NPS.42.13033) has now also successfully completed Boomerang training. This brings the number of pigeons trained in Boomerang up to three.

- Honeyset has been asked by MI14 (d) to compile a list of elite pigeons suitable for recruitment to the Boomerang training programme.

- Binks predicts that Columba will achieve revolutionary results if a large-scale implementation of the programme is authorised.

- Air Chief Marshall Tyrell was pleased to report Wing Commander Delaney's assessment that the ability of the RAF Special Duties Squadron to drop a pigeon at a given coordinate is improving with each drop.

- Captain Blackbourne presented the assembled with a detailed paper defining the ways in which the Germans follow the progress of Columba.

- Symonds confirmed that the number of pigeons to be dropped as part of Operation Crossbow is now likely to number eight hundred in total. It is planned that two hundred birds will be dropped from each Halifax bomber in the French regions of Dieppe, Cherbourg and Pas-de-Calais. This is to build on the very recent and successful bombing of the German secret weapon development facility at Peenemünde. Date of drop to be confirmed, but December is likely.

- Hobbs confirmed Columba pigeons would be required to assist with the deception operation Cockade.
- Latymer has authorised the 'Contamination Plan' after it was proven by specialists in the field of engineering that a faux Wehrmact pigeon ring could be attached to a British pigeon with no visible solder joint evident on the ring. This is only possible due to the development of a new, and as yet, unpatented type of solder.
- Professor Courteney provided those present with a copy of a letter forwarded to him by Honeyset. The author of the letter, Lady Darrick-Sinclair, is a valued pigeoneer and, as such, Honeyset requests that her concerns regarding pigeon welfare be taken seriously by the assembled. Honeyset warns that to lose L-DS's support means, in real terms, that Columba loses her pigeons. Honeyset also asserted that L-DS is well respected in the pigeon world and enjoys a good deal of influence over her fellow pigeoneers. Should L-DS withdraw her birds from Columba, it is feared others will be swift to follow suit. Given the quality of L-DS's loft, and the lofts of her compatriots, this might seriously impede the objectives of our operation, as well as endanger agents in the field. Professor Courteney highlighted the following passage from L-DS's letter as particulary salient and read it aloud:

'Given the colour and texture of the droppings produced by some of my brave boys and girls upon their return home, it is clear to me that many of the humans tasked with caring for them abroad lack basic pigeon husbandry, contrary to what I have been assured in the past. A dropping that is green, and hydrous in consistency, is a sign that a pigeon is off-kilter and should not be flown. Is it really too much to ask that your boys and girls only fly my boys and girls if my boys and girls are producing light brown droppings tinged with a white the colour of apple blossom? I would like to reiterate that a green dropping can easily be avoided by handling my boys and girls gently at all times, and by offering routine caresses and verbal reassurances during transit.'

Other business: None.

Motions:

- All those present agreed to assist Binks in thwarting any attempts by SIS to terminate Columba.
- All those present agreed to campaign for an extension of Boomerang.
- All those present agreed that future pigeon operations should do all that is practicable to prevent the Germans from becoming too Pigeon-Minded.
- All those present agreed that increasing our stock of pigeons should be a priority especially since, as Operation Crossbow suggests, it is envisaged that pigeons will play a vital role in locating the launch sites of the deadly German V-2 Rocket.
- Hobbs agreed to ascertain the number of pigeons required for Operation Cockade.
- In furtherance of the 'Contamination Plan', substandard pigeons are now being recruited in their hundreds to infiltrate German lofts and disrupt enemy pigeon operations.
- 'CD.' agreed to brief SOE operatives on Lady Darrick-Sinclair's directive; Professor Courteney agreed to send a polite reminder to all others involved in the handling and distribution of Columba pigeons.

Assessment of Meeting:

Going forward, it was agreed by all those present that conferences to discuss Columba should now be arranged on an ad hoc basis to reflect the increasing significance of the operation.

Meeting adjourned at 15:34 hours.

Minutes submitted by secretary, Winnifred Spearing.

23.

'It pains me to say this, dear, but I'm afraid you do rather go on about some things while virtually ignoring others,' complained Joyce. 'It's as if you lack the capacity to give all events equal consideration. It's as if you prefer some parts of the story to others.'

'File,' I corrected.

'Pardon?'

'You said 'story', Joyce, I'm not relating a story, I'm relating the contents of a file.'

'I think you're splitting hairs, dear, that's what you're doing.'

'I can only relate the documents that are contained in the file. If a document is missing, or scant in terms of the information it provides, I can hardly relate it to you. It seems to me that you're suggesting I invent what isn't there; that I give free reign to my imagination to fill in the narrative gaps, as it were. But to do so, Joyce, would reduce the entire file to nothing more than a contrivance, a figment of my imagination.'

'I have never thought of you as particularly imaginative, dear, really I haven't.'

'On what grounds, Joyce?'

She took a second to consider this. 'The gifts you buy: handkerchiefs for your father and bath powder for your mother.'

'Is this an oblique way of saying you don't like the gifts I buy *you*?'

'I was talking about your parents, dear. I'm perfectly content with the unvarying bottle of scent every Christmas.'

'Now look here, Joyce, I buy according to the lists provided. In so doing, I believe I buy gifts that are desired. '

'I believe most people enjoy a surprise,' she ventured.

Joyce's pronouncement did not reflect the facts as I knew them, and for this reason I chose to ignore it. Besides, I'd already completed my Christmas shopping; the *Soir de Paris* had been hiding among the socks in my underwear drawer since October. 'In terms of your other accusation…,' I began.

'Accusation, dear?'

'Alright, for the sake of argument, let's call it a rebuke…'

'I would hardly call it that either.'

'What would you call it, Joyce?'

'I'm not entirely clear to what we are now referring but whatever it is, I would describe my comment in relation to it as, *constructive criticism*; something I must confess I knew little about until you took great pains to lecture me on the subject.'

'Objectivity is the subject here, Joyce. I always approach a file and the documents it contains with complete and utter objectivity. Why should I prefer one document to another?'

'Simply because…'

'I'm afraid that was a rhetorical question, Joyce.'

She snorted. 'Was it? How was I to know?'

'Perhaps from the context of all that preceded it,' I suggested.

'There was no context to signal that your question was rhetorical. You're imagining a context that simply wasn't there, dear.'

'And yet you accuse of me having no imagination.'

'Perhaps you employ your imagination as and when it suits you?'

'Employ my imagination?'

'It could be an unconscious utilization, dear, just as it could be a conscious supression, or vice versa. That's a conundrum only you can solve.'

I was almost lost for words until I noticed that she was holding a book. 'Now just a minute, Joyce, I'm not the author of any *file* I'm tasked with classifying, any more than you are the author of the book you're holding.'

Joyce was reading an Isherwood novel, *Goodbye To Berlin*. Something about the expression on her face and the angle of her head as she opened her mouth to reply reminded me of the cat next door. 'Let's consider this novel,' she said, raising it as if it were evidence of some great magnitude in court proceedings and I was the arrogant defendant confident of acquittal in the heinous case.

'I'm afraid I cannot consider something I haven't read,' I said, which was consistent with the point I'd been attempting to make thus far.

She ignored my protest completely and went on, 'I prefer the character Otto Nowak to the character Sally Bowles just because I find him more interesting.'

'But you haven't finished the book; how can you possibly make that judgement?'

'Is that a rhetorical question, dear?'

Instead of replying, I imagined Dottie whispering a warning from Lady Marian that went, *'Every minute you're here, you're in danger'*. I'm happy to report that I heeded the warning and did not reward Joyce's facetious question with a response.

'If you were familiar with the structure of Isherwood's novel, dear, you would regard your question as irrelevant at best.'

I pondered all the responses I could give to this reproach, but settled for none.

She went on. 'If I were to retell Isherwood's story, not only might I give Otto more words than Sally, allot more space on the page as it were, but my depiction of the former might also be more favourable than that of the latter. In short, dear, not all of us can evade our own bias.'

'Since you're admitting that you're incapable of, to paraphrase your opening accusation, *giving all events equal consideration*, might I suggest that by accusing me of the same, Joyce, you're merely projecting your own shortcomings onto me?'

'No, you may not suggest this, dear. As I said, not all of us can evade our own bias. My hypothetical retelling of Isherwood's story was only intended to be illustrative. In reality, I'm conscious of my bias for Otto and, consequently, would do all that was necessary to counter that bias in any retelling.'

Joyce's claim was about as difficult to swallow as a two inch nail. 'But would you invent things about Otto that you had not read in the novel?' I demanded.

'That's a separate issue, dear; I think you may be getting in a muddle.'

'I think you're evading the question, Joyce.'

'Given your contentious dictum on what constitutes a rhetorical question, do you blame me, dear?'

I chose to categorize her question as a rhetorical one.

'But to answer your question,' she said, 'of course I invent things about Otto. It's expected of the reader by the author.'

'I don't think you can speak for all authors, Joyce,' I scoffed.

Crossly, she opened her book and from it, with almost no hesitation, read the following extract, *'Where's Lothar and Otto?' I asked. 'Don't know. Somewhere about...They don't show themselves much nowadays – it doesn't suit them, here...Never mind, we're quite happy by ourselves, aren't we, Grete?'* She stopped reading, closed her book and raised her eyebrows. 'Where are Lothar and Otto, do you think, dear?' she asked.

Since I had not read the book, we both knew I could offer nothing more than a shrug: I took the path of least resistance. With an arched eyebrow, she administered what she clearly thought would be the death blow. 'This is where I pause reading and begin to ponder Lothar and Otto's whereabouts. Then, based on all that I have previously learned about these characters from Isherwood, I infer where Lothar and Otto might be, and what each of them might be doing. In other words, dear, I fill in the...what did you call them? Oh yes, I have it, *narrative gaps*. As to whether Isherwood wishes for me to make this particular inference, I cannot say for sure since, as you've pointed out, I cannot possibly know what is in Isherwood's mind, but given that the subject of their whereabouts is not revisited, what other course of action is available to me? My feeling is this, if Isherwood did not wish me to engage in the production of inferences, he would be more explicit about the location of his characters.'

(Only Joyce could open a book to a random page and immediately chance upon a scrap of text that illustrated her point. I'm still of a mind to check Isherwood's book for the missing information. But, even if Joyce is correct and Isherwood doesn't return to the question of Lothar and Otto's whereabouts in the remainder of the book, it's obvious to me that the ommision is less about spurring the reader to make an inference and more to do with Isherwood deeming the whereabouts of these characters trivial.)

None of what Joyce had argued was relevant to her original complaint, the precise details of which I was fast losing track of. 'I've simply been trying to say that if I have less to say about one event than I do about another,' I said, 'it's because the *file*, Joyce, the *file*, has provided me with more information about that one event than it has about the other. If certain details are missing from the file then, unlike you, I'm not at liberty to replace those details with fantastical inferences.'

'But I never accused you of making things up, dear,' she said. 'And I would never advocate complete fabrication as you imply I have. But, even if I were to do so, I would only recommend it to someone with a healthy imagination,' she added, before firmly closing the subject by snapping open her book.

24.

Without any sort of preamble, I must reveal that Rose did not write in her diary for the duration of Lance Corporal Clarke's week-long leave. To be clearer still, there is no indication that an account of this horrific week was produced but later censored, either by her or by any other individual. There is no redaction of the diary, just as there is no obvious evidence to support the theory that the pages covering this spell were systematically ripped from the binding or exsected hence with a stanley knife and forensic precision.

Nonetheless, the distinct lack of personal testimony for this period is anomalous when the diary is considered as a whole. Prior to this dark chapter in Rose's life, very rarely did she leave a day unappraised. Naturally, she wrote more on some days than others, but flicking through it now, in a bid to ensure that I truly haven't missed anything, I can, in fact, find no other days, excluding the days of her father's leave, that are represented by a blank page or indeed, a missing one.

However, I can reveal that by the time her father arrived home, a jar of Golden Shred *was* waiting for him in one of the kitchen cupboards. The preserve was impossible to miss since it was waiting in solitary confinement. Further scrutiny of the shelf harbouring the marmalade *suggests* that for the Clarke family there had been more bountiful times in the past, if not happier ones, but the evidence for this might also be described by some as fanciful: a viscid black ring of treacle, a resinous bead of honey, a dusting of nutmug, a sprinkling of flour, scattered granules of spilled salt and sugar, an errant raisin backed in one corner like a spider under threat, enough grains of pudding rice to fill a teaspoon, a strand of saffron, a ribbon of dried lemon peel, a suggestion of suet, and white pepper accumulated over time and pinched into small heaps by bored young fingertips.

The Golden Shred sitting as it was in a cupboard stocked only with the remains of other edibles, for some reason, called forth an image I thought I had long since buried. Immediately, I saw a man wearing striped pyjamas, lying on a wooden shelf in a human sized cupboard. He'd lost the buttons to his pyjama top with the result that his chest was exposed, and the bone at the base of his sternum, later referred to as the xiphisternum by the attending doctor, looked as though it would pierce the taut skin that covered it. Prior to discovering this poor fellow, I had not known that this bone existed in the human body, and though he'd been alone in this miserable cupboard for some time, above, beneath, and beside him were the blankets and pyjamas of all those that had been murdered before him. I removed my Greatcoat and placed it over his chest for there was nothing else to be done. His eyes flicked open, very briefly, as if to acknowledge me, or at least the warmth of my coat on his skin, before his Adam's apple rolled away, seemingly to the back of his neck, and his last breath went meekly in the direction of the damp wooden slats above.

There were three shelves in the kitchen cupboard housing the Golden Shred. Rose had placed the jar on the middle shelf. The reason for this was manifest: here, the jar appeared at eyelevel, ergo it could not be missed and by extension, provoke wrath. But, contrary to all expectation, it had not been required on the first day of her father's leave, in spite of the professed desperation for it, because, as you might have hoped, he got waylaid at the home of that person living several streets away. We don't always get what we wish for and so it follows, the wish that he wouldn't bother coming home at all during that leave, that he would stay with the other woman, at the other house, was not granted. He finally stomped through the front door of the Clarke family home on Easter Sunday. The first dint he made was not to the jar of Golden Shred.

The only thing I can be reasonably sure of regarding Lance Corporal Clarke's week-long leave is that during it, Rose was responsible for putting all meals on the table. A Ministry of Food War Cookery Leaflet appears slap-bang in the middle of the gap in her diary. Of the recipes featured – Pilchard Pancakes, Scrambled Egg Salad, Salmon Savoury, Cauliflower Hollandaise, Chow Tan and Cabbage and Bacon Savoury – I believe it's most likely that she attempted the Pilchard Pancakes for it is here that a small bloodied fingerprint is faintly discernable.

Pilchard Pancakes

1lb. Potatoes	2 tablespoons chopped Parsley
2 Pilchards, mashed.	1 dried Egg, reconstituted.
1 tablespoonful chopped Leek	Pepper and Salt

Peel, cook and mash potatoes, add pilchards, leek, parsley, dried egg and seasoning. Mix all together and drop dessertspoonsful of the mixture into hot fat. Brown on both sides.

25.

A .-	J .---	S ...	1 .----
B -...	K -.-	T -	2 ..---
C -.-.	L .-..	U ..-	3 ...--
D -..	M --	V ...-	4 ....-
E .	N -.	W .--	5 .....
F ..-.	O ---	X -..-	6 -....
G --.	P .--.	Y -.--	7 --...
H	Q --.-	Z --..	8 ---..
I ..	R .-.		9 ----.
			0 -----

Fullstop .-.-.-
Comma --..--
Query ..--..

Message on: Operation Attar
Message Status: Highly Confidential
Message Transmitted: 30 March 1944, 03.53 hrs
From: Earthstar
For: SOE/F Section
Message As follows:

... / -.- -. . .-- / --. .. .-.. -... . .-. - / .- ..- -- ---
-. - / .-.-.- /
.... . / .-- .- ... / .- / -- . -- -... . .-. / --- ..-. / - ....
. / ..-. .-. . -. -.-.
.... / .-. . ... - .- -. -.-. . / --. .-. --- ..- .--. /
--..-- / .-.. . ... /
--. . -. .... / .--. .-. . ...- .- .-.. . -. - / .-.-.- / .... .
/ .--- --- .. -. . -.. /
.-.. --. .-. / .-- .... . -. / .... / ..-. .- -- .. .-..
-.-- / .-- . .-. . /
... - .-. .- ..-. . -.. / -... -.-- / - .... . / --. . . .-. --
.- -. .... / .. -. /
.---- ---. ....- ..--- / .-.-.- / .... . / .-- .- ... / .... .-
-. --. . . -.. / -... -.-- / ..-. .. . .-.. -.. / -- .- .-. ...
.... .- .-.. .-.. / ...- --- -. . / . ... -. /
--- -. / ----- -... / .-.-.- / ----- ..--- / .-.-.- / ....-
....- / ..-. --- .-. /
.--. --- ... . --- -. / --- ..-. / .- / -.-. .-
.-. .-. .. . .-. /
.--. .. --. . --- -. / .-.-.- / .... . / .-- .- ... /
.---- ----- / -.-- . .- .-. ... /
--- ..-. / .- --. . / .- - / - .... . / - .. -- . / --- ..-. /
.... /
-... . . .- - - .... / .-.-.- message end

26.

I have to confess that what I know about pugilism could be written in full on the bare knuckle of a teenage hand. However, one need not be Sugar Ray Robinson to predict the outcome of a boxing match in which one teenage boy takes on three older teenage boys. I realise that my construction of the preceding sentence implies that the showdown between Konstantin and the three unknown residents of Amiens was suggested by the former and jointly organised with the latter. Of course, it was no such thing. Konstantin was ambushed by the masked youths in the woods, as he walked home from a long and enjoyable day fishing for trout on the Somme.

Though an accomplished boxer, having been trained in the sport at various Hitler Youth summer camps and having bloodied many an Aryan nose in boxing competitions at countless jamborees the length and breadth of Germany (and been congratulated for doing so by father, opponent, spectator and boxing promoter alike), in this boxing match, Konstantin failed to throw a single punch, such was the element of surprise unleashed upon him by these bigger boys.

Once on the ground, his tactic was to curl up like a woodlouse and cradle his head in his hands, a manoeuvre he knew would spark ire in his father had he been there to witness it, but one that gave him the greatest chance of avoiding injury to his brain and other vital organs. The blows rained down. Kicks followed when the arms tired. Each fresh assault was issued with every conceivable insult imaginable, insults I can generally sum up in one or two words, regarding his race (dog excrement); his ideological allegiance (pig excrement); his godfather (donkey's vagina); his father (excrement); his father's mistress (siphilitic lady of the night); his name (ridiculous); his long legs (lanky); the particular blue of his eyes (girlish); his imagined sexuality (homosexual); the blond shade of his hair (girlish); the imagined size of his genitals (minuscule); his command of the French language (laughable); his uniform – in particular the woggle – (stupid); the position he adopted once on the ground (cowardly); the size and number of his catch (pathetic); and everything else about him not listed here but insulted at the time and with, I note, an increasing lack of originality (girlish and/or homosexual). To each, Konstantin made no response save the non-verbal sounds his body made when the wind was knocked out of him, the cartilege in his nose cracked, and a substantial portion of an upper incisor sheared off (although only Konstantin heard the last injury, amplified as it was by the onset of sudden deafness to all external sounds, a deafness I suppose one must anticipate following a mighty kick to the ears). The combined blood of his nose and mouth pooled in the dimple of his chin and the sun-kissed skin of his face was lost beneath mud, leaf, other organisms generally found on a French woodland floor, tooth, and the spit and sputum of his assailants (who periodically lifted the scarves from their mouths to issue the latter). No part of his body went unpunished and every part reacted predictably, including his consciousness which began to flicker like a film poorly projected onto a screen.

There was a pause in the beating to enable one of the youths to effect a rough search of his pockets. From Konstantin's shorts, a penknife was removed.

A treasured inheritance from his maternal grandfather, its handle was made of ivory into which a wolf had been carved howling on the summit of Zugspitze – the tallest mountain in Germany – and its blade, made of silver, had been engraved first with his grandfather's initials, and then, following his grandfather's death, with his own. It was a possession that, if the fight had been fair, for example, one-on-one, he'd have fought to the death to keep.

Konstantin spent the lull in proceedings being violently sick. Another of the youths waited until he had finished before rubbing his face in it and then suggested they use the penknife to cut a swastika into his cheek. Quite unable to hear the suggested plan, he guessed it as the middle-sized youth, having taken ownership of the blade, was merrily slashing swastikas into the air by way of demonstration. He watched the boots of his assailants jostle for position: one would be surgeon, the other two would assist. Seconds later the blade changed hands and he felt its tip upon his cheek and his chin clamped in what was presumably the strongest of the hands present, although it was an unjustifiable restraint given his all but senseless condition. He closed his eyes and willed himself away to somewhere altogether more pleasing, his mother's embrace, I suspect. In went the knife and out poured another furious stream of blood. He near bit his tongue in half with the pain of it and his mouth filled up once more, giving his newly imperfect teeth a fresh coat of brilliant red. The surgeon led the blade along the line of his cheek bone to render the first arm of the swastika. The resultant incision emerged as a jejune squiggle. A heated debate ensued: a decent rendering of the swastika as a whole was considered unlikely if the surgeon was not replaced. A decision was made: the blade changed hands as did Konstantin's chin. It was a gratuitous delay to the inevitable.

He drifted off, as if in a river with a strong current. Over rocks and through narrow channels he glided, face down in the water, unresisting, for miles, until he arrived at a deep pool. The water there was brown and cold and tasted of iron. Jagged rocks loomed on all sides. Then muted voices penetrated the water. His chest tightened. The sun blinded. In went the tip of the blade again. The voices fell away with the rocks. Down he went into the void. Gently pulled by someone unseen, his mother, I suspect, to an unfathomable depth. There he remained, held in suspension until the bubbles arrived appearing as glass lutz marbles, a curiosity he once collected, at first tiny in size but growing larger with time to a size he'd never had the good luck to acquire for his collection. They rushed over his arms and legs, bounced over his uniform, rolled through his hair, filled his pockets and slowly, slowly, buoyed him upwards, to the surface, where the trees were visible, and also, another set of boots, much smaller than any of those belonging to his assailants.

The voices went back and forth but the blade was removed from his cheek, although not returned to his pocket. The second arm of the swastika had not been fully realised and this is how it would remain. The bigger boots were leaving. They dragged their feet along the ground, postured wildly at one another, and spat into the bushes as they left.

Konstantin gasped not unlike the trout he'd caught before he whacked them on the head with a stone. The boy with the small boots, shabby clothes, small nose, full lips, and freckles assayed the mess that was Konstantin's face before crouching and dribbling water over it from his canteen. '*Merde*,' he said. 'You're covered in puke.' It was an outstanding observation.

Konstantin's French, contrary to what had been implied by his assailants, was impeccable. His hearing, however, was still somewhat impaired. 'Pardon,' he said, with a swelling tongue that was set to fill the entire cavity of his mouth and was already affecting the authenticity of his French accent.

The boy helped him to sit. '*Merde*, you'll need stitches in your face,' he said.

'Yes.'

'*Merde*, they kept your knife.'

'Yes.'

'*Merde*, was it valuable?'

'Yes.'

'*Merde*, you'll never see it again.'

'Yes.'

'*Merde*, they broke your rod.'

'Yes.'

'*Merde*, you look like…*merde*.'

'Yes.'

'Do you know any other French than *oui*?'

'Yes. Do you know any other word than *merde*?'

The boy hid his smile by retrieving Konstantin's woggle. He handed it to him but pressed the accompanying neckerchief onto his cheek. 'Keep the pressure on,' he instructed.

Konstantin was sick, but not on himself this time. The boy kept the pressure on for him, but at a distance.

'Do you know who I am?' said Konstantin eventually.

'Yes,' said the boy, but how he understood the question, the boy alone knows.

'How?'

'Your *merde* uniform gives you away.'

Konstantin's small smile was more of a grimace. 'My father insists I wear it.'

The boy said nothing, then marvelled at the state of his tooth. 'Not much you can do about that,' he said, as if there was something Konstantin could do about his father's insistence that he wear his uniform in a country that despised it.

'Why did you stop them?' asked Konstantin.

'That's a stupid question.'

(It was one I'd have asked.)

'Could I have some of that, please?' asked Konstantin, nodding at the canteen.

The boy handed it over. Konstantin rinsed his mouth and discharged muck and debris onto the fallen leaves of the Norwegian Maple beneath which they were sitting.

'It wasn't a fair fight,' said the boy, 'that's why.'

'Do you know them?'

'That's another stupid question.'

'That means you don't,' said Konstantin.

'It does mean I don't,' confirmed the boy. 'Keep the pressure on,' he repeated, leaving the wound to Konstantin.

Wearily, Konstantin did as he was bid. 'I'm Konstantin,' he said offering the boy his spare bloodied hand.

'I know,' he said. 'I'll never shake the hand of a German.'

'How about the hand of a very grateful Boche?'

This made the boy laugh. He gave Konstantin's hand the very briefest of shakes before shoving it away. 'What will you tell your father?'

Konstantin considered the question then said, 'I fell out of a tree.'

'He'll never believe that,' said the boy.

'He'll prefer it to the truth.'

The boy frowned. 'Why?'

'He already considers me a disappointment. He doesn't require more proof. He'll think I should have won that fight.'

The boy shrugged. 'Can you see me?'

'No,' said Konstantin. 'Have you seen the state of my eyes?'

The boy smiled. 'No, have you?'

Konstantin smiled then winced.

'I'll see you to the château,' said the boy, standing. 'Well, to the edge of the woods, anyway.'

Konstantin also stood but felt faint. He leaned against the trunk of the Norwegian Maple. He remembered the marzipan in his breast pocket. 'Do you like marzipan?' he asked.

'No,' said the boy, 'but since when did that matter? If you weren't so battered, you'd see I can't afford to be choosy about what I eat.'

(Note to Joyce: What did I say about marzipan? Note to the reader of this file: how satisfying it is to have one's assertions upheld.)

The marzipan wasn't just any old marzipan. It had been shaped into fruits, hand-painted with food colouring, then wrapped in foiled paper. The boy took a marzipan plum in the end. It was squashed from the beating. 'This is what your eyes look like,' he noted with glee.

'I can't see,' said Konstantin. 'Remember?'

The boy shook his head and helped himself to another. Konstantin moored a marzipan banana alongside the gum that was least sore and left it there to dissolve of its own accord as he'd seen his father do with those strange tasting vitamultins of his.

'Tell you what, those fellas were spot on about your fish,' said the boy, inspecting Konstantin's creel. 'That really is a pathetic catch you've got there.'

'You think you can fish better?'

'I know I can.'

'Do you want to bet?'

'Time to go.'

'I don't know your name,' said Konstantin.

'You don't need to.'

'I'd like to know.'

'Why?'

'I owe you.'

'A beating?'

'No,' said Konstantin. 'My life.'

'I'll settle for the fish,' said the boy.

'I thought they were pathetic.'

'They'll do for a snack.'

'They're yours.'

'Sure you don't want to fight me for them?'

'Not today,' said Konstantin.

'My name's Gilbert,' said Gilbert. 'Gilbert Aumont.'

27.

Transcript of Interview. Operation Attar.
Date: 15/09/44. Time: 09.00 HRS. Interview 5/7.
Informant: Konstantin von Essen. Interviewer:
Saunders. Also present: Acting Guardian: Hesketh.
Location of debrief: Combined Services Detailed
Interrogation Unit, Latimer House, nr Amersham,
Buckinghamshire.

Interviewer: I'm very sorry to hear that Mrs
Bloomfield is feeling a little delicate this
morning, Konstantin.
Informant: Yes, Mr Saunders, it is most unfortunate.
However, please do not be alarmed; Mrs Bloomfield
is confident of being fully recovered of her health
by lunchtime.
Interviewer: Is that so?
Informant: This is what Mrs Bloomfield has said.
Interviewer: I see... (PAUSE) Well, that is good news.
Informant: So, we will wait for Mrs Bloomfield
before we continue, Mr Saunders?
Interviewer: Er, I don't think that'll be necessary,
Konstantin. Fortunately for us, Hesketh has very
kindly agreed to step into Mrs Bloomfield's shoes,
as it were, and act as your temporary guardian.
Informant: (PAUSE) I...
Interviewer: Of course, as soon as Mrs Bloomfield is
feeling up to sitting in on the interviews again,
Hesketh will...

Acting Guardian: Go back to making the tea.

Interviewer: Indeed. Nobody makes a finer pot of tea than you, Hesketh.

Acting Guardian: (INAUDIBLE)

Informant: Mrs Bloomfield believes her stomach upset was caused by something she ate, Mr Saunders.

Interviewer: Oh, that sounds most unfortunate, Konstantin, not to mention exceptionally surprising.

Informant: Mrs Bloomfield believes that the cook made a very large mistake while preparing the Woolton Pie.

Interviewer: Surely not, Konstantin? A mistake? That sounds highly improbable to me.

Informant: I am very sorry, but, yes, Mr Saunders, this is what Mrs Bloomfield believes.

Acting Guardian: I think Mrs Bloomfield must be mistaken, me laddie, I had the Woolton Pie and I've not got dicky guts.

Informant: I am very sorry, Mr Hesketh, but I do not understand the word dicky, nor can I remember the meaning of the word guts, though it is ringing my bells.

Acting Guardian: It rings a bell, me laddie.

Informant: It rings a bell. Thank you, Mr Hesketh.

Interviewer: Hesketh is referring to Mrs Bloomfield's upset stomach, Konstantin. Dicky guts, well, it's what we call a colloquialism.

Informant: As you know, Mr Saunders, in German we have a similar word to 'colloquialism' and so I am familiar with this word and its meaning. However, could you please tell me if I would be expected to say that I have dicky guts if I receive a stomach upset in the future?

Interviewer: No, Konstantin, you should say upset stomach. I would not say dicky guts.

Informant: Thank you, Mr Saunders.

Acting Guardian: For the record, me laddie, I didn't have an upset stomach after eating the Woolton Pie.

Interviewer: Also for the record, Konstantin, I do not speak German. Thus, I did not know that a similar word to 'colloquialism' exists in the German language.

Informant: (PAUSE) I am very sorry, Mr Hesketh, but do you have a problem with eating fish?

Acting Guardian: Fish? No, me laddie, but...

Interviewer: (CHUCKLE) There isn't any fish in Woolton Pie, Konstantin.

Informant: Yes, Mr Saunders, this is what I have also been led to believe, but Mrs Bloomfield discovered some fish in her pie.

Interviewer: Fish in a Woolton Pie? If true, that's most peculiar, Konstantin.

Acting Guardian: Did you have the Woolton Pie, sir?

Interviewer: Yes, Hesketh, I most certainly did.

Acting Guardian: Did you come across any fish, sir?

Interviewer: No, Hesketh, I most certainly did not.

Informant: I too had the Woolton Pie, Mr Hesketh, and I also did not find any fish. Mrs Bloomfield is the only person I know to have found fish in the Woolton Pie. This is very unfortunate because I remember Mrs Bloomfield telling you that fish makes her ill. I have been wondering how it happened, Mr Saunders. I wondered if there had been some accidental cross-contamination...

Interviewer: Cross-contamination? Now there's an impressive word, Konstantin.

Informant: Thank you, Mr Saunders, I found it in my dictionary last night.

Interviewer: Your English appears to be improving, quite literally, by the day, Konstantin. Some might describe the rapidity of your acquisition as astounding.

Informant: (PAUSE) I've been studying my dictionary, Mr Saunders. (PAUSE) A lot.

Interviewer: Evidently.

Informant: (PAUSE) I also committed the menu to memory, Mr Saunders, and the only other available option for the main course last evening was Potato

Jane. I've since discovered that Potato Jane contains potatoes, leeks, carrots, cheese, and milk. It does not contain fish. Consequently, accidental cross-contamination seems unlikely.

Interviewer: You have a very good memory, Konstantin.

Informant: (PAUSE) Thank you, Mr Saunders, it has helped me to conclude that there was no reason for a fish to be in the kitchen, and therefore in any of the prepared dishes.

Interviewer: Did you question Cook regarding the exact ingredients of the Potato Jane, or indeed the Woolton Pie?

Informant: No, Mr Saunders, I know that I'm not permitted to go beyond my room unaccompanied. I questioned Mrs Bloomfield as she was being sick from the fish she had eaten. (PAUSE) I questioned her through the door of our adjoining sleeping quarters.

Interviewer: (WATER POURED. SOUND OF DRINKING) I see.

Informant: I still do not know how any fish got into Mrs Bloomfield's pie.

Acting Guardian: Well there you have it, me laddie, Mrs Bloomfield *must* be mistaken.

Informant: But Mrs Bloomfield is always right, Mr Hesketh.

Acting Guardian: (LAUGH) Is that what Mrs Bloomfield told you, me laddie?

Informant: No, Mr Hesketh, it is not. It is an observation I have made.

Interviewer: (PAUSE) (TAP OF FINGERS ON DESK) I'm very sorry, Konstantin, but if Mrs Bloomfield is not mistaken, the unfortunate incident will just have to go on record as a complete and utter mystery, I'm afraid. (CLEARS THROAT) Perhaps, Hesketh, we could make Cook aware that Mrs Bloomfield must not, under any circumstances, be given fish in the future, either by accident or design. We certainly wouldn't wish for a repeat performance. We would all rather have Mrs Bloomfield present during this interview, would we not?

Acting Guardian: Yes, sir, and yes again.

Interviewer: So you needn't worry about Mrs Bloomfield any more, Konstantin.

Informant: Thank you, Mr Saunders, I am greatly relieved to hear that this will not happen again.

Interviewer: Lunchtime will be upon us before we know it.

Informant: Actually, Mrs Bloomfield said if she's feeling recovered before lunchtime, she'll rejoin us after tea-break, so she may be here sooner than expected.

Interviewer: (PAUSE) Interesting...and jolly good...obviously. Well... Okay... (CLEARS THROAT) (SHUFFLES PAPERS) Goodness, we've wasted a lot of time. Let's push on and return to the subject of the poster. This is the poster your father distributed to warn the people of Amiens that the penalty for possession of a pigeon was death. (PAUSE) In a previous interview, Konstantin, you stated that the removal of this poster was also punishable by death. You also stated that you didn't know if anybody had gone on to remove one of these posters. Could you please tell me if I have remembered all this correctly?

Informant: Yes, Mr Saunders, that is correct.

Interviewer: Thank you, Konstantin. (PAUSE) The thing is, we think at least one of your father's posters *was* taken down, *was* removed from display so to speak, by somebody not authorised to carry out such a task.

Informant: (COUGH)

Interviewer: What do you think about this, Konstantin?

Informant: (PAUSE) I am very sorry but I do not know what to think about this, Mr Saunders.

Interviewer: About the removal of the poster?

Informant: Yes, Mr Saunders.

Interviewer: But, now that you know a poster was removed, can you think of anybody who may have done it.

Informant: (PAUSE) No, Mr Saunders.

Interviewer: I would like to show you something, Konstantin. (RUSTLE OF PAPER) Is that alright?

Informant: (COUGH) Yes, Mr Saunders, I...think...so.

Interviewer: And I would like you tell me if you recognise it.

Informant: (COUGH) (SHARP INTAKE OF BREATH) I will...try.

Interviewer: It's the poster, Konstantin.

Informant: (LABOURED BREATHING)

Interviewer: Do take a look.

Informant: (WHEEZE)

Interviewer: Do take a look please, Konstantin.

Informant: (COUGH) (WHEEZE)
(GLASS OF WATER POURED)

Acting Guardian: (WHISPERED) Here, me laddie, have a guzzle.

Informant: Thank you, Mr Hesketh.

Interviewer: Could you please confirm that the poster I am now showing you is the poster your father had made?

Informant: (WHEEZE) (COUGH) (WHEEZE) (COUGH) (WHEEZE) (COUGH) Yes.

Interviewer: That the image on the poster of the three boys hanged from a tree is the same photograph your father instructed Madame Brugière to take?

Informant: (WHEEZE) (COUGH) (WHEEZE) (COUGH) (WHEEZE) (COUGH) (WHEEZE) (COUGH) (WHEEZE) Yes.

Interviewer: That the name of the smallest boy hanged from the tree was ten—year—old Gilbert Aumont?

Informant: (WHEEZE) (COUGH) (WHEEZE) (COUGH) (WHEEZE) (COUGH) (WHEEZE) (COUGH) (WHEEZE) (COUGH) (WHEEZE) (COUGH) (INAUDIBLE)

Interviewer: Sorry, Konstantin, was that a Yes?

Informant: (WHEEZE) (COUGH) (WHEEZE)

Acting Guardian: He's nodding his head, sir.

Interviewer: That the name Gilbert Aumont was, contrary to your previous claims, not just a pseudonym fabricated by you to keep your true identity from us, but rather, the name of a real boy?

Informant: (INAUDIBLE) (CRYING?)

Interviewer: That you were the person who removed this poster?

Informant: (WHEEZE) (PAUSE) (SILENCE)

Interviewer: We know it was you that removed the poster, Konstantin, because this very poster, the one I'm now showing you, was found by Troop Sergeant Major Bloomfield hidden in a pillowslip on *your* bed in the château. So, not only did you remove the poster from display, but you also kept it.

Informant: (WHISPERED) Yes.

Interviewer: Now I want to know why, Konstantin? Why did you do these things?

Informant: (WHEEZE) (SNIFF) (COUGH) (WHEEZE) (PAUSE) (WHEEZE) (WHEEZING)

Interviewer: Why did you remove the poster, Konstantin?

Informant: (SILENCE)

Interviewer: Why did you take Gilbert Aumont's name?

Informant: (SILENCE)

Acting Guardian: Come on, me laddie, best you answer the questions now.

Interviewer: Why did you embark upon this course of action, Konstantin?

(DOOR OPENS, MRS BLOOMFIELD BURSTS INTO THE INTERVIEW ROOM)

Guardian: Cooee, I'm back everybody. (CHUCKLE) Fish in the Woolton Pie, Mr Saunders; who'd have thought it? (TUTS) (THE NOISE OF GENERAL HUSTLE AND BUSTLE) How it got in there I'll never know. Good job I spotted it before I ate the whole lot. (RUSTLE OF KNITTING BAG?) (PUFFS) Might have been bob and

dick for days if that had happened. Then what would
you have done, eh? What have I missed? Anything?
Interviewer: (SILENCE)
Acting Guardian: (SILENCE)
Informant: (COUGH) (WHEEZE) (SNIFF)
Guardian: Oh my sainted aunts, what the blazes is
going on here? Konstantin, whatever's the matter?
Have you been crying? Oh my gawd what a horrible
picture. Is that the poster you two were going on
about the other day? Five minutes I'm gone and what
happens, but a right old carry on by the looks of it.
Well I'm very sorry, Mr Saunders, but it won't do:
why have you upset my boy?
Interviewer: INAUDIBLE

Interview Suspended: Date: 15/09/44. Time: 09.25
HRS. Interview 5/7.
**(Informant: Konstantin von Essen. Interviewer:
Saunders. Also present: Acting Guardian: Hesketh.)**
Location of debrief: Combined Services Detailed
Interrogation Unit, Latimer House, nr Amersham,
Buckinghamshire.

An Unnarrated Event
The Adulterer and The Thief

KONSTANTIN WISHED TO BID HIS FATHER GOODNIGHT. HE KNOCKED ON THE DOOR AND ENTERED ...

AS USUAL, KONSTANTIN FOLLOWED HIS FATHER'S ORDERS.

28.

"Ici Londres! Les Français parlent aux Français.
S'il vous plaît avant de commençer écoutez-bien ces messages
personnels"

Monsieur le Gendarme Faucheux, vos poules reviennent se percher. Trop de jus a gate les boulettes. L'arc en ciel a ete peint par Bonnie a midi. On recommande avec insistance que la trousse contienne des pansements. Le sable de la plage est rentre dans les sandwiches. Composez le concerto des que possible. Le potager a ete devaste par la tortue, il ne reste plus de laitues. Bon anniversaire, Severine, sept ans aujourd'hui. Le pretre a celebre la messe en latin. Maintenant chaque nerf est joint a chaque disque. Le comble de l'excursion c'etait les croissants au cafe. Le soleil reflete dans le miroir de la salle de bains. Devinez deux fois et demie mais le dixieme essai est juste.La chenille jaune est apparentee au papillon brun. L'avocat trouvera les profits dans la grange a foin. Garcon ordinaire, le Pere Noel apporte des jouets mardi. On repete - garcon ordinaire le Pere Noel apporte des jouets mardi. Dans la cimetiere chaque fantome agitera les chaines. Le vin rouge est bouchonne, buvez donc le blanc. La recolte a ete detruite, ne mangez pas de haricots verts.

"This is London! The French speak to the French. Before we begin, please listen to some personal messages.

Gendarme Faucheux, your chickens are coming home to roost. Too much gravy has spoiled the dumplings. The rainbow was painted by Bonnie at midday. We urgently recommend that the kit contains bandages. The sand from the beach went in the sandwiches. Compose the concerto at your earliest convenience. The allotment was raided by the tortoise: no more lettuces remain. Many happy returns, Severine, seven today. The priest said the mass in Latin. Every nerve is now attached to every disk. The highlight of the excursion were the croissants at the café. The sun is reflected in the bathroom mirror. Guess two-and-a-half times, but the tenth guess is correct. The yellow caterpillar is related to the brown butterfly. The lawyer will find the profits in the hayloft. Ordinary boy, Father Christmas brings toys on Tuesday. We say twice, Ordinary boy, Father Christmas brings toys on Tuesday. Every ghost will rattle the chains in the graveyard. The red wine is corked so drink the white. The crop has failed: do not eat the green beans.

29.

28 March, 1944

Regarding Operation Attar, a second message has been received from the informant claiming to be Gilbert Aumont. For the sake of continuity, I shall continue to refer to this informant as Aumont since his true name has not yet been established. All aspects of its delivery are identical to the first message, that is a) pigeon used to transport the message from France to Britain b) from Britain, message sent in a Basildon Bond envelope addressed to me and in the same handwriting c) hand-drawn rose and dot motif included on the seal of the envelope d) smudged postal mark on the envelope indicating that the message was posted from a town that begins with the letter C or possibly the letter O.

Against my better judgement, tentative enquiries continue with the General Post Office with regard to the postal network in a bid to identify the mystery postal town. However, even if the postal town is identified, I'm acutely aware that a two-man team conducting twenty-four hour surveillance on each and every postbox therein is a colossal surveillance commitment that, realistically, cannot be realised by the resources currently at our disposal. Even if the requisite resources were available, short of our people jumping on every man, woman or child observed posting a letter, I believe there remains very little prospect of pinning down the exact location of the British-based sender, and it occurs to me that this line of enquiry amounts to nothing less than a search for the proverbial needle in a haystack.

In relation to the identity of the pigeon, Aumont's second message has certainly provided us with food for thought. Binksy in MI-14(d) has now read the opening passage and agrees that Aumont appears to describe a pigeon trained in Boomerang, albeit unknowingly it would seem. Records show that of the three pigeons we trained in Boomerang, two are listed as confirmed dead, while the third, Ethelred the Unready, known to Binksy and the rest of the elite piegon community as Ethel, is listed as missing presumed dead.

Since SIS point-blank refused to extend the Boomerang programme, it is Binksy's assessment that Aumont has somehow acquired Ethel from Earthstar, the SOE agent to which he was originally assigned in Northern France, and is using him to fly his messages from Amiens to Britain. Earthstar reported Ethel missing in February. Ethel's owner, Lady Darrick-Sinclair, also reported Ethel missing in February. Discreet enquiries indicate that Lady Darrick-Sinclair remains ignorant of Ethel's apparent ressurection. Furthermore, it has been confirmed by Archibald Haines, leader of The Surrey Sprinters pigeon group, that there has been no sign of Ethel at his home loft in Surrey since Lady Darrick-Sinclair originally reported him missing.

Consequently, we are satisfied that Lady Darrick-Sinclair is not the British-based sender of Aumont's messages; this is a sensible conclusion given that she and I are not acquainted and further, that she has, without exception, always passed on Ethel's messages via the formal channel. We have taken the decision not to inform her that Ethel lives as it may do more harm than good, particularly since we cannot offer any guarantee that his welfare is a priority for those who currently have possession of him.

Expanding upon what he has concluded regarding the identity of the pigeon used by Aumont, Binksy has subsequently offered two theories in relation to the possible identity of the British-based sender 1. The sender is a casual stranger who came upon Ethel by chance and 2. The sender is a member of our security services who targeted Ethel for use in a clandestine operation of their design, and for reasons unknown.

If the sender is a casual stranger it suggests that, following his release by Aumont, Ethel got lost or fatigued during the journey back to Britain and landed somewhere alien to him (Binksy says this could be anywhere in Britain). Once the stranger found Ethel, rather than hand him in to the nearest police station as would be expected, he or she opened his message canister, posted Aumont's message to me, sent Ethel back to Aumont, and repeated the entire escapade a few weeks later. There are so many snags with this theory I hardly know where to begin, but the greatest of them has to be, why would this casual stranger have knowledge of me, my position in MI5, and my address? Furthermore, why would Aumont, with all the danger it entails, continue to send sensitive information to a stranger? Also, is it really likely that a stranger would know how to care for a pigeon, let alone a pigeon of Ethel's calibre? If, perchance, they were a pigeoneer, it is unikely that they would ignore protocol and retain Ethel in this way. This theory simply doesn't hold true.

If, on the other hand, the sender is a member of the security services, it means they've sanctioned the purloining of Ethel from Earthstar, SOE's agent already based in Amiens, then, presumably with the assistance of Aumont, re-trained Ethel to boomerang between two new locations: Aumont's location elsewhere in Amiens and the rogue agent's location somewhere in Britain. It also means that they've not only managed to recruit Aumont but have also become his handler without our knowledge. Why would a member of our own security services go about acquiring and disseminating intelligence in such an arse about face fashion? Furthermore, why would they undermine a pre-existing

179

intelligence gathering operation? (SOE are, understandably, rather miffed to hear that Ethel is being used by somebody other than Earthstar.) Also, why would this agent maintain anonymity with me given that I'm clearly the chosen recipient of their intelligence?

The truth of the matter is, neither of the two scenarios proposed by Binksy can be judged sufficiently plausible to warrant further investigation along these lines. I rather suspect that the truth of the matter lies somewhere between the two, but which of the inherent hypotheses are fact, and which are fiction, is anybody's guess. Though I suspect we'll never unmask the British-based sender, I have permitted myself one last throw of the die by fowarding a copy of the rose and dot motif to a world-renowned Professor of Semiotics at the University of Edinburgh for analysis. I await her reply with bated breath.

The intelligence in Aumont's first message has now been verified, and much in the way of tactical ground has been gained by us as a result. Generalfeldmarschall Dieter von Essen has been identified as the 'senior German officer' of Aumont's messages. Earthstar, via a contact in Les Gens Prévalent, confirmed that von Essen requisitioned the Château des Beaux Anges last July and has been the Commander for Operations in the North Zone ever since. Notwithstanding von Essen's senior rank, hitherto Aumont's contact with us, von Essen seems to have avoided our radar to some degree. In the cold light of day, this is, of course, rather astonishing. Expeditious enquries with Willie Stevenson, the former British assistant military attaché in Berlin, reveal that von Essen is a close friend of Hitler and, furthermore, that von Essen's appointment in France was at the behest of Hitler himself.

After receiving Aumont's first message, our initial response was to remove von Essen from the picture via a targeted aerial attack. However, this was, as reported by Aumont, ultimately a failure with the unfortunate, and most regretable, loss of French civilian life. The present position is to leave von Essen in situ at the château to safeguard not only French civilians, but also Aumont and the priceless intelligence he continues to bestow. In terms of dealing with von Essen, I'm in favour of the softly, softly, catchee monkey approach: in the future, Aumont's messages will serve as useful evidence against von Essen for complicity in 1) crimes against peace 2) crimes against humanity 3) war crimes.

I remain extremely doubtful that Aumont is an ordinary boy as he coninues to claim. I went over to discuss his so-called 'ordinariness' with CD. of SOE. CD. said, 'Ordinary my eye', or words to that effect. Aumont's second message reveals that he has access not only to von Essen's office and the highly sensitive military documents housed therein, but also, von Essen's personal correspondance. This sort of access can only be described as exceptional, although I'm mindful of the other words that might also apply. His request for a Minox camera, secret ink and supply of rice paper not only reads like a seasoned spy's Christmas wishlist, but also demonstrates a degree of strategic perspective that is wholly at odds with what can be expected from an ordinary boy. And we are still very much in the dark as to why Aumont made his pseudonym the name of a murdered boy. Any French name, or indeed any name, would have done in the circumstances. I deliberately include 'any name' here because it occurs to me that Aumont is not French. His diction puts me in mind of the German prisoners-of-war we currently hold at the Combined Services Detailed Interrogation Unit (CSDIU) at Latimer House near Amersham...

'By the way, Daphne, that's Latimer spelled with an 'I',' broke off Latymer, 'not with a 'Y'.'

'So this Latimer House in Buckinghamshire is not your stately pile then, Mr Latymer?' she joked, taking the pause in proceedings as an opportunity to rotate her hands and alleviate the ache in her wrists.

Latymer used the pause to light his pipe. 'Good lord, no,' he said, taking her seriously, 'merely a coincidence.'

On the third rotation, Daphne sneaked a peek at her watch: she was supposed to be meeting Bunny at a dance after work.

The irritating thing was, she wasn't sure Latymer should be keeping a diary at all. The sensitive information he, and by extension her, typed onto these pages night after night was the sort of information she, and doubtlessly the Official Secrets Act of 1911, was convinced oughtn't to journey further than one's head.

It's fair to say that very little escaped Latymer and this included Daphne's glance at her watch. 'Shouldn't be too much longer,' he said, without removing his pipe from his mouth. 'I've got an engagement to keep, too, though I sincerely doubt mine will be any where near as fun as yours.'

Daphne blushed. The opportunity to insist he was mistaken and that she had nothing better to do than sit for another few hours taking his dictation was up for grabs, but she desperately wanted to dance with that flight lieutenant so she ignored it, smiled, and tilted her head to one side to show that she was ready for his next sentence.

```
Moreover, when Aumont writes of the female German spy
posing as a Belgian artist in England with the code-
name MOPS, he states that the word 'mops' is the German
word for a breed of dog, which, incidentally, we have
assessed to be a pug. This little boo-boo reveals two
things 1. the letter received by von Essen about MOPS
was written in German, which initself is unsurprising
and 2. in order to understand the contents of the
letter, Aumont must be proficient in the German
language. This, given the claim that he is an ordinary
French boy, is very surprising indeed. Aumont goes on
to state that the English translation for the German
word 'mops' cannot be found in his dictionary. The only
dictionary in which Aumont could reasonably expect to
find an English translation for a German word is within
a German to English dictionary. This begs the question:
Why would a French boy be in possession of such a text?
This slip-up, when combined with all the other oddities
```

of this case, utterly undermines Aumont's avowels regardng his identity. Hence, CD. and I agree that Aumont is a German boy. As a matter of extreme urgency, BEEKEEPER will make contact with Earthstar to determine if von Essen has an adolescent son or other young male relative living with him at the château.

In relation to the intelligence offered by Aumont in this second message, I remain cautious, particularly in light of what we now suspect regarding Aumont's true nationality, but because additional intelligence from Garbo substantiates Aumont's claims in relation to Normandy, I have nonetheless a) passed on the coordinates for the ammunition depots to Bomber Command at Naphill as well as Hillside at Hughenden b) organised a drop of the items requested by Aumont in the field specified. (Rice paper is included in the package although my position on the matter is that, in Aumont's case, loo paper works just as well.) However, due to mist this first attempt was unusucessful c) arranged with Binksy for the requested items to be dropped with a Columba pigeon in an attempt to cut out the BASILDON BOND middle man d) arranged for today's BBC broadcast to France to include a message for Ordinary Boy alerting him to the revised drop date for the requested items e) begun checks on all married British official war artists for foreign spouses purporting to be Belgian nationals. Queerly, the code-name MOPS sounds familiar, but as it stands the reason for this escapes me.

I have also now shared Aumont's intelligence with C. of SIS, partly because I consider it impolitic to keep him ignorant of its existence, and partly because it substantiates what we have argued all along in relation to the pigeons involved in Operation Columba: they are worth their weight in gold.

In other matters, in the luggage of Jasper Nifterick, a small piece of note paper was found. Initially thought to be devoid of script, closer scrutiny revealed the presence of secret ink and the following list of words: 'Adelbert, Kleermaker, Gala, Tellurian, Pioneer.' X has deciphered this as follows: Adelbert is Adalberto. Kleermaker is the Dutch for Tailor and means Schneider. Gala means 'Ober', Tellurian means 'Sturm', and Pioneer means 'Führer'. Hence, Adalberto Schneider, Obersturmführer, who is a Gestapo officer in the Sicherheitsdienst in Amsterdam.

Also, I have arranged to meet with Emese Bárány this evening, Bárány being the mistress of Laszlo Bartha, on the pretext of wishing to improve my vocal range from baritone to tenor. Of course, the real reason for visiting Bárány is to get hold of Bartha's phone number. I hope that my voice will not betray me, and further, that Bárány is as gullible as they say she is, and does not see through my chronic deception.

An Unnarrated Event
Gone Fishing

'Time's up,' says Konstantin.

'Another half-hour,' demands Gilbert.

'No way,' says Konstantin. 'I've won fair and square.'

'You don't know that.'

'I saw how many you pulled out.'

'You went for a pee.'

'I wasn't gone all day.'

'Maybe it was long enough…'

'To catch another two? You're kidding me?' says Konstantin.

'I wouldn't joke about this.'

'Rubbish, you joke about everything.'

'Let the count decide,' says Gilbert.

Konstantin shrugs and says, 'Okay, my friend, let the count decide. I take it you can count to two?'

'Ha, ha, *trou de cul*. You won't be so cocky in a minute.'

'One,' counts Konstantin, and throws a trout on the grass.

'One,' counts Gilbert, and does the same.

'Mine's bigger,' notes Konstantin.

'Maybe I'm saving the best till last.'

Konstantin laughs. 'Two.'

'Two,' says Gilbert.

'Th..re..ee,' says Konstantin.

'Three,' says Gilbert.

Konstantin frowns at the third of Gilbert's fish.

'Keep going,' says Gilbert.

Against his better judgement, Konstantin does. 'Four,' he says. 'I win.'

'Four,' says Gilbert, producing another fish from his creel.

'What? No way. You did not catch four, Gilbert. You didn't even catch three. You caught two.'

'What are these then?' says Gilbert, waving his third and fourth fish at Konstantin. 'Figments of my imagination?'

'Suspicious, that's what they are.'

'And what is this?' says Gilbert, producing a fifth fish. 'It's five, is it not?'

'You're a cheat,' laughs Konstantin.

'How is it possible?'

'You caught the last three fish yesterday and brought them along to the competition.'

'Where's your proof?'

'I saw you pull two fish from the river today. You definitely didn't catch five.'

'You went for a pee, and while you were away, I had tremendous success because you weren't scaring away my fish with your big mouth.'

'You're such a liar, Gilbert.'

Gilbert grins. 'Winner takes all.'

'I was going to let you have mine anyway, you idiot.'

'Next time, Konsti, pee in the river like I do and you won't miss a thing.'

'Next time, I'll check your creel before we begin.'

'You're a bad loser, Konsti.'

'And you're a cheat, Gilbert.'

'See you tomorrow,' says Gilbert.

'See you tomorrow,' says Konstantin.

30.

It was fair to say that Konstantin was not expecting to receive a letter from a boy named Oliver and a girl named Polly. He re-read Oliver's letter and made the following deducements:

1. Oliver was not actually a boy, but a girl. Therefore, Oliver was not the real name of his new pen friend. (Touché, Joyce.)
2. Since Oliver was a pseudonym, Polly was too.
3. Oliver's emblem revealed that Oliver's real name was either Rose or a variant of Dota, Dotzie or Dorathea since, in Germany, these names were frequently shortened to Dot.
4. Polly's real name was the name that remained of the two.
5. Oliver wasn't much cop at spelling, but wrote full and interesting letters.
6. Oliver asked a lot of questions.
7. Oliver's father was both the very important man in London and Father Christmas.
8. Oliver wanted the pigeon's name to remain Kenneth.
9. The word 'Howdy' was not in the English dictionary and, as such, was a strange invention/inclusion.

Konstantin stowed Kenneth in the loft he'd built for him in the woods, readjusted the camouflage netting he'd pinched from the stores weeks before to make Kenneth's dwelling invisible, and began work on his reply. I must point out that Konstantin had yet to take delivery of the toys he'd requested from Oliver's father, hence he did not have the rice paper and so reverted to the loo paper as his stationary of choice. I must also point out that loo paper was something he habitually carried to facilitate the answering of complex calls of nature while in the woods, particularly since he spent most of his time there. Further, Konstantin did not intend to send the letter to Oliver and Polly until he had some microfilm to send with it as it wasn't fair on Kenneth to send him back and forth over the Channel, particularly given the risks (earlier expounded by the great bird himself).

First, he translated each of Oliver's questions as follows:

1. Does Kenneth belong to Father?
2. Do I have a different name for Kenneth?
3. Will I tell Polly that Oliver thinks the history book written by A.J.P. Taylor is boring?
4. Why didn't I colour my map?
5. Do I have colouring pencils?
6. Have I considered requesting an artist's box for my birthday?
7. Is Mops an artist?
8. What career would I like in the future?
9. What happened to Mops' teeth?
10. What is wrong with Mother?
11. Where do I really live?
12. Did the Germans really behead the British agent?
13. Do I know the fate of King Henry VIII's wives?
14. Did I witness the execution of Bettina Agnes Rutter?
15. Why are children and Jews being sent to Poland?
16. Is Poland large? (Konstantin translated 'swell' as *large* rather than *splendid*.)
17. Is secret ink a figment of my imagination?
18. Can I provide a physical description of myself?
19. Have I begun puberty?
20. Do I like school?
21. Is rice paper made of rice?

Then he put a line through all the questions he conveniently didn't understand, questions 11, 12, 14, and 15, as it happens. Then he began writing a letter, deliberately throwing in a bit of Gilbert here and there for added authenticity:

Salutations, Oliver and Polly,

Thank you for writing to me. It was a lovely surprise. I will try to answer as many questions as I can but my Anglais is not very good and I do not understand all of your questions. Here are answers to the questions I do understand.

1 Kenneth does not belong to my Papa.

2 I do not have a name for Kenneth. I like the name Kenneth.

3 I will not reveal your opinion on A.J.P. Taylor's book to anybody.

4 I didn't colour my map because I didn't have time.

5 I don't have many colouring pencils.

6 It is a good idea to ask for an artist's box for my eleventh birthday.

---

7 Mops is an artist, as far as I know.

8 I would like to be a gamekeeper when I am a man.

9 I don't know what happened to Mops' merde teeth. She was probably born with them like that.

10. My mother has a serious problem with her lungs.

11. I don't know much about merde Henry VIII or his wives.

12.Poland is smaller than France, but bigger than Britain.

13. Secret ink is authentique.

14. I am short like you, with straight black hair and dark brown eyes. I don't have freckles or dimples but I do have small teeth with gaps between most of them. A large part of my left thumb is missing after a wild boar bit it off. I am also hairy and it is dark hair. I like fishing and particularly enjoy cheating in games and fishing competitions.

I am very brave.

15. I am only ten. I do not have a man's voice, but it will be very deep when I do get one.

16. I don't go to merde school.

17. Rice paper is made from rice. I enjoy eating it. Next time I write to you, I hope to do so on rice paper. Please consider eating my next letter. I think you will like it.

Thank you for sending my messages to the important man in Londres, and for your kind sentiment in relation to my drawing ability, and my failure to die in the attack on the château. I am glad you are able to warn your mother about the merde Boches. I am sorry to hear about the merde evacuees. I think a green and yellow eye is very unusual.

I have not seen an eye like this before. Please could you tell me the meaning of 'howdy'? I cannot find it in my merde dictionary.

I hope Polly permits you to write another letter to me.

I hope we both receive our papas soon.

> Viva La France!
> Adieu mon ami,
> Gilbert Aumont

P.S. Merde, I am very sorry, but I do not know the meaning of this 'bust a gut'. I do not know how this is done. I am very sorry but I do not think it sounds like a good idea.

After he had finished the letter, he bid Kenneth a good night, secreted the letter (together with the rough work) in Madame Brugière's pilfered brassiere, and trod a reluctant path back to the château, just in time to dine with his father and that *merde* woman.

31.

This file has taught me that, in certain circumstances, a pigeon could be regarded as a very dangerous animal indeed, even by a sensible person. And, unlike Mrs Bloomfield, I'm not referring to hypersensitivity pneumonitis, also known as Pigeon Breeders Lung, when I say this. In point of fact, I would almost go so far as to say that by 1944, a pigeon was as dangerous to handle as any of the explosive weapons being cooked up in Station IX by Dudley Newitt et al, for deployment by SOE agents, such as Earthstar, in enemy occupied territories, such as France.

Yes, my statement may be considered controversial: even I can concede that, unlike a rat bomb, a pigeon was not liable to explode in one's hands. And, whilst I'm also willing to concede that pigeons are pigeons and generally come in one recognizable form – unless they've fallen victim to any one of the job hazards outlined by Ethel in his anthropomorphic monologue – and come in very few sizes, what I have learned from reading this file is that a pigeon could come in more than one guise. One such guise being the Gestapo pigeon; a pigeon much utilised by *Generalfeldmarschall* Dieter von Essen during his tenure in France.

When I told Joyce about the Gestapo pigeon she described my use of the term as 'misleading'. She said I made it sound as if the Gestapo pigeon were a variety of pigeon one could specifically breed if one were so inclined. To appease Joyce, I would like to make it absolutely clear that a Gestapo pigeon was fashioned, not begot. Furthermore, when I make use of the term I am but referring to any old pigeon, rarely an elite pigeon, dressed up by the Gestapo to look like Ethel or his compatriots. To labour the point further, and labour it is for I'm working up quite a sweat on this clarification I assure you, while you could ascribe these nouns to a Gestapo pigeon: *impersonator, charlatan, masquerader, poser,* or *trickster,* you could not, under any circumstances, ascribe these nouns to a Gestapo pigeon: *strain, genus, type, kind,* or *sort.* More to the point, what Joyce had missed as a consequence of her rant on my so-called 'consistent tendency to deceive' was the incontrovertible truth that, unless you were German, handling a Gestapo pigeon in enemy occupied territory would almost certainly cost you your life, and more often than not the lives of others to boot.

So, imagine you had no experience of pigeons, how would you tell the difference between a Gestapo pigeon and an Allied pigeon if, for example, you innocently stumbled upon a pigeon cooing away in a container as you hungrily scoured a farmer's field in Amiens for a stray potato? As you may have guessed, the telltale indicator of a pigeon's nationality/allegiance was the brand of cigarettes they carried with them. For example, Pall Mall cigarettes were a British brand, ergo, if you found a pack of Pall Malls in the container, you could be sure the pigeon was British. So, you breathe a sigh of relief that you haven't just tripped arse over tit on a Gestapo pigeon, you soothe your severely frayed nerves with a Pall Mall, assuming you smoke, before pocketing the remainder of the pack and removing the friendly pigeon from the container. Whereupon, you discover a canister strapped to its leg carrying a message that reads:

> Greetings to the French. Allied invasion imminent! Help us to rid France of the German enemy. We request the names and addresses of all those willing to lend us a hand. We can only succeed with your assistance. And if you know of anybody willing to give shelter to Allied airmen should the need arise, please do let us know where we may find them. Répondez s'il vous plait. Vive la France!

About time too, you think, and then you start listing all the names of those you know that fit the bill on the supplied paper, using the supplied pencil. Before you can say, think twice, you've named the French equivalent of Fred from the allotments; Jean from number 7 with the dormant talent for playing the spoons; your old drinking buddies, Bert and Ned; Bert's sister from up the road; not to mention Bert's sister's husband, who never says much, but you assume he's keen; Father Bruno who, by contrast, says a good deal, especially on Sundays; nonagenarian Nancy the greyhound breeder with the gammy leg and penchant for pickled eggs (which she sucks noisily, even in company); Donald the hothead and famed maker of the swish tin baths; the Jones' who are already hiding the Calmers – a Jewish family of five; Mrs Scullion the widowed primary school teacher who hugs every child as they enter the classroom whether they like it or not, and blows tremendous smoke rings at parties; Arwel and Lynwyn the jolly shopkeepers whose proportions and disposition appear entirely unaffected by rationing; and last but not least, yourself, and every member of your cherished family. And yes, you add that any one of those listed would be only too happy to shelter a stranded Allied airman should the need arise. You sign off with a V for Victory in keeping with the fashion of the time.

It's quite a list and you feel very satisifed with yourself for having done your bit, so much so in fact, you help yourself to another Pall Mall. And as you puff, you stuff: inside the container goes the list, up to the sky goes the pigeon, and weather permitting, just hours later, into the hands of the British your intelligence lands. As evening falls, you relax by the fire with the last of the Pall Malls, if your habit is as filthy as mine, and the imminent Allied invasion you've all but been promised has you periodically rubbing your hands together with anticipation, not to mention relief.

Now, if it really were the case that I exhibit a 'consistent tendency to deceive' as per Joyce's allegation, would I not leave this sunny supposition here? As I keep having to remind Joyce, and it's a painful business, believe me, I'm not telling a story, I'm relaying the contents of a file. Unlike the Gestapo pigeon, the facts in this file were begot, not fashioned, and well before I joined the War Office, I might add. Therefore, I'm no more guilty of deception for not always offering the happy ending I suspect Joyce secretly desires, than I am of adultery merely because I chose to surprise her with half a dozen sprays of freesias last month. To be once again clear, the concoction of a happy ending for this anecdote or any other contained in the file, is not part of my job description, hence I do not concoct them.

And, whilst we're on the subject, there's no such thing as a free pack of smokes either: the pigeon with the Pall Malls isn't British, it's Gestapo, and you've been had. As you relax before the fire smoking the last of the trap, out race the Gestapo to viciously round up Fred, Jean, Bert, Ned, Bert's sister, Bert's sister's husband, Father Bruno, Nancy, Donald, the Calmers family, the Jones', Mrs Scullion, Arwel and Lynwyn, and last but not least, you, and your cherished family. This is a net haul of 27 prisoners for the enemy (I erred on the side of caution and made you a family of four; I hope to goodness your family doesn't number more), 27 people to be wiped from the earth by means of the guillotine, the scaffold, or the firing squad (the latter method of execution being the most likely in this scenario for the occupying force love nothing more than a spot of collective punishment). I'm quite sure you've gifted somebody in the Gestapo a promotion, especially given that five Jews and a priest were part of the haul.

Your only consolation, if you think it'll make the scenario more palatable (although it's no lemon sorbet so wouldn't be enough to cleanse my palate), is that it was an easy mistake to make. After all, Gilbert Aumont who did know a thing or two about pigeons was likewise ensnared. The problem is, he wasn't. Not quite like you, anyway. Yes, he was hanged for being In Possession Of An Enemy Pigeon, but the key word in the proven offence is the adjective used to describe the pigeon: Enemy. It's a topsy-turvey state of affairs but for your sake, as well as Joyce's, I will attempt to elucidate them. To a German soldier, an enemy pigeon was an Allied pigeon. To a patriotic French boy, an enemy pigeon was a Gestapo pigeon. Gilbert knew the difference between an Allied pigeon and a Gestapo pigeon even if the Gestapo pigeon was living it up in an Allied container with a pack of British fags. With regard to the latter he would do as his oppos in Les Gens Prévalent advised: he would smoke the fags and eat the pigeon. With the Allied pigeon, he would hide it until he could safely hand it over to his commanding officer. The problem was, *Generalfeldmarschall* von Essen wasn't the idiot that, Joyce for one, privately wished he was. He knew the portly Gestapo pigeons were no longer pulling the wool over Les

Gens Prévalent. That's why he captured an Allied pigeon — a poor old Columba pigeon to be exact – and planted it, container and all (but with no giveaway Pall Malls), in the potato field. After that, it was just a matter of waiting and watching to see who would take the bait. And, well, we all know what happened next, don't we?

Come now, take it from me, it doesn't do to dwell on the events that distress us.

Ordinarily, the *Generalfeldmarschall's* office was strictly out of bounds to all but him and invited guests. But his office, for reasons of convenience, was also where the post tray lived. Consequently, Konstantin devised a special modus operandi for snooping in his father's office. In fact, it was a prerequisite for snooping in that particular place: before embarking on a snoop, he would arm himself with a letter he had written to his mother. That way, if he were ever caught in the act by the man himself, or spotted entering or leaving the office by any one of his father's spies, the largest of which were Madame Brugière and his father's Chief-of-Staff/Chief henchman, *Oberleutnant* Hans Krebs, he would simply claim that he was there to deposit his letter in the post tray. (Prior to the office being designated an office, it was a library and in that function a lock on the door wasn't deemed necessary. With hindsight, I imagine the *Generalfeldmarschall* regarded the lack of a lock as a catastrophic oversight.)

The frequency of Konstantin's snooping required the writing of a lot of letters to his mother. The *Generalfeldmarschall* routinely discovered these letters sitting in the post tray. The ubiquity of them irked him since they were clear evidence of the boy's excessive emotional dependency on his mother. And yet, he didn't outlaw them. Neither did he tear them in two and throw them in the wastepaper basket as one might expect. To the contrary, he allowed them to be posted, and by extension, delivered to the sanatorium in Bradenburg. Then he drove them from his mind with the help of a few Pervitin, and by this point in the file, his *Führer's* favourite opioid, Eukodal.

If the post tray had been located anywhere else in the château, Konstantin would not have had legitimate cause to enter his father's office and snoop. It's a sobering thought but had it not been for a post tray, none of Konstantin's intelligence – intelligence described by Latymer as *game-changing in the war against Germany* and prompted a full-scale speech from Winston Churchill – would have made it across the Channel. No doubt Joyce would accuse me of exaggeration if I dared to suggest that a post tray had been instrumental in ending World War Two, but, as you well know, I'm not given to exaggeration and further, I allow the facts of this file to speak for themselves.

Konstantin found it difficult writing so many letters to his mother simply because he had very little to say. Each day in France passed in much the same way as the day before: he studied, he helped his father with odd jobs, he kept out of his father's way, and now that Gilbert was what Gilbert was…(dead), the hours between these activities were spent entirely alone trapped in a very private hell. And of course, he could hardly tell her about Kenneth, Polly and Oliver, and his great plan to reunite the von Essen family by lassoing himself and his father back to Germany, and freeing her from the sanatorium.

Though his mother hadn't replied recently, in accordance with her physician's advice that she wasn't to excite or exert herself with the writing of letters, it wasn't as if Konstantin had received a message from her physcian politely requesting that he refrain from boring her to death with his daily account of life in France, either. So, he continued to write, compensating the unfettered minutiae with fabricated anecdotes of fun, frolics and fishing with his many French friends. I note that Gilbert, though…(dead), was the fellow protagonist in most if not all of these yarns.

On this reconnaissance mission, Konstantin focused on the ginormous maps layed out on the desk. Helpfully, the maps had already been secured at the corners with a number of Devil's Toenails; these fossils, originally found in Florac, in Southern France, must have been discovered by one of the château's anterior owners during a summer holiday. His father must have been studying the maps early that morning, or sometime during the night, either time equally plausible since he slept so rarely. Regardless, it was helpful. Konstantin was undoubtedly brave but he wasn't stupid. The noise associated with unrolling several maps of this size would have represented a risk too far, particularly given that he was ignorant of his father's precise whereabouts. Also, the office door was larger than its frame so didn't close firmly. (With hindsight, I suppose that was the reason for the lack of a lock.) If the scheduled delivery of the requested toys by Father Christmas had not been made impossible by Tuesday's mist, he'd have whipped out the Minox camera and photographed the lot. For even he knew that what confronted him was a coup de grâce in terms of intelligence for the Allies, if he could successfully relay all that they revealed.

The first of the maps showed the locations of the production facilities and launch sites of the German V-2 rockets along the coast of France. Marked locations included Brecourt, Sottevast, Eperlecque and Roquetoire. The second map illustrated the dispositions of his father's Wehrmacht command, Army Group D, which numbered some 50 odd divisions in the Pas-de-Calais region and clearly substantiated what Konstantin had previously reported: the Germans were expecting the Allies to attack this region and not Normandy. The third, fourth and fifth maps detailed the precise locations of the German coastal defence batteries. The sixth and final map was much smaller than the others – about the size of an elbow patch – and printed on silk rather than paper. It seemed to reveal some sort of escape route, but for whom, it was unclear. Likewise, the precise route since to an untrained eye the route appeared as a meaningless jumble of colourful squiggles.

The sixth map aside, Konstantin's hands began to shake with the enormity of what he was viewing: these weren't just maps, these were currency, a currency strong enough to buy back his family. He felt nauseous, but whether from excitement or fear I know not. I suppose if someone were to hold a gun to my head and demand to know which I thought most likely: excitement or fear, I would suggest fear. Though Konstantin had an excellent memory, it wasn't a photographic one, at least not so far as I know, and the sheer amount of detail in these maps would require the latter if they were to be successfully relayed. Added to that was the very real possibility that by the time he had taken delivery of the camera from Father Christmas, the maps might have gone walkies. These were issues that had the potential to weaken his currency. And there certainly wasn't enough time to make notes on the maps, if that's what you're wondering: he still had a letter to snoop through. It had been hiding beneath the maps and was from *der Wüstenfuchs,* the Desert Fox, *Generalfeldmarschall* Erwin Rommel. Konstantin skim-read it while periodically glancing at the door and listening out for footsteps, a creaking floorboard, or a patriotic whistle in the hallway beyond. I'm quite sure it's impossible to grasp the speed with which his eyeballs moved and the degree to which this did not help his nausea.

While the snoop of the century was going on downstairs, the *Generalfeldmarschall* was sitting in his bedroom writing a difficult letter to his Führer.

Château des Beaux Anges
Amiens
Picardy
France

Berghof
Berchtesgaden
Obersalzberg
Bavaria
Germany

15 April 1944

<u>Happy Birthday, Mein Führer!</u>

Mein Führer,

Happy Birthday! I hope this letter reaches you before Thursday. I am most disappointed that Konstantin and I are not able to share your special day with you as we have done many times in the past.

However, we shall be with you in spirit and celebrating all your wonderful achievements; although, truly, there are not enough hours in the day to do them all justice!

I also wanted to take this opportunity to thank you again for taking care of the arrangements for Gerda. Your counsel in this matter was greatly appreciated and your decision that I remain at my post in France was both wise and proper. The interests of the Fatherland must take precedence above the interests of any one man. I would be most grateful if you could pass on my eternal gratitude to Eva for supervising the supply of Gerda's wardrobe.

Lastly, as Konstantin's godfather, I humbly request that in the event of my death, Lieber Führer, you take charge of his upbringing and education. As you know, Konstantin is a very bright boy but I fear Gerda's overindulgence of him may have done him a great disservice. Nothing would give me greater peace of mind than to know that, in my absence, Konstantin will be guided by a loving but firm hand. In your guardianship, I know that Konstantin will become a man worthy of the Third Reich.
 Sig heil!
 Your dear friend and most loyal of servants,
 Dieter von Essen.

The *Generalfeldmarschall* placed the letter in the envelope, tidied up his tunic, which he hadn't bothered to take off for the forty winks he presumed he must have had at some point in the preceding twenty-four hours, and made for the post tray.

When the *Generalfeldmarshall* burst into his office, as was customary, the von Essen men, if I may call them that, locked eyes and drew their respective letters like Lügers.

 'What are you doing in here?' the *Generalfeldmarschall* demanded.

 'I'm posting a letter to mother,' said Konstantin. 'Is that a letter for mother?' he asked, gesturing at the letter his father was holding.

Konstantin was far too hopeful for his father's liking and it was bloody irritating. 'No, son, this is none of your business, that's what this is. Have you written to your godfather lately?'

Konstantin couldn't remember the last time he'd written to his Onkel, but he didn't play clever by suppressing the frown that instantly communicated this.

'For God's sake, boy, have you forgotten that it's his birthday on Thursday?'

It had completely slipped Konstantin's mind. 'No,' he said. 'Of couse not, Father.'

'So you were just about to write, were you? Just about to wish him the most glorious of days? Is that right, son? Is it?'

Konstantin avoided his father's glare, but it was like a hand around his throat.

'Why are you writing yet another letter to your mother when you should be writing to your Führer?'

'I'm sorry, Father, I shall write a letter today.'

'Oh, I know that, son, and you'll do it now.'

Konstanin glanced at his father's desk. It was designed to be read as the question: *Where shall I write it?* But, it was orchestrated to allow him to check that he hadn't left any of the documents out of place. One tiny corner of the Desert Fox's letter was newly exposed. He lunged for the post tray, launched his mother's letter at it with a good deal of flourish and surreptitiously forced Rommel's letter back into hiding with a nudge of his hip. It was a strange perambulation, but fortunately for him his father's perspective was becoming nicely skewed by the narcotics he'd just taken.

'Write the damn thing on the floor,' he shouted, finally losing his patience.

Konstantin flew at the hand-made rug like cannon fodder diving for the trench then realised he didn't have any paper. 'Could I have some paper please, Father?'

'What?'

'My writing set is in my room.'

'*Verflucht noch mal,*' his father shouted. '*Geh mir aus den Augen,* you little *scheißekerl.* Get out, get out, get out.'

You'll be very relieved to know that Konstantin did as he was told and bolted from the room as if under sustained live fire. The *Generalfeldmarschall* attempted to slam the door after him (but without success thanks to its shoddy condition) then set about clearing a space on his desk in order to write a letter to Madame Brugière, the contents of which I cannot relate since the letter is not on file, but understand contained many declarations of love and devotion.

Château des Beaux Anges
Amiens
Picardy
France

Berghof
Berchtesgaden
Obersalzberg
Bavaria
Germany

15 April 1944

Lieber Onkel,

Herzlichen Glückwunsch zum Geburtstag! I wish you the most glorious of days on Thursday. How will you celebrate? I am most excited to know.

I wish to reassure you, lieber Onkel, that I have been **Silently Fufilling My Duty**, trying my very best to **Be Useful At All Times**, and every day **Striving To Be Most Obedient And Faithful To My Father, My Mother, And To Germany.** I am taking every opportunity **To Behave Honourably**, and **To Imitate The Brave Soldiers** I see all around me, here in France.

That I will one day come **To Fight For The Fatherland Is The Greatest Joy Of My Existence**, lieber Onkel; may that day come soon.

I Will Always Serve You Gladly, Mein Führer,

Your loving godson,
Konstantin.

An Unnarrated Event
Friendly Fire

Lance Corporal Clarke is known as Nobby to his mates. (Believe it or not, he has plenty of them. Well, he has Jack anyway.) He sits next to Jack on an American steam locomotive bound for Tunisia. The train is overloaded and he wishes he were smaller. No part of him seems able to escape a body part belonging to another; more than one person has fallen on his lap amid cheers and taunts of *queer*. He's wasted no time in shoving them off again and pointing out his wedding ring − something he only just remembered to replace on his finger following his last quick visit to that person living several streets away during the final hours of his leave − but nobody seems interested in the truth. He feels the back of someone's head upon his own, and butts it until the head moves. He is irritated by Jack's thigh muscle. It won't stop twitching. He can feel it through his trousers. The windows won't open and the carriage is thick with smoke and the tang of unwashed bodies, dehydration and cheap red wine. Old men with skin like parcel paper peddle the wine from the platforms out of whitewashed containers; he suspects they previously contained petrol, but it hasn't stopped him having a few himself. The thin white garments they wear remind him of dust sheets and billow in a breeze he can see but can't feel. Packed up tight in a long-sleeved shirt and a coarse woolen tunic he feels like a side of spoiling meat in comparison. His knees ache from being confined. A drop of sweat pools on his upper lip, another zooms down his temple. He doesn't know where to put his hands. He decides that the carriage smells like pig blood. He remembers that he once lived near an abattoir. On Tuesdays, the pigs were slaughtered. The smell of their blood spread from the abattoir, settled over the nearby streets and lingered like a trapped fart. His mother didn't do washing on Tuesdays. In the summer, the stench was worse. Pig blood used to give him a headache. He thinks he has one now. He leans forward and feels the insides of his head shift and settle like sand in seawater. The carriage is too loud, like a party with everybody laughing, shouting, singing and joke-telling. It doesn't sound like a train journeying to war. It makes him angry. He wishes he could get off at the next station. He leans back. The reunion of his clammy spine with the slick leather surface of the seat makes him shiver with discomfort. He regrets the move; it feels as if it's raining inside his uniform. He springs out of his seat and pushes his way to the aisle. Jack warns him that it's a mistake to give it up.

'I've got to stretch my legs,' shouts Nobby. 'I've got to move.'

'Bloody hell,' says Jack, and follows as if he has no choice.

Nobby stands in the aisle swaying with the motion of the locomotive and wondering, like a child, how many more miles there are to go. He wonders whether it's worth trying to force his way to a door, if there will be enough time to dart out at the next station and grab some air before the locomotive moves off again. He thinks about what would happen to him if he got left behind on the platform. Would they think he'd deserted? Would they shoot him? Why don't the windows in the carriage open? If he could just sit by an open window, he thinks he could stand months of travelling in this carriage but with them shut, he's not sure he can stand another five minutes. He imagines the officers lounging in a carriage with the windows down, their shirt sleeves rolled up to their elbows, the breeze on their skin. Then he thinks about smashing the carriage windows with his boot. A soldier with red hair barges past him and then stands between him and Jack like a slice of curling luncheon meat. Red Hair is shorter than him but taller than Jack. He wonders what the penalty would be for kicking in the windows when he feels another layer of heat on his back. Red Hair grips his shoulders and breathes on his neck in hot rapid gusts. 'What you playing at? Get off me,' he says. He twists and turns but Red Hair stays put. 'Get your bloody hands off me,' he demands with as much menace as he can muster, vaguely wondering whether this is some sort of homosexual advance. 'Get him off me will you, Jack,' he shouts.

'Get off him, you nutty bastard,' says Jack, trying to wrench Red Hair's hands from Nobby's shoulders. Then everybody stops moving and all the noise in the carriage dies down to nothing more than the mechanics of the train as a soldier with black hair and artesian wells for facial pores, appears at the carriage entrance with a rifle pointed at Nobby's chest.

'There you are, you little ████r,' says the gunman gleefully.

'Oh ████,' whispers Red Hair.

'Christ Almighty,' shouts Nobby at the gunman. 'You're pointing that ████ thing at me.'

'Get off him,' says Jack.

'No chance,' says Red Hair.

'He's going to shoot me,' says Nobby.

'That's the idea,' says Red Hair.

'What?' says Nobby.

'Rather you than me.'

'Don't shoot,' says Nobby, raising his hands in surrender.

'If you don't want to die, get out of my way,' says the gunman.

Nobby drives the heel of his right boot into Red Hair's shin, and Jack tugs at Red Hair's waist but it's a pointless exercise. The gunman advances down the aisle. An officer with shirt sleeves rolled up to his armpits comes storming into the carriage demanding answers to questions he has frightful trouble articulating.

Like a blanket, Red Hair slips from Nobby's shoulders. Somebody further down the carriage vomits.

The officer orders somebody else to clean it up.

Nobody in the carriage understands one single word of the order. And everybody denies being the somebody else. All of these developments are lost on the gunman.

'Jesus wept,' shouts Nobby. 'Somebody do something.'

But nobody does.

Well, not of any consequence.

Well, not in time, anyway.

32.

The *Generalfeldmarschall* was something of a linguist. In addition to his mother tongue, he spoke French, English, Russian and a smattering of Dutch. (He was also learning Spanish on the old q.t.) Consequently, he relished a French listening test like no other, specifically the kind provided by the BBC with its daily programme, *The French Speak To The French*. You could argue that the *Generalfeldmarschall* was one of the programme's greatest fans, and was terribly put out if, for whatever reason, he missed it. In a dedicated notebook, he'd systematically record every nonsensical phrase broadcast. Then, because he had a proclivity for puzzles, he'd spend the entire evening (if at liberty to do so) endeavouring to decode them.

To the uninitiated, the BBC broadcast appeared to bring the von Essen family together: father, mother, and son. Conjointly, and, for the most part, unwittingly, they enacted a scene straight off a Goebbels' poster: the *Generalfeldmarschall* all but sitting on the wireless transcribing apace, crossly shushing all external noises; Madam Brugière draped over him, or quietly capturing him lost in thought with her revered Leica G; and Konstantin before the fireplace, sitting cross-legged on the floorboards, bulling his boots or field-stripping his father's Lüger on an old sheet of propaganda.

At the end of the broadcast, the *Generalfeldmarschall* would read aloud the jotted messages and invite his loved ones to share their thoughts on their meaning. It was a game in which Madame Brugière revelled, but didn't excel.

'*Bernard est trop intime avec Valentine,*' he read. (*Bernard is overly familiar with Valentine.*) 'Well, what do we think? You first, Blandine.'

'Hmm,' said Madame Brugière, with a twiddle of her camera lens. 'I think Bernard loves Valentine more than Valentine loves Bernard. Poor Bernard. He is spending too much time on Valentine, *non*? It is a very sad story of unrequited love, *non*?'

The *Generalfeldmarschall's* laugh was long and loud enough to conceal Konstantin's despairing sigh. 'It's no such thing, Blandine,' he said benevolently, smiling into her camera. 'What say you, Konstantin? You're usually quite good at deciphering these.'

'Smile, Konsti,' ordered Madame Brugière, pointing her camera at him.

Konstantin did no such thing and said, 'A British agent code-named Valentine is being warned not to trust a member of the French Resistance code-named Bernard. Bernard has overplayed his role. The British suspect that Bernard is working for us. Bernard will soon be found dead in a ditch somewhere, with his eyes gouged out, and his genitals cut off, I expect.' At the thought of a knife being used against Bernard's body, Konstantin remembered the wound on his cheek. His fingers travelled to his face. Now that the dressing had been removed, he could play with the thread of the stitches at will.

'*Sacré bleu*, truly, Konsti, that is a horrible story,' said Madame Brugière, clutching her camera to her chest as if the instrument were a talisman.

'Leave that alone,' warned the *Generalfeldmarschall*, pointing at Konstantin's wound. 'It'll get infected if you don't, and you'll lose your looks.'

'You are a very handsome boy, Konsti,' said Madame Brugière.

Konstantin ignored the compliments.

'Dieter, we must warn this chap before it's too late,' she added.

'Blandine, how can I possibly do that? I don't know the true identity of the silly sod,' he snapped.

'Oh dear, poor Bernard,' she exclaimed.

The von Essen men ignored the lament. The *Generalfeldmarschall* made a note of Konstantin's analysis, but did not grade it. He turned his attention to the next message. '*Dans la place la statue demande un mouchoir en papier,*' he read. (*The statue demands a tissue in the town square.*) 'Well, Blandine?'

Konstantin wished he could put his fingers in his ears. He hated the way she spoke, and the nonsense she uttered. Everything she said was vacuous. It was clear for all to see that Blandine *was overly familiar with Dieter.*

Madame Brugière stood over Konstantin and photographed the top of his head, juxtaposing (one supposes) his youth with the gun he held in hands. 'Ah, this one is easy,' she said. 'The landmark is in a state of disrepair, *non?*' She winked at the *Generalfeldmarschall* and added, 'It wishes to be serviced, *non.*'

The *Generalfeldmarschall* smirked into his notebook, then fished in his pocket for his tube of Pervitin. 'The statue requires some maintenance, Blandine.'

'That's what I said, *non?*' She all but stuck her camera in Konstantin's face. 'Smile,' she implored.

Konstantin refused.

'Son?' said the *Generalfeldmarschall* with traces of methamphetamine between his teeth. 'What's your theory?'

Konstantin turned away from the camera and said, 'The mayor of some town or other is aware of the illicit activities of the townspeople and is demanding money in return for his silence.'

'Or, perhaps, it's an order to execute the mayor?' said the *Generalfeldmarschall*, his jaws still working on a pill that was long gone from his mouth. 'Because, as you say, he's bribing the townspeople and they don't have the funds to pay, or they don't want to pay.'

'Possibly, Father,' said Konstantin.

'Who is the mayor?' asked Madame Brugière.

'How should I know, Blandine?' said the *Generalfeldmarschall*.

'Surely you know everything, *non?*' she insisted, capturing his odd expression on film.

'Nobody knows everything.'

And so it went on, until the *Generalfeldmarschall* murdered Gilbert Aumont. Following that, Konstantin seemed to lose his interpretative powers. Every subsequent invitation from his father to offer his opinion on the personal messages he simply declined with a shrug of his shoulders and/or the words, 'I am very sorry, Father, but I do not know the meaning of this message.'

By the time Konstantin was listening out for his own messages on the BBC programme, the *Generalfeldmarschall* had given up asking him for his opinion. Indeed, at this juncture, Konstantin hardly registered with his father at all.

'*Garcon ordinaire, le Père Noël est coincé dans la cheminée. Faites le sortir jeudi je vous prie? On repete – garcon ordinaire, le Père Noël est coincé dans la cheminée. Faites le sortir jeudi je vous prie?*' read the *Generalfeldmarschall*. (*Ordinary boy, Father Christmas is stuck in the chimney. Would you mind letting him out on Thursday? We say twice, Ordinary boy, Father Christmas is stuck in the chimney. Would you mind letting him out on Thursday?*) 'You know, Blandine, they've sent this so-called *Ordinary Boy* a message before,' he said, leafing through his notebook for confirmation.

Madame Brugière was using a photographer's loupe to magnify the tiny details of a photograph she'd recently taken. 'They have?' she said, distractedly.

Konstantin continued to bull his boots. Round and around the toe of his boot went his cloth covered finger: in the polish, in the water, back on the boot, round and around.

'Yes, here it is. Initially, they told this so-called Ordinary Boy that Father Christmas would deliver his toys on Tuesday. This obviously didn't happen, did it?'

'Did it not?' she said.

'Well, no, Blandine, it obviously didn't because now, you see, *now*, they're telling this little *Scheiße* to expect the delivery on Thursday.'

'I didn't hear anything about a delivery,' she said, considering a different photograph. 'I understand that something is stuck in a chimney and they'd like it freed on Thursday, *non?*'

'Maybe. Maybe not. I don't know,' said *Generalfeldmarschall*.

'What do you think of this photograph, Dieter?' she asked, raising an image of a massacre that the *Generalfeldmarschall* had overseen three weeks earlier. 'Will it do, do you think?'

It showed 70 dead French men and boys lying beside a mangled railway line. Each had been shot in the back of the head in reprisal for a train derailment, and, more specifically, the delay it had caused a large convoy of Hitler Youth. Madame Brugière had been tasked with producing another of her anti-espionage posters. (The pigeon poster

209

had proved very successful at undermining Allied pigeon operations in the area.) The *Generalfeldmarschall* briefly considered the image, nodded his approval then said, 'What sort of *Scheißkerl* calls themselves an *Ordinary Boy*. Who wants to be ordinary? And another thing, have you noticed that the BBC always repeat their message to him?'

Madame Brugière shook her head. 'What does it mean, Dieter?'

'It means this *Ordinary Boy*, whoever he is, is either deaf, stupid, or both.'

'Who do you think this *Ordinary Boy* might be then?' she asked.

The *Generalfeldmarschall* shrugged. 'All I know,' he said, 'is that he's a *kleiner Scheißkerl.*'

'Would you describe this Dieter von Essen as a character that inclines towards stereotype or caricature, do you think, dear?' asked Joyce.

I lowered my newspaper and inclined my head.

'It occurs to me that your character is one or the other,' she added, taking a sip of her tea. 'Could he be both?'

I inclined my head further.

She nibbled her Garibaldi and went on. 'I mean to say, he's *exceptionally* unpleasant. You tell me he murders defenceless little *children* as well as innocent adults. Not only that, but he positively seems to *enjoy* luring these impoverished youngsters to their deaths with these unsuspecting pigeons and frightful cigarettes. Then you show him commiting *adultery* with this Frenchwoman while his *poor* wife is coughing up her lungs in a sanatorium hundreds of miles away in some German *backwater*. And just look at the way he treats his *only* child. Really, the names he calls his son, dear, well I've never heard you say such words. When you talk of this Operation Attar affair, I simply don't recognise you; it's as if you're the one swallowing those dreadful tablets and succumbing to their terrible effects. You know, dear, before you began regaling me with this tall tale, I had not the slightest idea about methamphetamines, as you call them, and opiates, and all the other exotic pharmaceuticals you seem to have invented and introduced me to. And, if I'm being perfectly honest now, dear, I'm sure I really don't wish to know about such things either. I rather suspect that when it comes to this Dieter von Essen character, you've allowed yourself to get a little carried away.'

A wiser man than I might simply have raised his Financial Times and enlisted the market data therein to quell the folly of Joyce's appraisal, at least in his own mind if not audibly in his own sitting room. However, my summation of that day's market data was that it was going to be wholly incapable of neutralizing the inequitable suggestion that Dieter von Essen, far from being a real person, was nothing more than a dramatis personae in a fictional tale of my own making. More vexing still was that Joyce, not content with accusing me of making Dieter von Essen up, was further implying that the man was also a stereotype and/or a caricature.

I drained my teacup then said, 'I've often found it to be the case, Joyce, that when an individual is confronted by an unpalatable truth, they simply dismiss it as *untrue* or *exaggerated*. You cannot dismiss *Generalfeldmarschall* von Essen as a character simply because you find his behaviour repugnant. I assure you the man was as real as you and I.'

Joyce frowned at my saucer because it was without its cup. I retrieved the cup from the arm of my chair upon which it balanced and replaced it in the saucer. She sighed as if all was well in the world when I would have argued most strongly that it wasn't. She went on, 'I suppose what I'm saying is that, in addition to all the unpleasant features of your tale...'

'Facts of the file.'

She waved my objection away and continued, '...you might have said whether this von Essen fellow played the piano or danced the foxtrot or something akin. In short, dear, you might have told me something surprising about the man to give him some flesh, so to speak.'

'Tell me, Joyce, do you really find it so difficult to believe that a senior Nazi and close personal friend of Hitler was an unpleasant man?'

'I suppose it's just that when I think of these Nazis I tend to think of them as being all the same: all terribly wicked and equally capable of performing evil deeds. But, can this really be true in every single case?'

'I'm afraid I cannot answer your question, Joyce, since I was not acquainted with every single Nazi during the war. I was, however, one of the first to liberate Bergen-Belsen and saw with my own eyes what the Nazis did…'

'I know, dear, I know. You mustn't upset yourself. Please don't, dear, please. '

I swallowed the lump in my throat and said, 'Of *Generalfeldmarschall* von Essen, I can only relate of the man what I have found in the file. The truth is, Joyce, I don't know if he played the piano or danced the foxtrot.'

'No,' said Joyce, putting her arms around me, 'of course you don't. And, you're quite right to leave the facts to speak for themselves. I see you've finished your tea, dear, how about another cup?'

In truth, it wasn't Father Christmas that delivered the toys to Konstantin during the early hours of Thursday morning, it was a Lizzie. This time, she, and her pilot, were not defeated by mist, although, truth be told, it wasn't the perfect weather for a supply drop either. Anyhow, Konstantin watched a small container drift to the ground and let it sit in the middle of the field until such time as he was sure its delivery had not been witnessed by the Wehrmacht, or the French Resistance.

He'd chosen a small field, next to a country lane, miles away from the château, and miles away from anywhere. It offered little cover by way of a bordering woodland, dense thicket, or hedgerow, and few escape routes in the event of a sting. For this reason, it was a risky location for a delivery of spy materials. But its apparent unsuitability as a drop site for Allied supplies and spies to the French Resistance was what made it the perfect drop site for Konstantin, since, for the reasons stated, it had never been considered worthy of patrol by his father's men.

It'd been a long and slow cycle ride in the dark to the field. Konstantin set off just before ten but did not arrive much before midnight. He wore black clothes in place of his uniform, Madame Brugière's brassiere beneath his shirt to conceal the toys, and a knitted balaclava to conceal his blond hair. Once at the field, he lay his bike on the ground and threw some of that camouflage netting over it, as well as over himself. From a distance, crouched as he was, and with precious little moonlight to illuminate him, he may have been a small boulder, or a mound of earth such as you might find at the entrance to a badger set, but certainly nothing more.

When he finally did feel confident enough to break cover and recover the container, he was at once reminded of Gilbert. In addition to the Minox camera, microfilm, suitcase for the microfilm, secret ink, and rice paper, Father Christmas had also sent another pigeon. But this pigeon had not survived the landing. If Gilbert had been alive, Konstantin would have given him the pigeon to eat. Then again, if Gilbert had been alive, Konstantin would not have been standing in this field retrieving these toys.

He buried Kenneth's comrade in a shallow grave beneath a bush, and marked the spot with the pigeon's container. Before he got back on his bike, he popped an aniseed ball into his mouth; the quarter of sweets in the white paper bag were an unexpected gift from Father Christmas (via Witts' Stores) and tasted a damn sight nicer than marzipan.

33.

Would you find it impossible to believe that in the space of one day, you could receive the worst news of your life immediately followed by the best news of your life?

When Rose walked in from school on this particular day, she was immediately confronted by the sickening and headache-inducing smell of gas. She didn't wrinkle her nose in complaint, nor did she call for her mother to question the source of the smell. She just dropped her satchel and flew down the hallway, past the front room, and the back room, and into the kitchen. There, she found the lower half of her mother spread-eagled upon the kitchen floor. She was lying in a puddle of urine. Her head was holed up inside the oven, lying in a plash of vomit.

Without any sort of utterance, Rose crashed over the unwashed baking pans and oven racks that her mother had removed from the oven to make room for her head, and had left scattered about her, and dived for the switch. She dragged her mother from the oven. She cleaned the vomit from her mouth with a dishcloth. She removed her knitted school cardigan and placed it beneath her mother's head. She threw open the kitchen window. She opened the back door. She fell to her knees and put her cheek beside her mother's mouth to see if she could feel a breath. It was feeble, but it was there.

She raced out into the back yard and screamed for all the street to hear, 'Help, help me, help,' but nobody came. She snatched a towel from the washing line. She ran back into the kitchen. She covered the lower half of her mother with the towel. She ran into the back room and hauled the cumbersome mattress from the day bed. She ran with it, as best she could, back into the kitchen. She rolled her mother onto her side and wedged the mattress at her mother's back to keep her from rolling onto her chest or back and choking on the vomit that was yet to spill out. Then she ran out of the kitchen, back down the hallway, past the back room, past the front room and into the front garden. For all the street to hear she screamed, 'Help, help me, help,' but nobody came. She ran back into the house, down the hallway, past the front room and the back room and back into the kitchen. She fell to her knees and held her mother's wrist between her fingers to check for a pulse. It was weak, but it was there. She kissed her forehead and whispered, 'I love you, Mother. I'm sorry. Please don't die.'

She heaved herself up, panting, crying, spreading snot all over her face and the back of her hands and ran out into the back yard, through the back gate, into the alleyway and down the alley three doors to where Lawrence (*of all people*) kept his bicycle. And, even though his bicycle was far too big for her comparatively much shorter legs and she could barely reach the pedals, she rode the old boneshaker down what remained of the alleyway, out into the street and all the way over to Dottie's house.

At Dottie's house she threw the bicycle to the ground, ran up the garden path and hammered on the door. Ferret and Badger were standing at the window of the Morning room, having been put into temporary quarantine for attempting to bite Dottie the moment she arrived home from school.

'Rose,' shrieked Juniper through her tears. She didn't like quarantine one bit, and here was a potential saviour or, failing that, a second victim.

'Hose,' shrieked Jinny, and smeared the window with whatever was on the end of her pointed finger.

'Where's the fire,' shouted Mrs Darby, as she arrived at the front door.

'My mother…' stammered Rose, white-faced and shaking.

'Rose?' said Mrs Latymer, appearing behind Mrs Darby. Mrs Darby moved aside. 'What's happened, sweetheart?'

'Accident,' said Rose.

'What sort of accident?' asked Mrs Darby sharply.

Rose gave the answer to Mrs Latymer. 'A very bad one,' she admitted.

Mrs Latymer took hold of Rose's shoulders and marched her down the hall. She bent down to Rose's ear and whispered, 'Tell me, sweetheart.'

Rose whispered into Mrs Latymer's ear, then near collapsed.

'Sugar,' exclaimed Dottie, coming upon her mother and Rose in the hall. 'How swell.'

'Not now, Dottie,' warned Mrs Darby. 'I don't know what's happened exactly, but I do know this isn't a social call.'

'What in the heck's happened, sugar?'

'Never mind that now, Dottie,' said Mrs Latymer, as she heaved Rose back to standing. 'Just you listen to me, okay?'

Dottie nodded.

'Take Rose to the telephone box on the corner of Park Street with Park Road. You got that?'

'Yes, Marmee,' said Dottie.

'Rose, sweetheart, when you get to the phone box, dial 0 for the operator and tell the lady what's happened. Ask her to send an ambulance to your home address right away. Is that understood?'

Rose turned to Dottie.

'Yes, Marmee,' said Dottie, grasping Rose's hand. 'I got it.'

'Dottie, as soon as you're sure the ambulance is on its way, take Rose to her house, and meet me outside. Outside, Dottie. Is that clear?'

'Yes, Marmee.'

'Go,' she said, gently pushing the girls outside.

Dottie yanked Rose down the path and said, 'Come on, sugar, we gotta run.'

Mrs Latymer watched them go then turned to Mrs Darby. 'Please take care of Juniper and Jinny.'

'Yes, of course, Mrs Latymer,' said Mrs Darby, glancing at the door to the Morning room with a degree of trepidation that was so tangible one could have removed it from her face and fed it to the little blighters.

Mrs Latymer nodded. 'Keys to the motorcycle,' she said, cryptically.

'Motorcycle?' repeated Mrs Darby, frowning.

'Never mind,' said Mrs Latymer racing from the house to the garage (in her high heels). 'I've remembered,' she added, her voice growing smaller. 'Under the flowerpot.'

'What motorcycle?' shouted Mrs Darby after her.

Within minutes, her question was answered. Mrs Latymer appeared on the driveway revving up a 1930 Norton Model 20. Naturally, it was the landlady's pride and joy and its use by the tenants was strictly prohibited. 'I'm sure she won't mind,' shouted Mrs Latymer, referring to the landlady. 'It's an emergency.'

'I'm sure she will mind,' muttered Mrs Darby. 'Do you know what you're doing with that thing?' she asked, gruffly.

'How hard can it be? It's just a bicycle with an engine,' she said, doing her best to turn her skirt into trousers. 'Don't you agree, Mrs Darby?'

Mrs Darby's experience of contraptions ceased when she fell out of a wheelbarrow as a tot. You could say that she was ahead of her time since from that misadventure onwards, she travelled solely by **Shanks' Pony** (which meant she never went very far as she didn't just **Walk Short Distances**, she walked all distances). 'I'm not sure you should be doing it in those shoes,' she said, pulling a long face.

'Missy Darby,' shouted Juniper.

'Dissy Dardy,' echoed Jinny.

'Children should be seen and not heard,' responded Mrs Darby to the door of the Morning Room.

'I do everything in these shoes,' shouted Mrs Latymer.

I imagine the emerging query given the times is: Was there sufficient petroleum in the motorcycle to convey Mrs Latymer to the Clarke abode? All I can tell you is that Mrs Latymer arrived in good time and in one piece at the tragic scene and found Mrs Clarke exactly as Rose had left her. 'Oh, honey,' she said, kneeling beside her. 'What in the Sam Hill have you done to yourself?'

It was as she unfurled Mrs Clarke's hand to hold it in hers that she found the Mis—Fortune Teller. Naturally, she assumed it was Rose's to begin with; Rose must have been playing with it in the seconds before she discovered her mother and dropped it. Whilst her mother, at some point, must have temporarily regained consciousness and grasped it, perhaps as a source of comfort. That Mrs Clarke appeared to have temporarily regained consciousness gave Mrs Latymer hope. Until, of course, she played the thing: Pick a colour. Blue. B—L—U—E. Pick a number. Five. One. Two. Three. Four. Five. Pick another number. Three. Oven. 'Dear God, no,' said Mrs Latymer, finally grasping the full extent of the situation. She placed the Mis—Fortune Teller in the pocket of her skirt and said, 'Let's see if we can't get you fixed up a little, honey.'

She kicked shut the oven door and dashed up the stairs in search of an eiderdown to keep Mrs Clarke warm, but as we know there wasn't one to find. She pulled the sheet from Mrs Clarke's bed, followed by the sheet from Mr Clarke's bed, and ran back down the stairs. She mopped the urine with Mr Clarke's sheet, and used the towel to wash the floor, throwing both in the sink when she was finished. Then she covered Mrs Clarke with the remaining sheet and set about bathing her face with a combination of the kitchen dishcloth, as Rose had done, and her own hankie with the Latymer family crest embroidered on one corner (heraldic cross, dove, escallop, crescent and cinquefoil). She tenderly combed Mrs Clarke's hair with her fingers and was distinctly distressed by the amount that came out in her hands. Not knowing what else to do with it, she pulled the Mis–Fortune Teller from her pocket, tucked the hair inside, lifted the sheet covering Mrs Clarke, and this time, placed it in the pocket of Mrs Clarke's shift. Then she covered Mrs Clarke again, tucked her in the sheet as if she were a child being put to bed, stroked her cheek, and told her over and over again that everything would be alright, and that she wasn't to worry one jot about Rose. 'She'll stay with us,' she assured her, 'just while you're getting better, honey.'

After she'd done and said all this, Rose and Dottie arrived, both flushed, grasping their knees and gasping for breath.

'The ambulance is coming, Marmee,' yelled Dottie.

'Stay outside, girls,' instructed Mrs Latymer.

'But, Marmee, Rose wants to see her mother.'

'Just Rose then. You wait outside for the ambulance, Dottie. Flag it down as soon as you see it.'

'Yes, Marmee.'

'It's okay, honey, Rose is here now.'

When Rose appeared, Mrs Latymer moved towards Mrs Clarke's waist and patted the floor beside her head. She said, 'Take your mother's hand, sweetheart, and give me your other one.'

There the three remained, holding hands until the ambulance women arrived to take Mrs Clarke to the Cottage Hospital.

And as Mrs Clarke was conveyed by stretcher from her kitchen to the rear of the ambulance, the neighbours that Rose had earlier called for in vain, appeared, as if by magic.

'What's happened now?' tutted Number 55.

'Always some carry on or another,' said Number 59.

(The Clarkes lived at Number 57.)

'Isn't there just,' said Number 55.

Numbers 42, 48 and 52 agreed.

Nodding at Rose, Number 59 said, 'I must admit, I did hear old Fanny-Ann there calling for help, but didn't think much of it.'

'Well, you don't,' said Number 57.

'No, you don't,' agreed Number 59.

'What's happened?' said Number 42.

Then up popped Lawrence (from Number 51) to say, 'Oi, Stench Bomb, what have you done with my bike?'

And Mrs Latymer, in a Southern accent that had never belonged to her, nor any of her ancestors since she and they hailed from the Northern states, was heard to drawl to them all, 'How now, ladies an' gentlemen, it's a cryin shame one of your number ain' aimin' ter come sooner. Ah'm sure Rose coulda used yer help jes' as soon as Mrs Clarke done gone and slippt on the wet kitchin floor and clean broke her head in two. Pray fer her now, bekase you aint done no more fer her.' Then taking Rose's hand and turning to Lawrence she added, 'Why, who is this ninny standin afore me with talk of a bi-sickle at a time like thee-is? He jes' soundin plain silly.'

Well, the neighbours, and Lawrence, scratched their heads in collective confusion as to what, precisely, this (apparent) Alabamian was saying. And the longevity of their confusion, I have to say, did much to ensure that Mrs Latymer was the subject of the neighbourhood gossip in place of Mrs Clarke, and long after the principal players had left the stage. (Hurrah for Mrs Latymer. I say twice, Hurrah for Mrs Latymer.)

And so now that we've had the worst news of Rose's life, we ought to turn to the best news of her life. It was as the ambulance was pulling away and Mrs Latymer was long gone finishin lickin them buzzards (apologies for this turn of phrase, but imitation is the sincerest form of flattery) that the Angel of Death, otherwise known as the Telegraph Boy, arrived. He handed Rose the following telegram and said, 'I'm very sorry,' as he slowly wheeled his bicycle away.

POST OFFICE
TELEGRAM

Prefix.   Time handed in.   Office of Origin and Service Instructions.   Words.

82

THE WAR OFFICE REGRETS TO ANNOUNCE THAT YOUR HUSBAND L/CPL
LYNDSEY CLARKE 6118968 HAS BEEN KILLED IN ACTION. LETTER TO
FOLLOW. (MAJOR GENERAL GREENE, 6TH ARMOURED DIVISION.)

No doubt you'd have preferred to have had all this straight from Rose, but it would have made for an extremely short read as her diary entry for Friday 28th April, 1944, went something along the lines of:

Today was the worst day of my life: Mother had a terrible accident and will have to spend a long time in a special hospital getting well again.

Today was also the best day of my life: Father is dead and will never again be able to hurt poor Mother.

P.S. Or me.

P.P.S. I have agreed to help Gilbert Aumont end the war.

34.

School of Divinity
New College
University of Edinburgh
Mound Place
Edinburgh
EH1

PO Box 500

10 April, 1944

<u>Semiotic Analysis of Rose and Dot Symbol</u>

Dear Mr Latymer,

Many thanks for your letter dated 7 March. I'm only too glad to assist with your query. Apologies for not having replied sooner, but I recently suffered an asinine misfortune: I fractured my radius wrangling Brenda, a 14 foot Burmese python, during a life drawing class. Brenda was a prop that got out of hand having spied the caretakers sonsy tabby lolling on the windowsill. Alack, rationing has turned Brenda into a self-serving snake and terrible danger to all cheets. Anyhoo, traction supervened and kept me from my office and your letter until yesterday afternoon. I do hope my predicament has not impeded your inquiry; it has certainly impeded my research (I'm now having to take a gestaltist approach to pictorial semiotics, corrie-fisted). Och, the life of a Semiotician; I would'nae wish it on another living cratur!

Your rose and dot symbol is not one I've encountered previously, Mr Latymer. For this reason, I shall consider the signification of its independent components, that is, the rose, and the dot/s, singly, before going on to consider how each may act as a vehicle of meaning within the conglomoration as it has been anonymously presented to you. (I note that you do not wish to receive a theological, scientific, or numerical analysis of your symbol; though intriguing this is, given ma current difficulties, it's a relief.)

I will begin with a consideration of the rose. Historically, the rose has been used as a sign to communicate censorship and secrecy. You may be familiar with the term 'sub rosa' which literally refers to an action done on the quiet to maintain confidentiality. This might mean that your messenger believes their communication with you invites some sort of peril into their life. Hence, the application of a cryptographic signature in place of an apellative one. Alack, since you've not enlightened me of the full circumstances in which you received this symbol, I can'nae speculate further on this.

Interestingly, your messenger has not chosen to colour their rose in a hue ordinarily associated with this particular flower such as red, orange, yellow, white, or pink, but instead, grey. It's possible that the absence of a vibrant colour here signifies a passivity or an attitude of inaction in the person represented by the rose i.e. they're not the chief of the operation, but the subordinate. Then again, given that the rose looms largest in the symbol when considered as a whole, the opposite may also be true. Alternatively, the decision to colour the rose grey may be a reference to the horticultural certitude that grey roses do not naturally exist in nature, but are made grey by the human hand, so to speak. This could mean that something terrible has happened to the individual represented by the rose and it is this that has compelled the messenger to make contact with you. The colour choice might also serve as a message or warning: since a grey rose does not strictly exist, it can'nae be found, likewise the individual it represents, and indeed the messenger, if they are one in the same. Though arguably simplistic, the analysis must also note that a dark-coloured rose is often used to represent death; a rose, albeit it a red one, is the floral symbol of England; and thorns protrude from the stem of a rose which may be a reference to the character of the individual it represents i.e. they are prickly, guarded, difficult to grasp etc,. Here, what the rose may be telling you is that, in addition to being a difficult English woman, the individual it represents may also serve as a portent of doom.

222

Similarly, the rose is also drawn in full bloom. This may indicate the age of the English woman it represents i.e. geriatric, or if not particularly advanced in years perhaps coming to the end of her life. If so, this is, of course, another communication of death. Consequently, it may indicate that they have contacted you because they've nothing to lose. On the other hand, a grey rose might also mean that your poor wee messenger does'nae have any coloured pencils in their pencil box.

I will now consider the significance of the dot/s. A dot implies the end of something. In this symbol, it clearly communicates the end of a sentence. The many dots represent the many possible endings to either one sentence (of course ignoring the punctuational use of three dots to signal an ellipsis), or numerous sentences, each with their own ending. In simple terms, the dots represent the liminal space between the written and the unwritten: the full stops are present, but the attendant sentences are absent. Thus, the messenger has many, many, things to tell you, but for whatever reason they can'nae communicate these things to you. Now, I don't know if you're aware of this, Mr Latymer, but the North American term for a full stop is a period. We have 12 periods in this symbol (unless my cataract has worsened, and there's every chance it has), and I can'nae help but be struck by this. For us, the term period relates to the menses. On average, Mr Latymer, fertile women menstruate 12 times a year. Thus, the period in your symbol may well be a signifier for the fertile feminine as well as for the continent of North America. Och, it's just a thought, but it is worth bearing in mind...

If I were you, Mr Latymer, I'd certainly wish to ask some very pertinent questions of your symbol, and I would specifically direct those questions at the rose and the dot/s. For example, what, if anything, is rose communicating to dot, and vice versa? Are we being told that the rose has more power than the dot in the relationship because it's so much larger than the dot? Or, conversely, is the ratio of dot to rose more significant, the ratio, as I've already said, being 12:1? If so, is the symbol attempting to transmit the message that dot outranks rose? If the answer to this is in the affirmative, then we might also regard the wreath formation of the dots as a sign that the dot, either consciously or subconsciously, is runing an infinite number of rings around the rose. Again, without further information regarding the document upon which you received this symbol, I'm afeart I can'nae speculate nor provide a more considered answer to any of your relevant questions.

Having just had another wee look at your symbol, I've a strange feeling we're doing the circular presentation of the dots a grave mischief if we continue to regard it as a mere mechanism for keeping the dots in order. Afterall, if the circle was simply selected by your messenger for its aesthetic value, why not select a square, triangle or diamond for that matter? As I've already said, Mr Latymer, a circle is infinite, it has no beginning and no end. In your symbol, I'm of the opinion the circle of dots has been drawn to signify the sun. (If you have cataracts, Mr Latymer, it's quite easy to view your symbol as the sun. If your eyes are not thus encumbered, just screw them up and the effect is the same.) The sun gives us light. Light is related to truth. These ideas amalgamated suggest that your messenger is sending you a truth or truths as opposed to, let's say, utter nonsense. We know that once the sun is depleted of hydrogen, and in turn, helium, it will die. Similarly, your messenger will continue to dispatch their truth ad infinitum until such time as their truth, whatever it may be, is fully spent. I'm now also convinced that you should think of your circle, in addition to what I've already said of it here, as a signifier of a coterie of individuals: Rose, Dot/s and Circle.

In conclusion, it is my professional opinion that your symbol, although drawn by one individual (probably the dot), certainly speaks for two, and possibly even three individuals. The rose can be read as a female English woman in difficulty (probably older than the dot, though not necessarily more powerful). The dot can be read as a female fit to burst with the unspoken, and with origins in North America, possibly. We tend to think of a circle as masucline as the following tune proves: The sun has got his hat on/hip-hip-hip-hooray/the sun has got his hat on/and he's coming out today, and in your symbol, Mr Latymer, we can also think of the sun as representing the masculine, but I dinna ken from whence your sun may hail.

It's a braw symbol you have there, Mr Latymer, and, if I were permitted to consider its significance from a theological, scientific, and numerical frame of reference, one on which I believe I could write an entire paper. That said, you should probably note that I do tend to overanalyse things and so you may wish to take all that I've written with a hefty pinch of salt. Please dae let me know the true meaning of the symbol if ever you chance upon it.

Semiotically yours,

Lizzie Carnegie

35.

True to her word, Mrs Latymer added Rose to her clutch and bunged Mrs Darby a bit extra to cover the additional work. For the first time in years, Rose was the child. She didn't cook. She didn't clean (as such). She most definitely didn't do the laundry. Her chores, as Mrs Latymer termed them, were minimal: going about the cornices with the feather duster once a week, and lighting the fire in the Drawing Room of an evening (if it were cold, which it wasn't because this was all taking place in the spring of 1944). And at night, when she went to sleep, tucked up with Dottie in a large double bed with Dottie's arms invariably around her as if she were a teddy, she'd never felt so safe or loved. And though you might argue that what I'm about to tell you verges on the predictable, you must know by now that I'll only report what I've read: Ferret and Badger just adored her.

They brushed her hair, they practised the business of doing up buttons on her cardigan, and they stuck her shoelaces up their noses and in their ears to make her laugh (though it didn't make her laugh). Jinny was even learning how to say the letters T and R under Rose's semi-patient tutelage. When Rose showed the twins how to make daisy chains, they responded by harvesting every last one of the weeds from the back lawn and making jewellery sets for everybody, including Dottie the Omega wolf. Rose was the person they insisted should bathe them in the kitchen sink post tea-time, and put them to bed with a story. Rose picked the story: a few pages of A.J.P. Taylor's, *The Habsburg Monarchy 1809–1918*. It always knocked them out without any fuss. And when Rose told them off for biting Dottie, and made them promise to never do it again, they well-nigh kept their word. Though Juniper didn't find

The Promise easy to keep, and Jinny didn't find The Promise easy to say, even with the tuition.

Mrs Darby couldn't believe her luck. In some respects, she felt as if she were getting paid more for doing less. Needless to say, she also thought an awful lot of Rose, but it was Rose's ability to tame a wild animal that really endeared the waif to the charlady.

That said, Mrs Latymer still had her concerns about Rose. By letter, she expressed them to her husband. Here was a child who had, to all intents and purposes, lost both her parents in one day. And, in the case of her mother, had witnessed the event itself. What should she do about this? What should she say? Mr Latymer didn't have the answers and advised his wife to seek medical advice. Which she did, as the following transcript testifies:

Mrs Latymer: Doctor, should I speak to the child about her mother? About the circumstances? About what her mother has suffered? I've seen the child staring at the oven sometimes.
Doctor: I wouldn't advise raising the matter, Mrs Latymer.
Mrs Latymer: To be quite honest, Doctor, the child's often staring at the oven.
Doctor: I shouldn't worry about that. I suspect she wishes to assist you with the cooking, Mrs Latymer. She is a girl after all.
Mrs Latymer: Hmm... And what about the child's father? They buried him in Tunisia. Do I tell her?
Doctor: Best let sleeping dogs lie, Mrs Latymer.
Mrs Latymer: But what if the child asks questions?
Doctor: Has she asked any questions?
Mrs Latymer: No, Doctor, not yet.
Doctor: A sore doesn't heal if it's picked, Mrs Latymer.
Mrs Latymer: So, your advice is to...
Doctor: The best advice I can give to you, Mrs Latymer, is simply to *Keep Calm And Carry On.*
Mrs Latymer: Right, that's your expert medical advice on the matter?

Doctor: Indeed, Mrs Latymer... and, perhaps let the child assist you with the cooking. I'm quite sure her husband will thank you for it in the future.

Mrs Latymer followed the doctor's advice as far as the **Keeping Calm and Carrying On**; as for his advice in relation to the cooking, well, there's no polite way to say what she did with that.

As far as Mrs Latymer was concerned, a sure-fire way to **Keep Calm and Carry On** was to take Dottie and Rose to the Regal Cinema to see a rerun of *The Adventures of Robin Hood* at the earliest opportunity. Yes, the girls were old enough to visit the cinema alone, but as I've already stated, Mrs Latymer thought a great deal of Errol Flynn. And it wasn't as if she was going to be seeing her other love, Mr Latymer, any time soon: a new Operation, Operation Attar, was now likely to keep him in London for the foreseeable future. On the walk home from the cinema, and after Dottie had recited most of her favourite lines, with a little help from her Marmee, she remembered that she still hadn't mentioned the German soldiers posing as Allied soldiers in the British countryside.

'And for that reason, Marmee,' Dottie insisted, 'we have to start locking the doors at night.'

Mrs Latymer laughed. 'Oh, honey,' she said, 'where do you get your funny ideas?'

Dottie looked at Rose. Rose dropped out of the line to warn Dottie with a slow shake of her head not to give anything away.

'It's not an idea, Marmee, it's a fact, plain and simple. There's a very good chance these Germans will try to get inside our house. So, will you lock the doors?'

'Where did you hear this, honey? I've certainly not heard it. It must be one of those silly rumours.'

'I just heard it, Marmee, and it sure isn't a rumour.'

'From your daddy, I expect. That's just the sort of thing he would say. As a joke, honey. Something he heard at his Club. Well, if it makes you feel safer, sweetie-pie, that can be one of your little chores. You can go around the house and check all the doors are locked before you head on up the wooden hill to Befordshire.'

'Swell,' said Dottie.

Rose smiled: Dottie resented having to do any chores and now she'd earned herself another.

'Can we go and play?' asked Dottie.

'As long as you're both back in time for dinner.'

'What are we having for dinner?'

And thinking of the doctor, Mrs Latymer decided that whatever it was going to be, it sure as hell wasn't going to be something that required cooking.

That Rose had not visited the den in weeks, was a topic that was never going to be discussed. But, as they lay in bed one night, Dottie did admit to Rose that they'd received a second message from Gilbert, a message she'd not only posted to her father as before, but one she had replied to with a letter on Rizla rolling paper. Before Rose could blow her stack, Dottie had said, 'You see, sugar, Kenneth is such a clever baby bird. He can fly back and forth between our den and wherever Gilbert lives in France. Isn't that the best darn thing you ever did hear?'

'No,' Rose had said truthfully.

'Well, but don't worry, I told him my name is Oliver, and your name is Polly.'

To which Rose had replied, 'Polly is the name you give a parrot. I'm not going along with that.'

Dottie thought she'd got off very lightly.

Naturally, Rose had wanted to know the contents of the second message. Dottie had to work from memory since the note was now held by the people her important Daddy knew.

She counted the contents of the message on her fingertips. 'Ah, you know, something about some wine and some fight, and someone getting drowned, and some co-ordinates, and some artist with a pug dog, and some spy with really bad teeth pretending to be from somewhere but really being from somewhere else, and some horse and foal winding up dead because of something in the air, and something about the BBC, and he wants us to send him a camera, and some secret ink, which I didn't know you could even get.'

'Wants *us* to send him a camera and some secret ink?' Rose had said.

'Not *us* exactly. He means the important people, you know, the people Daddy knows.'

'Secret ink?'

'I know, sounds kinda swell.'

'Sounds ridiculous to me.'

'I'm gonna ask Santa Claus for some.'

'You mean Father Christmas.'

'*You like potato and I like potahto/ You like tomato and I like tomahto,*' Dottie had sung. 'It's all the same to me, sugar. The old man with the white beard brings gifts.'

'If you're lucky.'

'If you're good, sugar. Luck doesn't come into it.'

Rose had sighed. 'And what did you write back to Gilbert?'

'Ah, not much. I just asked him a few questions about France.'

'What did you tell him about me?'

'I didn't tell him anything about you, sugar. Except, maybe, your age. I told him I hoped he got the camera he wanted and that he shoulda used more colours on his map. You can write the next letter, if you wanna?'

'That's assuming the pigeon comes back to us,' Rose had said.

'You think Kenneth won't? You think he'll never come back? You think he prefers Gilbert to me? You think he's dead?'

'Who knows?' Rose had said. 'Goodnight, Dottie.'

But luckily Kenneth had come back with, not just microfilm and a letter written in the secret ink for The Very Important Man In London (aka Father Christmas), but a letter for Oliver and Polly as well, to which, it should be noted, he'd added a retrospective P.S. *Please send the enclosed empty rice paper with the microfilm to the important man in Londres.*

'That's more like it,' declared Dottie of the content, though she thought it a darn shame he hadn't understood all of her questions, and had completely misunderstood the one about Poland. There'd also been some discussion on the blank rice paper. Rose assumed it must contain a message written in secret ink for the people Mr Latymer knew. Dottie was disappointed that Gilbert hadn't bothered to write their message in secret ink, or re-written their message on rice paper since his invitiation to try eating it had tickled her tastebuds.

'I expect Gilbert is saving his secret ink and rice paper for the men in London that your father knows.'

'Gee, he coulda used a bit of the stuff on us,' said Dottie. 'Was it really too much to ask?'

'I don't doubt you could eat an entire stack of rice paper, Dottie, but do you know how to read secret ink?'

'No, but...'

Rose folded her arms.

Tucking Kenneth under her armpit Dottie changed the subject. 'Some of these words must be French. How exciting, sugar. It means I can speak three languages: American, English and French. This'll impress the heck outta Edmund.'

'You can't tell Edmund a thing about it. You can't tell anybody, Dottie.'

'Shucks.'

'I think this word here is a rude word, anyway.'

'*Merde*,' read Dottie.

'Don't say it, Dottie, it'll get us into trouble. Correction, it'll get *me* into trouble if you say it because I'm the eldest and they'll say I'm a terrible influence. I might not be able to carry on staying with you.'

'Alright, sugar, alright. I promise I won't say it.'

Rose nodded and read the third of Gilbert's answers. '*I will not reveal your opinion on A.J.P. Taylor's book to anybody*. What does Gilbert mean by this? How does he know about my history prize?'

Dottie shrugged and fussed over Kenneth and his new and improved suitcase. It clearly had capacity for a letter of epic proportions if Dottie and Rose were of a mind to write such a thing, and Mrs Witts had a good stock of Rizlas.

'Well you obviously told him more about me than my age.'

'I can't remember, sugar, but I didn't say anything really bad about A.J.P. Taylor. Hey, Gilbert's only ten. Can you believe that? He knows a lot for a ten-year-old, don't you think? Although, he doesn't know much about Henry VIII or the wives. But I like him.'

'Even though, by his own admission, he cheats in games and fishing competitions?'

'He's brave,' countered Dottie.

'So *he* says,' said Rose. 'Are you really going to take his word for it? You don't even know him. It sounds like boasting to me. And I don't like cheating either. It isn't fair on the other person.'

Dottie shrugged. She didn't care if Gilbert was a boaster and a cheat. She didn't get many letters. She liked having a pen pal. 'You'll have to tell him what *howdy* means, sugar.'

'You can tell him.'

'I thought you were gonna write the letter?'

Rose shrugged.

'We're still gonna help Gilbert, right? You haven't changed your mind, sugar? You're not gonna turn Kenneth into the police, are you?'

Rose hadn't changed her mind. She was just trying to make sense of how Gilbert's sign-off made her feel: *I hope we both receive our papas soon.* It seemed that these words of Gilbert's made her feel uncomfortable. They made her think of her father, and then her mother covered in sick and urine and close to death with her head in the dirty oven. She coughed away the unpleasant image, and then the unpleasant feeling, and covered the offending words with her hand. Dottie offered her the milk bottle of stagnant rainwater to wet her whistle. Rose declined the offer and blinking away a tear said, 'I'm not going anywhere near the police. I'll write a bit of the letter, and you can write the rest.'

Dottie was relieved, then elated at the prospect of helping with the letter. With pipe in mouth, she immediately set about licking and sticking the Rizla rolling papers.

Meanwhile, Rose thought about what on earth she was going to say for herself, and then, whether it would ever be possible to unsee the worst thing she'd seen so far in her short little life.

36.

Transcript of Interrogation.
Interrogation: Date: 10/05/44. Time: 14.00 HRS.
Interrogation 1/1.
Place: Gestapo Headquarters, 84, avenue Foch, Paris.
Interrogation Room No. 2. Fifth Floor.
**Interviewer: Obersturmführer Adalberto Schneider
(Sicherheitsdienst, Amsterdam.)**
Suspect: *Generalfeldmarschall* Dieter von Essen
Suspected Offence: Treason Against the Reich

Schneider: Do you know why you've been brought to
Paris?
von Essen: A spot of lunch at *Maxim's*?
Schneider: (SILENCE)
von Essen: (YAWN) I'm afraid I haven't the foggiest,
Obersturmführer Schneider.
Schneider: You've been arrested on suspicion of
Treason Against the Reich.
von Essen: Yes, that I do remember. I'm not likely to
forget you barging into my house this morning. I
have a long and unforgiving memory for stuff like
that.
Schneider: Specifically, we have reason to believe
that you're in the pay of the British.
von Essen: (LONG LAUGH) *Jij bent ver weggekropen
van je Amsterdamse hol.*
Schneider: I don't speak Dutch, von Essen.

von Essen: Last time I looked, I was your superior officer. Where the blazes did the 'sir' go? *I don't speak Dutch, sir.* Why don't you give it a try, Obersturmführer Schneider?

Schneider: I repeat: You've been arrested on suspicion of Treason Against the Reich. This makes you a nobody, von Essen. I will address you as I please.

von Essen: Obersturmführer Schneider is a bit of a mouthful, isn't it? And I doubt the rank will be yours for much longer anyway, so let's do as you propose and stick to surnames. I will translate the Dutch for you, Schneider, but just this once mind. I said, 'You've crawled a long way from your hole in Amsterdam.'

Schneider: I repeat: You've been arrested on suspicion of Treason Against the Reich. Insulting me is not a wise move, von Essen.

von Essen: (SIGH) I've never had much time for repetition, Schneider. I've always regarded it as a sign of stupidity. Furthermore, I'm not entirely sure I'm in the mood to discuss strategy with a pen pusher, and I assure you, it's completely beyond me to make an unwise move.

Schneider: Oh I can do much more than push a pen, von Essen.

von Essen: Don't sell yourself short, dear boy: I'm sure your pen skills are exceptional. More so than your Dutch, anyway. Indeed, I imagine you push that pen into places I can only have nightmares about, but that's not really the point, if you'll pardon the pun. I'll only take advice on strategy from my dearest and oldest friend, our beloved Führer (PAUSE) Or from a man who's fought on the Front Line, at the very least.

Schneider: Your attitude is very disappointing, von Essen. This is a serious charge.

von Essen: (TUT, TUT, TUT) Schneider, Schneider, Schneider, it was your choice to play this tedious little game, was it not? Between you, me, and the bloodstained walls of this little room in which we sit, I can think of more productive ways to spend an afternoon, such as responding to a direct order from my dearest and oldest friend, our beloved Führer, to defend *Fortress Europe* against the imminent threat of an Allied invasion. Are you familiar with this threat, Schneider? Or is it just me because I'm in the pay of the British?

Schneider: You're admitting the offence, von Essen?

von Essen: (CLAPPING, LAUGHTER) This is most entertaining, Schneider, but war waits for no man, not even the stupid ones. So, on that note we'd better push on and get to the particulars of the alleged offence, not to mention the overwhelming evidence you possess of my wrong-doing. You know, my Treason Against the Reich. Does that sound like a good strategy to you? What will the pen decide, I wonder?

Schneider: Veronika Oursler. What do you know about her?

von Essen: Give me a clue?

Schneider: Code-name MOPS.

von Essen: And another?

Schneider: You recruited her in... (SHUFFLE OF PAPERS) the autumn of 1941.

von Essen: To do what?

Schneider: You tell me.

von Essen: Is this a trap, Schneider? Are you inviting me to spill the beans so that you can then accuse me of the offence? If you offer me a slice of gingerbread, don't expect me to bake it for you.

Schneider: (SIGH)

von Essen: No need to be like that. Had you asked me if I wanted to play this game, I'd have politely declined. As a general rule, I don't much care for games, especially silly ones. Shall we call it a day and get back to work?

Schneider: You recruited Veronika Oursler to spy on the British.

von Essen: Is that a bad thing?

Schneider: Only you and her handler knew about her role.

von Essen: You know, Schneider, I firmly believe that covert operations have a greater chance of success if the world and his wife remain ignorant of them. You've seen the poster: *Hush, You Put Me In Danger.* I rather like that poster. Like your pen, it has a point.

Schneider: So, you agree that only you and her handler knew about Oursler's role?

von Essen: What does your paperwork tell you?

Schneider: It tells me that Veronica Oursler was betrayed, that her cover was blown, that she was arrested by the British on May 1st. It also tells me that we have no idea where she's been taken, or indeed, if she's been executed.

von Essen: (SILENCE)

Schneider: Are you going to claim that this information is new to you?

von Essen: Actually, Schneider, I am.

Schneider: Somebody gave her up, von Essen, and I think it was you.

von Essen: Is that a question or an expression of fact?

Schneider: You tell me?

von Essen: (PAUSE) Veronika's not just an agent I've been running for nearly four years, Schneider, but a friend I've known for nearly twenty. The news that she's been arrested, and possibly murdered by the British is, of course, deeply distressing. But I've identified British agents operating in my jurisdiction because they looked the wrong way when crossing the road. Nobody gave them up, Schneider; they gave themselves up. Veronika was good at her job, but she was growing impatient. Her target wouldn't play ball as often as she wanted and it irritated her. In a recent letter to me, her handler expressed his concern that Veronika's desperation to deliver intelligence to us might prompt her to do something that would put her under the spotlight. I have retained the letter and can provide a copy. Desperation breeds mistakes, Schneider. You're a fine example of this: in your desperation to land what you quite clearly consider to be the catch of your career, you've forgotten to bring your bloody landing net to the river. You're not dealing with a member of the Maquis now, dear boy; you'll need solid evidence before you'll have the pleasure of putting me before a firing squad.

Schneider: (SHUFFLING OF PAPERS) What about the aerial attack on your Command Centre?

von Essen: (SIGH) What of it? I, as well as my son, was in the château at the time of the attack. This can be verified by my Chief-of-Staff, *Oberleutnant* Hans Krebs. If the price of being in the pay of the British is to sacrifice my son, as well as myself, even an idiot must surely conclude that the deal is not a good one for me. I think I'll stick with my own side, if it's all the same to you.

Schneider: The radio jammer in Amiens was attacked. The weapon stores in your jurisdiction were attacked. Many weapons stores located elsewhere in France have also been subjected to targeted aerial attacks by the British. You have knowledge of each and every one of these locations.

von Essen: You're grasping at straws, Schneider, and you know it. The Maquis also have knowledge of each and every one of these locations, not to mention hundreds of our own soldiers, and while I'm sitting here talking *scheiße* with you, the Maquis are preparing to sabotage more of our weapon stores, more of our radio jammers, and more of our railways. (CHAIR SCRAPING) If you're going to keep me from my orders, Schneider, it better be for more than just a hunch.

Schneider: (CHAIR SCRAPING) You should know that we'll be watching you, von Essen, and...

von Essen: You should know, Schneider, that I've had enough now and it's time for you to crawl back

to your hole in Amsterdam. Quite what you're doing in Paris I don't know, but if you travelled here just for this, you've had a wasted journey. If you ever obtain evidence that I've committed Treason Against the Reich, I'll rip out my own fingernails and put a bullet in my own brain to save you the trouble. But, if you ever haul me back here again on supposition alone, I'll do a lot worse than rip out your fingernails before I finally put you out of your misery. In the meantime, I'll be sure to pass on your regards to my dearest and oldest friend, our beloved Führer. (PAUSE) Heil Hitler!
Schneider: Heil Hitler!
(DOOR OPEN) (DOOR SHUTS)
von Essen: (SHOUTS) Krebs.
Krebs: Sir?
von Essen: Let's go. And don't spare the bloody horses. *Schnell!*

Interrogation concluded: Date: 10/05/44. Time: 14.10 HRS.

'*Sohn einer Hündin,*' roared the *Generalfeldmarschall,* once his Chief-of-Staff, *Oberleutnant* Krebs, had pulled onto the main road out of Paris and it was apparent they weren't being followed by the Gestapo. He punched the back of the front passenger seat until his fist complained.

'Sir?' said Krebs to the rear-view mirror.

'Leave me be, Hans,' said the *Generalfeldmarschall.* 'I need to think,' he added, taking several Pervitin.

'Yes, sir.'

It didn't take long for him to think of Konstantin and to remember all the times he'd found him skulking about his office, always with a letter for Gerda in hand, always ready with the claim that he'd only entered the office to post the letter. So many letters to Gerda. So many unauthorized visits to the office. Konstantin was such a lazy little *scheiße* and did so little with his day that he couldn't possibly have had that much to write. And such devotion to his mother was unnatural in a boy of his age. Konstantin's letter writing habit should have aroused his suspicion weeks ago. The little *scheiße* had probably been posting nothing more than blank sheets of paper to the Sanatorium. That was the price he had to pay for allowing his guilt over Gerda to cloud his judgement.

But, by Christ, what a price to pay.

He thought of all the documents that had lately graced his desk. The importance of them made him nauseous. He had to wind the window down. With the spring air blowing on his face and through his hair he thought of his desk as it appeared now, as he'd left it when that imbecile Schneider had marched into his office that morning, unannounced, clicking his fingers left and right at the *Generalfeldmarschall's* staff – at Hans, and at Blandine who misread the click in her face as an order to document the arrest with a photograph – waltzing in and out of rooms as if he owned the place, to arrest him on a trumped-up charge and cart him off to that godforsaken place in Paris. Schneider would pay. *Er würde bezahlen.*

Maps drawn for his eyes only were on that desk. Leaving them as he had, unguarded like that, well, he may as well have framed them and hung them on the wall for any old Tom, Dick, or Harry to view. If Konstantin were in the pay of the British, that stupid *Saukerl* Schneider had given him carte blanch to read those maps at his leisure.

If Konstantin were in the pay of the British, Germany's hand had just been shown to the enemy.

'Pull over,' he ordered.

'Yes, sir,' said Krebs.

When the car came to a stop, he opened his door, leaned out and was violently sick on the road.

Krebs was trained in impassivity and remained in the driver's seat with his eyes fixed on the road ahead, as if the vehicle were still being propelled and nothing unusual was happening in the back.

The *Generalfeldmarschall* fumbled in his pocket for the bottle of Eukodal and the tube of Pervitin and took a handful of each, even though neither was a preventative for sickness, and taken together were medically contra-indicative. But, once the pills had gone down and he'd spat into the road several times to empty his mouth of his stomach acid, he was able to pull himself together and instruct Krebs to drive on.

It was ridiculous to suspect Konstantin of being in the pay of the British. He was just a boy. He'd always been a sop for his mother. How many times had he told Gerda off for encouraging him? For babying him? Of course the boy wrote her letters. Out of his earshot, she'd probably begged the child to write to her daily before they'd left for France, and Konstantin being the boy he was, dutifully did as he was bid, no matter that he had nothing to write about. The thought of his son being in contact with the British was laughable. So, he laughed. Krebs smiled at the rear-view mirror. For one, how did he imagine Konstantin communicated with the British? By letter, via the post tray in his office? They had no links to Britain. There was not the slightest hint of Britishness in their bloodline; no long lost ancestor festering away in a thatched cottage somewhere, now or ever. Prior to the war, Konstantin had never even left Germany. So, what, now Konstantin is chummy with British Intelligence? It was laughable, so he laughed again, but this time hysterically.

Until he remembered Veronika.

The only thing that stupid *Saukerl* Schneider had been right about was that only two people, himself and Veronika's handler, knew the precise details of her mission, and her code-name. He'd spouted complete rubbish when he'd claimed that Veronika was growing impatient. That her target wasn't playing ball as often as she wanted. That she was irritated. That she was desperate and ripe for making a mistake. On the contrary, Veronika was on the verge of pulling off something stupendous. That was what the letter had reported: the excellent progress she'd made in relation to the agreed objective. Schneider had lapped up the bluff like a dog does its own vomit.

But that letter about Veronika had, without a shadow of a doubt, been read by Konstantin. He'd been caught red-handed with it. By the time the *Generalfeldmarschall* entered his office, following a swift and impromptu assignation with Blandine, Konstantin was on to the second page.

'I thought it was a letter from Mother,' he'd claimed, dropping the thing as if it were a live grenade.

'So, you had to read it to the end to be sure?'

'I'm sorry, Father, I picked it up without thinking. I was just looking for something to do.'

'And reading my private correspondence qualifies, does it?'

He'd ordered Konstantin out of his office with a string of expletives. Guilt about his affair with Blandine had kept him from dealing with him more stringently.

But now it was clear: Konstantin was the one committing Treason Against the Reich.

His own son was a traitor to the Fatherland.

He slid to the edge of the back seat and, as if he suspected the car had been newly bugged, whispered into Krebs's ear, 'I have a job for you.'

Krebs nodded.

'It's unofficial business.'

And Krebs, ever the loyal subordinate, simply nodded again.

37.

HIGHLY CONFIDENTIAL
Report on: Operation Attar
Report Status: Highly Confidential
Report Date: 3 August 1944
From: Troop Sergeant Major Bloomfield/1st Special Service Brigade
For: MI5/Director of Counter Espionage
Report As follows:
Arrived at the subject's address on the morning of 25/07/44. No German military personnel in attendance. As per orders, a thorough search of the property for *Generalfeldmarschall* Dieter von Essen was conducted. No trace found. As instructed, photographs were taken of every room in the property by Earthstar. (Film preserved, and submitted to C.O upon arrival in Portsmouth.) While photographing what is believed to have been the *Generalfeldmarschall's* bedroom, a quantity of dried blood on a rug situated at the foot of the bed was observed. (Bloodstain photographed by Earthstar.) No other blood discovered elsewhere in the property.

The subject was located in a small barred room in the cellar. The door to his cell was locked. The subject was lying upon the floor in dirty clothes and with only a thin blanket for warmth. His general condition was poor. He was undernourished and dehydrated, though a glass of water and a sandwich appeared untouched on a tray beside him. There was evidence he'd been subjected to sustained physical interrogation. Extensive bruising was apparent on his person, particularly his face and upper body. His nose appeared broken. The subject was uncommunicative, though compliant. Given his condition, 5mg of Benzedrine sulphate was administered before the subject was removed to the designated safe house. At the safe house, first aid was given and the subject invited to wash and dress in clean civilian clothes. Subject also consumed a small quantity of Bully Beef and several cups of weak tea.

During the homeward journey to England, the subject responded to basic questions regarding his welfare, but did not initiate conversation on any topic nor offer any information regarding the location of *Generalfeldmarschall* von Essen. The Subject was not directly questioned about *Generalfeldmarschall* von Essen. The Subject was observed drawing in a sketch book during rest periods. It was necessary to administer several more doses of Benzedrine sulphate in order to keep the subject moving and alert, particularly when rough terrain was encountered, and during the crossing of the Channel.

Given the subject's poor physical and mental condition, the C.O agreed that he be placed in the immediate care of Mrs Freda Bloomfield until a more permanent situation could be arranged. Mrs Bloomfield was notified via telegram. Following arrival in Portsmouth, the subject was directly conveyed to Mrs Bloomfield's home address in Kent (details overleaf).

Report End.

HIGHLY CONFIDENTIAL

38.

27 April, 1944

Regarding Operation Attar, Basildon Bond has forwarded a third message, written in secret ink, as well as a quantity of microfilm from Gilbert Aumont. This package constitutes the most exciting intelligence I believe I've ever seen, let alone received. The importance of what Aumont has gifted us is perhaps best illustrated by Churchill's reaction when I presented the deciphered message and developed microfilm to him at Chequers; he was speechless for a change, and blubbed for a good ten minutes, or thereabouts, in full view of the Commander of the 21st Army Group, General Montgomery, the Deputy Prime Minister, Clement Attlee, the Foreign Secretary, Anthony Eden, the Home Secretary, Herbert Morrison, and the Minister of War Production, Oliver Lyttleton.

Churchill has made it clear that no effort is to be spared in protecting Aumont in the aftermath of Operation Overlord and, should his father survive, reuniting the Aumont family. However, this directive is problematic. Earthstar has now confirmed that the true identity of Gilbert Aumont is the fourteen-year-old son of Generalfeldmarschall von Essen, Konstantin von Essen. Not just an ordinary boy, after all.

Owing to the fact that Konstantin von Essen is a bit of a mouthful, I will henceforth refer to him as KvE. Naturally, following the planned invasion of Normandy, and assuming we are successful, the Generalfeldmarschall will be sought for prosecution of the war crimes he has committed in France, Poland and the Soviet Union. Unfortunately, enquiries with Viola in Potsdam reveal that KvE's mother, Frau Gerda von Essen, died of TB during February of this year. Consequently, KvE will, to all intents and purposes, be left an orphan by the close of the war. Even if the Generalfeldmarschall survives the Allied invasion, he's unlikely to escape the death penalty for his crimes, particularly once the details of the Babi Yar Massacre have been made plain in court. In light of this, it has been decided that once the first phase of the Normandy campaign is complete, Troop Sergeant Major Bloomfield from the 1st Special Service Brigade will make every effort to rescue KvE from Amiens and bring him to Britain to begin a new life. Where necessary, Bloomfield, whom I'm told is a specialist in complex extractions of this kind, will be assisted by local members of the Maquis, specifically Les Gens Prévalent, briefed on the operation by Earthstar.

KvE's third message reveals that Generalfeldmarschall von Essen is scheduled to meet with Generalfeldmarschall Erwin Rommel sometime during the second week of May at von Essen's Command Centre, the Château des Beaux Anges in Amiens. Although the exact date of the meeting is currently unknown, KvE claims that the meeting was proposed by Rommel in a hand-written letter to his father that he saw lying upon his father's desk. KvE also reports that the precise agenda of the proposed meeting was not immediately clear to him, even though he was able to read the letter in full. Whether the following is merely a fanciful notion of an imaginative boy I cannot determine, but KvE believes the better part of Rommel's letter was written in some sort of code since the sentences appeared largely nonsensical to him in terms of what they expressed. Regrettably, KvE did not provide us with textual examples that we could have submitted to Bletchley for analysis. Happily for us though, KvE does appear to have had better luck with

Rommel's final paragraph. Therein, Rommel stated the proposed meeting would provide the two Commanders with a crucial opportunity to finalize the plan to put down the anticipated Allied invasion. Needless to say, it would be beyond useful for us if KvE could earwig on the meeting as and when it takes place.

To that end, I'm sending KvE a message via the BBC thanking him for all the intelligence he's provided thus far and requesting more of the same. However, I'm mindful of KvE's age and the inherent danger of his position. KvE reports that the opportunity to photograph the maps he sent to us arose only because his father was unexpectedly called to Paris to attend to some urgent business, the nature of which is unknown. If KvE's role as one of our greatest informants were to be discovered by his father, I'm concerned that kinship may not ameliorate the penalty. I can only hope that KvE does everything necessary to avoid detection until Troop Sergeant Major Bloomfield's arrival.

We have now identified the female German spy operating in England, code-named MOPS. Once again, KvE's information was spot on, even down to the teeth. Zurie Davidson, real name Veronika Oursler, a German national from Falkensee in Brandenburg, was discovered living in Hughenden with her husband, Maxwell Davidson, a cartographer working on Operation Hillside. Davidson, a civilian artist and alumnus of the Slade School of Fine Art, has been drawing maps at Hillside for nearby Bomber Command since Hillside's inception in '41. The couple met in early '42 and following what Davidson believed was a genuine whirlwind romance, married soon after. Davidson's claim that he was unaware of Oursler's true identity is accepted, but as a precaution he has, nonetheless, been relieved of his duties. The man has been left thoroughly distraught by Oursler's deception; he has lost his job, and what he believed was a loving wife, in the space of a few hours. All that remains of his former life is Oursler's pug, which I'm given to understand he's too distressed to retain with the result that, unless a suitable new home can be found, the pug will most likely be euthanized.

Though Davidson claims to have remained tight-lipped about the nature of his work to Oursler, pillow talk cannot be ruled out. Indeed, it is believed likely that Oursler obtained some information from Davidson that was useful to the enemy, since Hillside has consistently escaped Hitler's bombs, a fact that, heretofore, was regarded as oddly miraculous. Sadly, it now follows that with Oursler out of the picture, Hillside will be designated a primary target for the Luftwaffe by Reichsmarshall Göring. In a bid to protect Hillside from sustained aerial attack, numerous anti-aircraft guns as well as barrage balloons have now been installed throughout the Hughenden valley.

KvE's superb information on MOPS came not a moment too soon as, incredibly, Oursler was making a concerted effort to secure a role at Hillside on the basis of her own artistic ability, and the premise that she wished to work alongside Davidson. We'll never know if Oursler would have succeeded had her cover not been blown. Quite honestly, it doesn't bear thinking about.

Since her arrest and detention at Cockfosters Camp in Hertfordshire, Oursler has been interviewed a number of times. SIS believe that she should be under their sway meaning they should be given first dibs at pumping her for information. So far, I've managed to keep them out of it, but, quite frankly, the dispute's pointless since Oursler has refused to answer the majority of the questions put to her. The only information she has given up is that she was recruited by Generalfeldmarschall von Essen at a party in Berlin sometime in '41, and that the two were lovers in their youth. This is information I have shared with C. over drinks at The Rag.

To their credit, Bomber Command have always been pro-pigeon, but since discovering that a pigeon was responsible for delivering the intelligence on Oursler, are even more so now. Once again, we are all very grateful to Ethelred the Unready, though, I have to say, it's a shame the pigeon we sent to KvE didn't survive the drop. Regardless, I sincerely hope we shall be in a position to send Ethel home to Lady Darrick-Sinclair in the immediate future.

I've finally received a response from the Professor of Semiotics regarding Basildon Bond's rose and dot motif. While Professor Carnegie's analysis is interesting, not to mention entertaining, I find I cannot give it much credence. This is largely due to the Professor's cataracts, a self-confessed optical degeneration which has caused her to make an error of calculation in regard to the number of dots present. I have checked all three of Basildon Bond's motifs and each exhibits exactly thirty dots, rather than the twelve counted by Professor Carnegie. Sadly, this gross miscalculation on her part serves to undermine much of what she posits in her letter, such as a) the plausibility of a North American messenger b) the hypothesis that the dots represent menstruation and thus a female messenger c) that a power struggle is inherent in the relationship between the messengers involved in this case. With regard to the latter in particular, I see no evidence of a power struggle between KvE and Basildon Bond. Furthermore, while we've now confirmed that KvE is a male subject, I must confess that even when following Professor Carnegie's advice to screw up my eyes, I largely fail to see the rose and dot motif as a representation of the sun. However, in a recent conversation with an eminent ophthalmologist I chanced upon at The Caledonian Club last evening, I understand that, with cataracts, it's quite common to perceive a halo that doesn't exist.

Moreover, since there's a complete absence of evidence to support Professor Carnegie's theory that Basildon Bond when combined with KvE makes a team of three, rather than two, I'm of the growing opinion that Basildon Bond is in fact one individual with a fondness for a) roses b) decorative borders c) doodling in margins d) interfering in matters that don't concern him (although one must be grateful in this case). Regrettably, I find I must follow Professor Carnegie's advice and take all that she has postulated with a hefty pinch of salt. As a matter of course, I've written to thank her for her detailed analysis and have assured her of its value in relation to our case.

In other matters, Hector Brine informed me that Donald Vignali was terribly concerned about the Pansy fiasco. He had a powerful fancy that Parasol ought to be liquidated to protect Garbo from a German inquiry. Personally, I don't partake of his angst.

An Unnarrated Event
Love Letter to a Husband

The Grange,
The Avenue
Camberley

Surrey
Strand House,
Cheyne Walk
Chelsea

6 May 1944

Darling Hughie,

So sorry I didn't get around to writing to you last week. Things have been kind of busy around here. Before I forget, Mrs. Darby's broken the washing line again and try as I might, I just can't fix it. If I were just a few inches taller, it would help. Do you know when you might get around to visiting? Also, the twins had a close shave with the Epstein sideboard and I can't move it on my own, and I daren't ask Mrs. Darby for help. And another thing, the kitchen sink's slipped out of the frame, or the frame's rotted away, I can't tell, but it needs fixing.

You know, Dottie said the funniest thing to me the other day. She told me I had to start locking the doors and windows at night, even though it's beginning to warm up at last. She said it was because the Germans are roaming the countryside in British uniforms. She was deadly serious, darling, which made it even funnier, although I was careful not to laugh. I'm happy to say that summer's on its way, darling, but it's going to be kind of stuffy if I can't open the windows, especially at night. I've tried telling her it's nonsense, but she won't take it from me. I don't know where she gets these notions, but I think you ought to have a word with her when you next come home. I also think you need to be a bit more careful about the things you say in her presence. I have a feeling this is all your fault, darling.

Sorry, darling, I have to close now. The girls, twins included, are putting on a little show for Mrs. Darby and I, and Dottie's just yelled that the curtain's up!

I hope you're remembering to eat and sleep, as well as smoke.

Wish you were here,

Athena

P.S. Edmund's letter home was even shorter than the last, but he says he's doing fine, so I guess I will just have to believe him on this.

P.P.S. Dottie's decided to call the pug Pom-Pom, on account of her funny little tail, I suppose.

P.P.P.S. Please don't bring any more strays home, darling; I'm worried we might drive Mrs. Darby away. The house is now rather full.

🦃

"Ici Londres! Les Français parlent aux Français. S'il vous plaît avant de commençer écoutez-bien ces messages personnels"

La galantérie n'est pas morte. Le visage est chaud mais les mains sont froides. Tous les chiots sont malades. Garçon ordinaire, le père Noël adore vos tartelettes de Noël. Envoyez-en encore s'il vous plaît dès que possible. On répète, garçon ordinaire, le père Noël adore vos tartelettes de Noël. Envoyez-en encore s'il vous plaît dès que possible. La porte de devant est maintenant entourée d'une grille pointue. La flamme se dresse de manière imposante au-dessus de la brume. La dame élégante assistera au bal. La poudre pressée est trop pâle pour les pieds de Pascale. Le taux d'intérêt a influencé le marché monétaire. La faillite était pour de vrai et la génisse est coupable. Le poème était écrit en craie sur le poignet droit. Le cognac est sincère. La souris est ravie de sa petite réparation. Deux assiettes par

mois redescendront les bébés. Les fées sont
réceptives au juge.

"This is London! The French speak to the French.
Before we begin, please listen to some personal messages."
Chivalry is not dead. The face is warm but the hands
are cold. All the puppies are sick. Ordinary boy,
Father Christmas loves your mince pies. Please send
more as soon as you can. We say twice, Ordinary
boy, Father Christmas loves your mince pies. Please
send more as soon as you can. The pointed railings
now surround the front door. The flame towers
above the mist. The elegant lady will attend the ball.
The pressed powder is too pale for Pascale's feet.
The interest on the money has influenced the market.
The crash was real and the heifer is to blame. The
rhyme was written on the right wrist in chalk. The
brandy is sincere. The mouse is thrilled with its tiny
repair. Two plates a month will earth the babies. The
fairies are receptive to the judge.

39.

Transcript of Interview. Operation Attar.
Date: 17/09/44. Time: 09.00 HRS. Interview 7/7.
Informant: Konstantin von Essen. Interviewer:
Saunders. Also present: Guardian: Mrs Bloomfield.
Location of debrief: Combined Services Detailed
Interrogation Unit, Latimer House, nr Amersham,
Buckinghamshire.

Guardian: Do you know something, Mr Saunders,
when your automobile with the black windows
arrived at our place to bring Konstantin and me
here, well I wasn't sure what to make of it, if I'm
being honest. It's not often I get a ride out, and the
minute I do I'm not allowed to look out the windows.
Since you're asking, we couldn't understand the
point of painting those windows, could we, lovey?
Especially painting them black.
Informant: (PAUSE) No, Mrs Bloomfield, we could not.
Also, I don't think Mr Saunders asked about the
windows.
Guardian: Well, we thought, what a performance,
didn't we, lovey?
Informant: (PAUSE) Yes, Mrs Bloomfield, we did.
Guardian: Gawd knows what the neighbours made of
it. I mean to say, how many automobiles do you see
knocking about with black windows? I know it's the
war and all that, but how am I supposed to explain
it, Mr Saunders?

Interviewer: INAUDIBLE

Guardian: That's all very well for you to say, but I'm the one with the explaining to do. Mind you, it's given us a good little game, hasn't it, lovey?

Informant: I am very sorry, Mrs Bloomfield, but I do not understand. I am not aware that we have played any games except the one Mr Saunders gave to us.

Interviewer: The Snakes and Ladders, Konstantin?

Informant: Yes, Mr Saunders. I am very grateful for this game. I have enjoyed playing it with Mrs Bloomfield during my stay here.

Guardian: (CHUCKLE) Those blasted snakes. They seem to be everywhere. More snakes than ladders, I shouldn't wonder. And I don't like snakes. Ooh, just thinking about them makes me come over all peculiar. And I never seem to win, Mr Saunders.

Interviewer: I'm sorry to hear that, Mrs Bloomfield.

Informant: I am also very sorry about this, Mrs Bloomfield.

Guardian: (SIGH) Don't fret, lovey, it's not the end of the world. You know, Mr Saunders, my other boys didn't gave a hoot when I lost at Ludo. Though I never came last when Mr Bloomfield played the game with us. The only thing Mr Bloomfield can play is Snap, isn't that right, lovey?

Informant: I...

Guardian: But I've forgotten what we were talking about. As soon as you mentioned Snakes and Ladders, Mr Saunders, it went.

Informant: I am very sorry, Mrs Bloomfield, but I was the one that mentioned Snakes and Ladders.

Guardian: Never mind, lovey, it's water under the bridge.

Informant: I'm very sorry, Mrs Bloomfield, but...

Guardian: Never mind, lovey, I'll tell you what that means another time.

Interviewer: You were discussing the mode of transportation used to bring you here, Mrs Bloomfield.

Guardian: (CHUCKLE) So I was, Mr Saunders. That's right, the game. Yes, I remember now. Well, I said to Konstantin, I'm going to try and count how long it takes us to get to where we're going, didn't I, lovey, because I'm not as daft as I look, Mr Saunders, I've always been good with numbers. That's why I can knit so well, you see. I said, I'm going to count how long it takes us to get there and then work out where we are. You know, work out where we've been taken. Well, I counted a lot of pink elephants, Mr Saunders, I can promise you that. But do you know? I worked it out. Devon, I said. Didn't I, lovey?

Informant: Yes, Mrs Bloomfield, you did say Devon.

Guardian: I don't know exactly where in Devon, Mr Saunders, because I think that's asking too much, but I'm quite sure I've heard the sea when I've been drifting off at night.

Interviewer: Could that be your tinnitus, Mrs Bloomfield?

Guardian: Oh no, Mr Saunders, don't be daft. We're on the English Riviera. I'm right, aren't I, Mr Saunders?

Interviewer: INAUDIBLE

Guardian: Well, in the absence of anything else, Mr Saunders, I'll take that as a yes. Told you, lovey.

Informant: You are very clever, Mrs Bloomfield.

Guardian: Thank you, lovey. Not as clever as you, mind.

Informant: No, Mrs Bloomfield, I am not clever.

Guardian: (TUT) (CHUCKLE) I've always fancied the English Riviera, but Mr Bloomfield, well, he doesn't really want to go anywhere these days.

Interviewer: On that note, I'm quite certain you'll both be pleased to learn that today will be your last with us. Now that we've had a chat, Konstantin, I believe it's in your best interests to put this difficult episode behind you and begin anew. Sadly, Mrs Bloomfield, this does mean that you'll have to suffer the automobile with the painted windows once more, but it's for the last time and I hope that serves as some consolation. I've made arrangements with the headmaster of Rugby School for you to begin as a boarder after Christmas, Konstantin. Rugby School is an excellent school and Mr Lyon, the headmaster, is looking forward to meeting you. I'm quite certain you'll be very happy there. You can remain with Mrs Bloomfield in the interim. For reasons I hope you'll understand, you'll be given a new name...

Guardian: Wo, wo, wo, Mr Saunders, hold your horses for a just a minute, if you don't mind? I'm sorry, but me and Mr Bloomfield have been talking about this, and I've been meaning to talk to you about it, but it's been difficult to get a word in edgeways this past week. I don't mind if Konstantin goes to that fancy school of yours, Mr Saunders, really I don't, just as long as he comes home in the holidays. As for his new name, we've already got one for him. Davey said he'd be needing a new one. So, we decided he should have the name of the boy we lost. (PAUSE) (SNIFF) (BLOWS NOSE) We named him after my old dad. Ivo. That's short for Ivor, lovey, but as you know, we don't stand on ceremony in our house, so Ivo it is. And we don't pretend that you remind us of him either because he was only two when he died of Scarlatina, see, but, well, we think of you as one of our own, lovey, and, truth be told, Mr Saunders, we don't want to part with another one of our boys ever again. Our hearts couldn't take it. So, we were wondering if we could adopt Konstantin, you know, official so to speak. If that would be alright with you, lovey?

Informant: Oh yes, Mrs Bloomfield, yes. (SIGH) Thank you, Mrs Bloomfield, I would like that very much.

Guardian: So, Mr Saunders, is that agreed then? Ivo stops with us?

Interviewer: (CLEARS THROAT) I... INAUDIBLE.

HIGHLY CONFIDENTIAL
Report on: Operation Attar
Report Status: Highly Confidential
Report Date: 19 September, 1944,
From: Colonel Killian Dunne (AKA SAUNDERS), Combined Services Detailed Interrogation Unit
For: Hugh Latymer, MI5/Director of Counter Espionage
C., SIS
Report as follows:
The first thing to say about Konstantin von Essen is that I found him to be a most impressive young man. He's far and away the most intelligent boy I've ever met and I fancy he has a photographic memory. That he knows much more than he lets on is certain, not just about events in France, but also his own abilities. I imagine there are few academic subjects in which he doesn't excel.

He's adept at avoiding the question and keeping his own counsel, except when questioned on benign events; then, he is relatively forthcoming. In this respect, he would make a marvellous spy and, if I didn't know better, I'd say he's been trained in counter-interrogation techniques. He maintains ignorance in relation to the whereabouts of his father, but invariably refers to him in the past tense. It's pure speculation on my part, but I suspect he witnessed his father's death prior to his extraction from France. Whilst I believe the murder of Gilbert Aumont was the event that prompted Konstantin to make contact with us and betray his own country, I remain unclear as to why this specific murder sparked this remarkable response, given that many members of the Maquis in his father's jurisdiction met the same fate. He also maintains ignorance in relation to the name and location of his contact in Britain.

A review of the interview transcripts show that very little new information was obtained from Konstantin. If I'd not conducted the interviews myself, I'd have questioned the competence of the assigned interrogator. I've arranged for copies of the transcripts to be hand-delivered to you both for your consideration.
Report End.
HIGHLY CONFIDENTIAL

40.

As files go, this has been a complex one to classify. While Joyce might think I'm at liberty to classify my files at leisure, I'm not. What with the influenza and the willy-nilly handling of the documents following the fall of the file from my desk, I'm not up to scratch. You can imagine my horror when I was then informed that this file is actually one of two files. Just as I began to perceive palpitations of a vigour not previously experienced, and wondered aloud if I were, perhaps, suffering the onset of a heart attack, my colleague then realised that the second file remains Live, and as such won't require classifying until long after I've retired, I hope. So, though it's not ideal, I'm afraid I'll have to whizz through the remaining documents in order to meet my deadline. (My appraisal is due next week and I could do without a slap on the wrist for lack of productivity and dynamism.)

Oberleutnant Krebs's unofficial job was to conduct twenty-four-hour surveillance on Konstantin. The advantage he had over his target, aside from age and training etcetera etcetera, was that Konstantin was expected by his father to be home for dinner by 7, and to be tucked up in bed by 10. So, when Konstantin inadvertently led Krebs to Kenneth's loft the following afternoon, Krebs, unlike Konstantin, was able to mount a twenty-four-hour vigil for Kenneth's return. Inevitably, Kenneth was received by Krebs rather than Konstantin. As Konstantin wandered the land of nod, the *Generalfeldmarschall* was brought up to speed by Krebs. A dawn raid was effected on Konstantin's bedroom, Minox camera, secret ink and rice paper seized, and the boy taken to the cellar, where, for quite some time, nothing much happened to him.

Upstairs was a different story. It took a large quantity of Pervitin for the *Generalfeldmarschall* to make sense of Polly and Oliver's message. It was hardly the prose of British Intelligence. The very first thing Polly wished to make clear was that her real name wasn't Polly, it was something beginning with R, and that was all she was willing to say on the matter. Given the presence of the rose and dot motif, the *Generalfeldmarschall*, like his son, concluded that her name was Rose. The lesson on what her name wasn't, was all Rose was willing to write about this, or any other subject. This left Oliver with enough space on the Rizla stationery to go to town, and to town he went, to a town in Montana by the name of Great Falls where he regaled Gilbert with his plan to go there and become a sodbuster when he grew up. *What do you wanna do when you're fully grown Gilbert? Get married? Have loads of babies? Why not do something more interesting and be a cowboy instead? Any good with a gun?* (I can literally hear the tuts and sighs of Rose as she was forced to check Oliver's work for errors before Kenneth was sent on his way.) It occurred to the *Generalfeldmarschall* that this little *Scheiße* (which is evidence that, in relation to Oliver's gender he, unlike his son, did take Oliver at his word, as I'm quite sure he'd have called him something else had he suspected Oliver was really a girl) was not unlike the Führer with his obsession with the Wild West. The comparison inspired a wry smile.

As ever, Oliver closed the message by assuring Gilbert that they would pass on his secret note and microfilm to the very important man in Londres (though Oliver did point out Gilbert's spelling error: *Londres is'nt how you spel London, sugar.* This sentence must have escaped the censor, and I can only assume it was because Rose was crocheting another doily for the den at this point.). Had it not been for the inclusion of this sentence, a dose of Eukodal might have, once more, persuaded the *Generalfeldmarschall* that Konstantin wasn't a traitor to the Fatherland, but rather a complete and utter nitwit with poor taste in penfriends. Then again, *we* do have to remember that with an overdose of Pervitin *he'd* have likely remembered the seized items now sitting in the drawer of his desk. These, no matter how befuddled his brain, were undoubtedly the accoutrements of a spy, not a penfriend.

Eventually, the *Generalfeldmarschall* instructed his right-hand man to 'rough' Konstantin up a bit. *Try not to break any bones*, he suggested, *but feel free to draw blood.* This was a tricky order for Krebs. When it came to his hands, he was, I'm afraid to say, rather heavy-handed. However, whilst it's perhaps effortless to imagine Krebs entering Konstantin's cell fists flying, this isn't how his afternoon with Konstantin began. Proceedings commenced with a round of Krebs's favourite game: Mock Russian Roulette. As the name of the game implies, there's no actual bullet in the gun. Therefore, Krebs was not in danger of breaking any of Konstantin's bones, drawing blood or, indeed, blowing his brains out. But, Konstantin didn't know that. Of all the things Krebs did to him that afternoon and beyond, it was this little game that caused him the greatest pain.

Meanwhile, the *Generalfeldmarschall* zoomed off to Paris in the former Departmental Councillor of Amiens's Citroën Traction Avant. For a spot of lunch at *Maxim's*, you ask? Very plausibly, while the cartographer got on with drawing the false maps he'd been commissioned to supply. Three days later, microfilm of these maps (not produced by Madame Brugière because she'd gone shopping for a Hermès silk headscarf), maps that boasted a degree of manpower, armaments, Rommel's asparagus, air support, K-Verbände naval units, concrete gun emplacements, block houses, points of inland defences etcetera, etcetera, (you name it, they showed it) that simply weren't there in reality, were being thrust into Kenneth's container. Along with microfilm of battle plans purportedly drawn up by the *Generalfeldmarschall* and the Desert Fox showing that Germany was supremely prepared for an Allied Invasion largely anywhere along the French coast.

Needless to say, this was the sort of message one could be forgiven for hoping the messenger would be shot.

Only once Kenneth had been chucked into the air to deliver the *Generalfeldmarschall's* duplicitous intelligence to the British, and Konstantin had been allowed to fester in his cell for more than two months as punishment for his treachery, was he finally released. From there, he staggered up to his father's bedroom and had the almightiest row with him which, I might add, nobody overheard because the château was, by now, largely empty on account of Operation Overlord and the advancing Allies.

'What have you done with Kenneth?' he demanded.

'I didn't hear you knock,' said the *Generalfeldmarschall*.

'*Fich dich.*'

The *Generalfeldmarschall* walloped him around the face. 'Do you know what they do to those who betray the Fatherland?'

'*Fich dich.*'

'It's that all you've come to say for yourself?'

'You killed my friend.'

The *Generalfeldmarschall* laughed. 'Are you talking about Gilbert Aumont?'

Konstantin flinched at the sound of his name.

'You're lucky you didn't end up like him. Being hanged isn't always quick, son. The neck doesn't always snap. Often, death only occurs because of suffocation. By rights, you should be swinging from a tree just like that little French *Fotze.*'

'You're a murderer. You murder children.'

'You murdered Gilbert Aumont the minute you set that pigeon trap. In fact, if you hadn't recommended that field, I'd have set the trap elsewhere, but you knew better, didn't you, son? You knew the best place to catch a traitor. Gilbert Aumont picked up the pigeon you left for him. You're the murderer, son, and so I suppose that means that you're the one that can also be described as a murderer of children.'

Konstantin retched but nothing came up because the contents of his stomach had already covered the floor of his cell several times over, week in, week out. 'I'm going home,' he said.

'Home? Your home is with me, and, given what is now taking place in Normandy, we must find a new one. Again, your fault, son.'

'My home isn't with you. I'm going back to Potsdam to live with Mother. My home is with her.'

The *Generalfeldmarschall* doubled over with laughter. 'With your mother?'

'Yes.'

'With your mother?'

'Yes, my home is with my mother.'

'I could lie and say that what you wish is possible, but it *would* be a lie, son. I'm afraid your mother died some months ago. I should have told you, but I thought it was kinder to keep it from you. However, it's very clear to me now that you no longer deserve such kindness or consideration.'

Konstantin's face crumpled and his legs buckled.

'Given that your mother is dead, I would suggest that you have nowhere else to go. Is that not so, son? It seems we are now stuck with each other, and, since your betrayal of the Fatherland, time is now short for us. We must go.'

Konstantin grabbed hold of the dressing table for support. There he saw his father's Lüger.

But I shall allow the attached cartoon to fill in this narrative gap.

Afterwards, and with the Allied invasion in full swing, Konstantin returned to his cell, closed the door, and ran full pelt at the very spot on the cell wall where Gilbert Aumont had once carved his own name.

41.

They were back in the den and there was still no sign of Kenneth. 'Do you think that's it?' asked Dottie. 'Do you think he's finally decided to go home?'

Rose noted the tears in her best friend's eyes and said, 'Yes, Dottie, I think Kenneth may have gone home. But it's alright because he'll have gone home to his mother, I expect.'

'I know I should be happy about that, sugar, but I just feel sad.'

Rose handed Dottie her pipe and then put her arm around her. 'I know, sugar,' she said. 'You loved him, and I think he loved you, but you have Pom-Pom now, and me.'

And while it's very tempting at this juncture to allow Ethel to speak for himself and tell you where in the hell he'd got to, a promise is a promise, and so I'll do the talking. It would be downright absurd to suggest that Ethel didn't deliver the *Generalfeldmarschall's* false maps and battle plans because he understood the evil he was carrying and the disaster it would undoubtedly spell for the Allied invasion. The truth is, Ethel was doing his level best to fly to Dottie and Rose in the den. Indeed, he was last seen taking a breather on a chimney stack in Surrey.

But we would only know that if we were a bird in the sky, of course.

Redactors Note

I have to admit that Joyce is rather adept at mimicry.

'*Let it be known that I read the words of others, I don't write them,*' she mocked. '*I assess words, I don't embellish them,*' she mocked. '*And when I encounter words that you must never apprehend, I take my blue pencil and redact them with an even line that runs through the entire length and breadth of them,*' she mocked. Once she was finished mocking me, she added, 'Really, dear, there's precious little evidence of redaction in this file of yours. Perhaps you've decided that precious little of this file need be classified after all? In which case, one wonders why this file was deemed *secret* and was given to you at all.'

'To the contrary, Joyce,' I said. 'I most certainly will be taking my blue pencil to the better part of this file. You see, Joyce, this file is what we call a complex *secret* file. And one certainly doesn't redact a complex *secret* file on a first read. You should also note, Joyce, that I have a good deal of experience with complex *secret* files. No doubt, this is the reason I was assigned this file to classify. In short, Joyce, an experienced redactor assesses a complex *secret* file on the first read and redacts it on the second.'

'But what you claim doesn't make sense at all, dear. You've blatantly redacted the odd word, indeed the odd line, on your so-called 'first read' of your so-called 'complex *secret* file'.'

'Well, yes, Joyce, to an experienced redactor such as I it is patently obvious that some words, indeed lines, require no assessment, but rather immediate redaction and so redacted they are.'

'Such as, dear?'

'Invectives, for one, and indecorous activities for another.'

'But not when these invectives and indecorous activities are expressed in a foreign language? Is that right, dear?'

'I don't generally translate the foreign words on the first read, Joyce, therefore I'm not immediately clear as to whether they express an invective or an indecorous activity.'

'And yet you were a translator during the war. Were you similarly compelled to temporize while in that role?'

'I translated contemporaneously as per my orders, Joyce. I should also say that the role of a war-time translator is a world away from the role of a post-war redactor.'

'I'm afraid I can't help but regard your inclination to redact some invectives and indecorous activities on the first read rather than the second, but not all, as further evidence of your bias. Generally speaking, surely all words and activities contained in the file should be subject to an identical process of assessment and subsequent redaction?'

'I...'

'That was a rhetorical question, dear. Since your process is to assess on a first read and redact on a second, no blue lines should be visible on any of the documents in this file and yet...'

'Yes, Joyce, I take your point, but I'm afraid you're jumping the gun.'

'I'm afraid you jumped it first, dear.'

'I'm afraid you're splitting hairs, Joyce. Generally speaking, the entire file will be redacted in good time thereby eradicating any hypothetical bias.'

To illustrate my point, I permitted her to view the very first document of the file; a document I had not long finished fully redacting. (And, since it was fully redacted, I assessed that I was not in breach of the Official Secrets Act of 1911 showing it to her.)

Joyce reviewed the document.

CLASSIFIED
CONFIDENTIAL
Copy 3. Dossier on ███████████   23 September 1943
To: ██Head of S██████
From: N████████████████████████████████████

- We have ██████████████████████████s with
  ██████████

- ██████████████ now ████████████████████
  ██
  ██
  ████████████

- ██
██
██
██ s
████████████ ████████████ pigeons capable of
boomeranging between two consistent locations in
this way remains immeasurable and can no longer be
reasonably contested: Intelligence gathered in the
field can now be received by London within hours
rather than weeks or days.

- ██
████████████████████████

CONFIDENTIAL
CLASSIFIED

After I had shown Joyce the document, she was quiet for a long while. Eventually, she said, 'I believe I can still make out the word pigeon, here and there.'

Judging her criticism to be constructive, I simply replied, 'I shall draw a thicker line in future, Joyce.'

She nodded and said, 'Perhaps, dear, for the sake of our marriage, your files should remain in your office from now on.'

And taking back possession of the document, I said, 'Yes, Joyce, it may seem coincidental, but I've arrived at the self-same conclusion.'

'But I do have one final question, dear,' she said.

'Of course,' I said.

'Did Konstantin ever meet Dottie and Rose after the war?'

And I said, 'I'm terribly sorry, Joyce, but I'm afraid I cannot possibly say since that information is not contained in this file. It is possible that it may be found in the second.'

Epilogue

Surrey Advertiser

Wednesday, 29 September 1982

Decorated Hero Spy Pigeon Found in Surrey Chimney

The remains of the mystery pigeon, PS.42.13033, complete with green-coloured message canister.

Mr Hilliard stumbled upon the discovery of a lifetime last week when the chimney of his sixteenth-century farmhouse was swept for the first time in five decades.

Among the soot, twigs, and leaves, were the remains of what we now know to have been a very special World War Two carrier pigeon. Mr Hilliard said, 'Being a war baby myself, I knew as soon as I saw the green message canister attached to the leg bone, that what I'd found was not the skeleton of just any old bird, but quite possibly the skeleton of a war hero. It was so thrilling, I immediately called for my wife.' Mrs Hilliard said, 'We just had to open the canister. My hands were shaking with excitement. At first, the lid wouldn't budge, but with some soap and a run under the hot tap, we managed to get it open.'

Both agree that the canister initially appeared empty. 'Well we had to laugh,' admits Mr Hilliard. 'After all that anticipation, nothing.'

But it wasn't quite the end of the story. Mr and Mrs Hilliard didn't give up, and with the aid of a torch and a pair of Mrs Hilliard's tweezers, they managed to recover several lengths of microfilm. 'We couldn't believe our eyes,' said Mr Hilliard. 'It was a million times better than Christmas!'

The microfilm is now in the hands of MI5 who are said to be working on recovering and developing the war-time images. Whilst the identity of the sender of the microfilm remains a mystery, the identity of the pigeon has been solved thanks to the unique National Pigeon Service number still visible on the skeleton's ring. The National Archives have confirmed that the remains found by Mr Hilliard appear to be those of the elite carrier pigeon known as Ethelred the Unready.

Posthumously awarded the Dickin Medal for Conspicuous Gallantry in 1945, Ethelred the Unready, or Ethel as he was affectionately known by his owner, the late Lady Darrick-Sinclair of Eden House, Virginia Water, was reported Missing in Action in 1944. Lord Darrick-Sinclair, Lady Darrick-Sinclair's son, said, 'Mother simply adored Ethel. Although my sister and I were born after the war, we grew up on tales of Ethel's daring and bravery. Indeed, Ethel's photograph remained on Mother's dressing table right up until her death last year, and is now proudly displayed in my sister's drawing room. Mother always wondered what happened to him, and it is, perhaps, a blessing that his remains were not found during her life-time; learning that he'd most likely succumbed to fire fumes while resting upon Mr Hilliard's chimney stack, would have caused her untold distress. If Ethel hadn't tired at that precise moment in time, Mother might have got her beloved Ethel back.'

Meanwhile, Mr Hilliard's only disappointment was that the microfilm was not accompanied by a note. 'If only,' he said, 'but fingers crossed, the spooks will be able to tell us what's on the microfilm.'

Now that's a day we can all look forward to!

Chim Chiminy, Chim Chiminy, Chim Chim Cher COO!

The End

Morse code translations:
First message reads:

Target secured/./Boy in poor health/./Father not found/./Travelling to Blighty with Bloomfield/./V for Victory/./message end

Second message reads:

I knew Gilbert Aumont/./He was a member of the French Resistance Group, Les Gens Prevalent/./He joined LGP when his family were strafed by the Germans in 1942/./He was hanged by Field Marshall von Essen on 06.02.44 for Possession of a Carrier Pigeon/./ He was 10 years of age at the time of his death/./message end

Thank you

Mum, for the space to write, the will to keep at it, unending belief in me; Ig Dawson, for the time to write, illustrations, shoulder to grieve on; Rebecca Smith, for wise prompts and kind steers; Professor Will May, for saying sparkle and steely-eyed in the very beginning; Dr Ros Ambler-Alderman, Lizzie Killen, and Dr Suzanne Brunt, for kinship and boosterism; David and Ann Martin, for the pigeon bones; Terri Mayes, Dr Carole Smith and Yasmin Jackson, for the French; Minke Jonk, for the Dutch; Christina Westwood, for the German; Jan Kristensen, for the long list of medicines; Karen Ellis, Paul Reed, and Ian Nye for reading drafts and checking things; Patrick Knowles, for dressing NTWOAOB in a [bird] striking cover; Rose Drew, Alan Gillott, and Alex Bestwick at Stairwell Books, for saving Rose Clarke, Dottie Latymer, Konstantin von Essen, and Ethelred the Unready, from melting snow; Little Juno, for being my weighted blanket.

Author Information

Victoria L. Humphreys was born in Surrey, but now lives in Dorset. She has a PhD in creative writing from the University of Southampton, and has also studied at the University of Ulster, the University of Surrey, and the Moscow State Institute for International Relations. *Not the Work of an Ordinary Boy* was inspired by a newspaper article about the skeletal remains of a World War Two carrier pigeon found in a chimney. Attached to the pigeon's leg bone was a canister containing a coded message. Since then, she has been fascinated by the war-time flights of these intelligent creatures and the secret messages they once delivered.

Twitter/Instagram: @drtorhumphreys

Other novels, novellas and short story collections available from Stairwell Books

For further information please contact rose@stairwellbooks.com

www.stairwellbooks.co.uk
@stairwellbooks

Ingram Content Group UK Ltd.
Milton Keynes UK
UKHW011039270323
419232UK00001B/14

9 781913 432614